the Cold Palace

MELISSA ADDEY

THE COLD PALACE
Copyright © 2019 by Melissa Addey. All rights reserved.

First Paperback Print Edition: 2019 in United Kingdom
Published by Letterpress Publishing

The moral right of the author has been asserted.

Cover, formatting and map of China: Streetlight Graphics

Kindle: 978-1-910940-50-1
Paperback: 978-1-910940-51-8
Wide Distribution Paperback: 978-1-910940-54-9

For Linda and Rick
With love and thanks for all your support and
the joy you bring to my children.

Your Free Book

The city of Kairouan in Tunisia, 1020. Hela has powers too strong for a child – both to feel the pain of those around her and to heal them. But when she is given a mysterious cup by a slave woman, its powers overtake her life, forcing her into a vow she cannot hope to keep. So begins a quartet of historical novels set in Morocco as the Almoravid Dynasty sweeps across Northern Africa and Spain, creating a Muslim Empire that endured for generations.

Download your free copy at
www.melissaaddey.com

Spelling and Pronunciation

I have used the international Pinyin system for the Chinese names of people and places. The following list indicates the elements of this spelling system that may cause English speakers problems of pronunciation. To the left, the letter used in the text, to the right, its equivalent English sound.

c	=	ts
q	=	ch
x	=	sh
z	=	dz
zh	=	j

Therefore Lady Fuca would be Foo-cha and Qianlong would be Chian-long.

TERRITORIES OF THE QIANLONG EMPEROR, 1760

The Cowherd and the Weaver Girl

One of China's Four Great Folktales

THERE WAS ONCE A WEAVER girl named Zhinü (the star Vega), daughter of a Goddess, who fell in love with a mortal cowherd named Niu Lang (the star Altair), who loved her in return. They married and had two children. Alas, their love was forbidden, for a divinity may not marry a mortal. They were banished to the opposite sides of the Silver River (the Milky Way), where each was left to mourn the loss of their beloved: Zhinü sadly continuing her weaving, Niu Lang caring for their two children alone. But once a year, on the seventh day of the seventh moon (August), magpies all over the world took pity on the lovers and fluttered to Heaven to create a bridge between them, so that they could be reunited for one night. Because of this, a pair of magpies symbolise true conjugal love and faithfulness.

The Qixi Festival celebrates this story. On the seventh day of the seventh moon unmarried girls pray to Zhinü and Niu Lang for a loving husband and a happy marriage. They have competitions and create displays of their needle working skills. Newlyweds also worship the couple for the last time and bid them a fond farewell as they begin their own happy marriage.

China, 1730s

Snowfall

I WAKE TO THE PALE BLUE light that means snow has fallen. Outside I can hear excited shrieking, which can only be my younger sister, Shu Fang. Despite my thickly furred jacket and high boots, I shiver when I step outside.

"It's so deep! It is as high as my knees! Or even my waist in the snowdrifts!"

For once Shu Fang is not exaggerating, the snow really does come up as high as her knees, a little lower for me but still each step requires me to lift my feet very high. Our silly little dog Peach bounces around, leaping like a dolphin above the snow only to disappear beneath it again as she lands. Meanwhile her companion Star pushes with his nose, creating a tiny tunnel for himself through the drifts, his approach less enthusiastic but still determined.

Something hard and cold strikes the back of my head.

"Stop that, Shu Fang!" I yelp.

"It wasn't her," comes a laughing voice. I whirl round and look upwards, to the young man sitting on our rooftop, another snowball ready in his hand.

"How did you get up there?"

"Climbed."

"You'll fall off!"

"Will you catch me?"

"Why would I save a silly boy who has climbed somewhere dangerous?" I scold him.

"Out of love for a dear friend?" he teases back.

"What dear friend?" I ask, feeling my cheeks grow warm. "I can't see one. Can you see a dear friend, Shu Fang?"

Shu Fang is swinging under the old plum tree, its pink winter blossoms incongruous in the white snow. "Niu Lang! Isn't the snow beautiful!"

He laughs. "Your sister recognises me, at least."

"You'll break your neck," I say.

"Help me down and I'll be safe," he says, holding out a hand.

"I'm not sure young men are allowed to climb into our garden without permission," I say primly.

"Niu Lang, my dear boy, there you are." My mother, standing at the doorway, huddled in winter robes, smiles up at him. "Come inside and bring the girls. They haven't even eaten their breakfast. They'll freeze out there. I had the cook make honey buns, your favourite." She shuts the door to keep out the cold.

"It looks as though your mother knows who I am, too," says Niu Lang, edging forward on the rooftop. I hold my breath, watching him and gasp as he jumps down, rolling in the thick snow to soften the impact of his landing, then stands up gracefully, brushing snow off his robes. "Good morning, Ula Nara."

I let my breath out. "Are you alright?"

He grins. "So you do care what becomes of me. Here, I made this for you."

What I had taken for a large snowball in his hands is instead a tiny ice sculpture, beautifully carved. Two magpies, their bodies intertwined to form a spherical shape. I smile, turning it in my hands, not even feeling the cold from the packed ice. "Sparrows?"

"Magpies, as you well know," he says quietly and then raises his voice. "Shu Fang! If you don't come in at once your sister and I are going to eat all of the rice porridge between us. *And* the honey buns. There won't be a scrap of breakfast left for you!"

The snow lasts for days. Every time it begins to look as if it might be melting, growing dirty with footsteps and wet around the edges, a new snowfall returns it to its pristine beauty, unmarked and sparkling white. Every day Niu Lang creates an ice sculpture for me: some tiny, some huge. He has been building them since he was a little boy, taught by his father, who used to win competitions as a young man. He spends a whole day outside making the largest one; packing down snow with Shu Fang's eager help until it is ready to carve, then creating a full size man and woman, their robes fluttering, while all around their feet magpies fly.

"Isn't it beautiful?" says Shu Fang, clasping her hands in romantic wonder. "The Cowherd and the Weaver Girl, reunited for one night."

I stand silent. There is more than a touch of myself in the Weaver Girl that Niu Lang has carved. I recognise the style in which my hair is always pinned and her ice-white face has my nose.

"She is quiet for once, I think she must like it," says Niu Lang, winking at Shu Fang.

"It is lovely," I say softly and for once, I do not tease him or deliberately mistake what I am seeing.

Niu Lang waits for my tone to change and when I say nothing else he smiles. "Not as lovely as you, Ula Nara," he says and his voice grows a little thick. "Perhaps in a few years we will bid the Lovers farewell together, what do you think?"

I swallow and raise my eyes to his. "Perhaps," I say, my voice half a whisper while my lips curve to match his smile.

"Nothing against him," grunts my father when my mother broaches the subject. "Good family. Pleasant enough. Far too early though.

Years to go until she needs to be married. Barely sixteen, even. Years. Ridiculous woman, chattering about such things so early."

"He is a lovely boy," enthuses my mother, encouraged by my father's dour comments, which, after years of experience, she rightly interprets as a glowing endorsement of Niu Lang as my future husband. She nods at me conspiratorially, delighted at her groundwork having been received so well. "All in good time of course, all in good time, but there can be an understanding between our families. There will be no need for matchmakers for Ula Nara, no need at all. I will ask an astrologer to consult their charts in private, just to be certain there can be no objection. I already have all his details, his mother and I have known each other so long, why, we are almost sisters."

My father sighs. "No need for that nonsense now. I told you, all in good time. Besides, you're getting ahead of yourself. There's still the Imperial Daughters' Draft. She will attend this summer and if she's not chosen then there's plenty of time to discuss her marriage."

I swallow and tug at my mother's sleeve in sudden fear. "What if I'm chosen? What if they choose me and I have to marry into the Imperial Family and... and... Niu Lang..." I can't even formulate my sentences properly.

My mother waves my fears away. "Stop panicking. There's hundreds of girls at each Draft. Hundreds. And that's *after* they've whittled out most of them for being unsuited in some way, which you are not. Nothing wrong with you, though they may make something up, they are so fussy. You would be a perfect Imperial bride," she adds with satisfaction, forgetting for a moment in her pride that this is not what I want to hear. Catching sight of my expression she reverts to soothing me. "*Hundreds* of girls. And our Yongzheng Emperor is known for having barely half the concubines his father had. *And* he only has one son old enough to need any concubines, not like the old Emperor with his thirty-five sons. So there's only two men needing concubines this year, why, there's barely a chance of being chosen at all, even if you wanted to be."

"*I* want to be chosen," says Shu Fang. "I want to be an Imperial bride."

"Oh, shush," says our mother. "You won't be going for another three years."

Shu Fang pouts. "I'd like to be chosen," she insists. "Think of living in the Forbidden City. The clothes and the jewels… and being married to a prince or even the Emperor…"

"Such a romantic," sighs my mother. "You've no idea what it means to be an Imperial bride. The rivalries, the gossip, the expectations. Never seeing your family again. Never leaving the Forbidden City again."

"They go to the Summer Palace," objects my sister. "And the hunting grounds."

"Just the three places then? For the rest of your life?"

"*And* Southern Tours of the Empire," insists my sister.

"Every few years, *if* you're invited," retorts my mother. "No, you marry a good man where I can still visit you, my girl."

I take no notice of either of them. Let Shu Fang dream of a prince if she wants to, I am comforted by my mother's certainty that the chances of my being chosen are slim.

"You might be chosen as a lady-in-waiting," she reminds me. "But if you are you only have to serve a few years and make sure not catch the Emperor's eye, which can't be that difficult since he's so wrapped up in his paperwork, so they say. Then you'll be released from service and given a handsome sum to start your married life with Niu Lang."

Winter passes. Emboldened by our parents' approving smiles we hold hands as we ice skate with our friends and write one another poems inspired by our daily life: icicles and snowflakes giving way to the first buds of spring and nesting birds, certain that our love will be blessed. My mother returns beaming from the astrologer.

"'A great love,' he said," she announces. "'Undying faithfulness through all tribulations.'"

"What tribulations?" I ask, worried.

"All lives have tribulations," says my mother, unconcerned. "You'd rather face them with a great and faithful love by your side than on your own, wouldn't you? Besides, he also said that you were destined for a life of importance and that Niu Lang would be a man of wisdom. A famous scholar, perhaps," she adds, romanticising a different sort of man from her own husband's military career. "See, I told you that it was worth visiting the astrologer well before time."

My father only grunts.

Falling Blossoms

THE WOMAN SHAKES HER HEAD. "Malodorous," she snaps. The rejected girl's face flushes crimson in shame as she is led away, back to her family. Apparently, the smell from her armpits would have been offensive to an Imperial nose. Beijing at the end of the sixth month is unbearably hot, I'm surprised all of the girls here have not been rejected for this reason.

The sturdy woman approaches and gestures impatiently for me to raise my arm. I, like all the other girls here, have already had to shed my fine outer robes, made of the best silk my family could afford. I asked my mother to send me in something plainer, still afraid of being chosen, but she refused.

"I won't be shamed," she said huffily. "I know you don't want to be chosen, Ula Nara, but you will be examined by the Palace officials. They will see your father's name and our Banner on the paperwork beside your own name. I won't have them look down their noses at us just because you wouldn't wear the best we can provide."

And so I arrived this morning at an administrative hall in Beijing, just outside the Forbidden City itself. It seems we will not be allowed into its hallowed precincts until we have been selected as the most superior candidates. I am dressed in a beautiful robe, the best I have ever owned. It is a delicate blue like a spring sky, covered with intricate embroidery featuring fluttering magpies and trees heavy with golden peaches, all symbols for love and happiness, for longevity, prosperity and future sons, highly auspicious and appropriate for today. It was removed in moments. Eunuchs gathered around each girl in turn to disrobe us and leave us in nothing but our under-robes. The room we are in is large and stifling, full of girls disrobing and re-robing as they are inspected by stout older women elaborately dressed to show off their status as senior ladies-in-waiting, perhaps wives to important court officials. Eunuchs bustle about: some assisting with the undressing and dressing, some noting down comments made by the ladies on each girl and reminding them of every candidate's status and family. Perhaps a smelly girl will be reassessed if her family is very important, perhaps a lowly girl from an out-of-favour family will be marked down as malodorous as a good way of removing her from the possibility of being chosen.

I lift my arm as instructed and the sturdy woman assigned to my row puts her face against my armpit and inhales loudly. I look away in embarrassment and when I look back she is nodding briskly to the eunuch at her side, who makes a note against my name. It seems I do not stink. I look hopefully about for my robe to be given back to me, but instead the woman kneels in front of me and lifts up my under-skirts. I step backwards.

"Keep still, you stupid girl," she says. I stop moving and gaze down at her in horror as she sticks her face under the skirts, close to my private parts and I hear her inhale again. She emerges and nods to the eunuch, ignoring my now scarlet face. Apparently, every part of me must be found to be acceptable to the sensitivities of a possible Imperial husband.

By the time I have regained my composure and my robe, my hair is being checked for lice and my teeth scrutinised. The Court Physician takes my twelve pulses and examines my tongue before he pronounces me to be of a cold and damp disposition, something the Imperial kitchens will take into account when cooking for me, should I end up residing here.

"Bound feet? You have *bound feet*?!"

Heads turn. A girl has been found with bound feet, despite being Manchu. She looks terrified. We all crane our heads to see under her skirts, catch a glimpse of tiny pointed stubs encased in embroidered slippers and then quickly look away again. The head eunuch is appalled.

"Bound feet are forbidden! As you and your family are well aware. What were they thinking, a noble Manchu family copying the disgusting habits of the common Han Chinese? Your family will be fined and you and all your sisters will be rejected for any possible union with the Imperial Family."

The weeping girl is led away while we try not to stare. I wonder whether bound feet are worth having to avoid marriage to the Imperial Family but it's too late now, they would have had to have been bound when I was a toddler and my family would never have done such a thing.

More and more girls are dismissed. I start to worry, thinking there are not, after all, hundreds of us to choose from, before recalling that today is merely one of multiple preliminary rounds, when any small reason will have us sent home again. I hope to be sent home for something trivial, perhaps poor posture or an inelegant kowtow but as the day progresses I am still not dismissed. I am from a good family and a military background, any minor faults I have are perhaps being overlooked or minimised, allowed to slip through. They can't get rid of too many girls, they want a good showing when we are selected, after all. In-between being tested for our suitability a few of the girls talk to one another. A tiny delicate girl, barely thirteen, sits next to me while we wait for our turn to be scrutinised again for some other fault.

"I am Ula Nara," I say.

"Wan," she replies, her voice as delicate as she is. I feel protective towards her, she can't be much older than Shu Fang, who, being only twelve, has missed this year's Draft. But where Shu Fang is full of chatter and silliness, this girl sits in silence.

"Do you want to be chosen?" I ask, thinking that such a girl must surely be terrified by the idea of both marriage and the expectations of joining the Imperial Family. But her face lights up.

"Yes," she says. "I have been praying to be chosen."

"For the honour to your family?" I guess.

She looks away. "To leave them," she all but whispers.

"Are you not happy at home?" I ask.

She shakes her head and a quick tear falls.

I wonder at what kind of family she has if she wants to leave them so desperately, but I don't enquire further. "I hope you are chosen," I say comfortingly.

"You too," she says. "I will include you in my prayers."

I shake my head violently. "I don't want to be chosen," I whisper, afraid that someone here will take offence at me even saying such a thing. "I have a – a sweetheart. We want to be married."

Wan's eyes shine with a romantic light only matched by Shu Fang's when such things are discussed. "Oh!" she breathes. "How exciting! Then I will pray that I am chosen and that you return to your true love."

I nod and smile at her before we are hurried on to the next test. I lose sight of her and at the end of the day when I don't see her in the crowd I hope she has not been sent home to an unloving family for some minor fault.

My mother is proud that I have made it through to the final round, but she remains comfortingly convinced that I will not be chosen.

"They'll pick two or three extra concubines for the Emperor, if that," she sniffs. "Then they'll already have chosen someone high-ranking for the young Prince's Primary Consort and give him an extra few ladies. If they have vacancies, some girls will be chosen as ladies-in-waiting. That's all. Keep quiet, stand where you're told to and it will all be over soon enough. And then you can finish that embroidery you're supposed to be doing for the Qixi Festival, there's not long to go. And you need to pray to the Lovers for a happy marriage!" she says winking.

I can't help smiling. I have no need to pray for a happy marriage. If I am spared from the Daughters' Draft then I will marry Niu Lang and of course my marriage will be happy. We have known each other all our lives, we are best friends as well as sweethearts. He is the only man I could ever love.

On the day of selection I make my way through the side gates of the Forbidden City along with the other candidates. To my relief I see my mother is right. There are indeed hundreds of girls still left. I feel my heart lighten and look about me with interest. This is probably the only time I will ever see the Forbidden City unless Niu Lang becomes a court official or a very great scholar, as the astrologer suggested.

The spaces are vast. Even though we are hundreds of girls, surrounded by eunuchs and guards, we are dwarfed by the courtyards and gates we pass through, swallowed up as though we are ants. Everywhere I look I see the swooping golden-tiled rooftops indicating the presence of the Imperial Family. We pass gates and then more gates, temples and guard towers, huge courtyard after huge courtyard. I almost get the giggles wondering whether we will just keep walking forever, never reaching our destination in this unending complex. But eventually we find ourselves at a set of gates, which take us into a different part of the palace.

"The Inner Court," announces the eunuch accompanying us.

I have heard of the Inner Court. It is where the Emperor and his women actually reside, the Outer Court being reserved for public occasions and rituals, official, religious and administrative purposes. The space here is on a smaller scale, we pass multiple palaces and smaller courtyards filled with flowers or decorative trees. At last we reach a gateway and are ushered into a medium-sized courtyard with less decoration. We are left to our own devices for a short period, huddling in little groups or standing alone, lost and nervous, each of us perfect in our best robes, our hair pinned with fresh flowers and our mothers' best jewels, lent for the occasion. Now that we are all in one place I can already see that many daughters from lower-ranking families have been sent home, only the most beautiful remain, their looks elevating them above their less-than-noble or exalted backgrounds. My own family are middling ranked: important enough but not quite the very best. Then there are the girls from families who are only one step from the throne itself, who boast imperial connections throughout their generations, whose daughters are regularly chosen as brides and ladies-in-waiting. Among these it is easy to spot the very, very few who have been pre-selected, who will be astonished if they are not chosen. They have been groomed for the Imperial Family, everything about them speaks of a natural confidence in their destiny.

I spot Wan in the crowd and edge my way towards her. She beams when she sees me, as though we are already old friends.

"Ula Nara!"

"Hello Wan," I say. "You are still here."

"Yes," she says happily. "I am sorry you are, though."

"They have plenty to choose from," I say. "They don't need me." She nods.

"Daughters of the Manchu Banners! Line up!" shouts a eunuch.

We form somewhat disorderly lines before several eunuchs hurry through our ranks, ensuring perfect composition and a precise geometrical layout. A few girls are shifted about so that a too-tall girl does not stand next to a very short one, spoiling the overall impression of uniform womanly perfection.

"That's Fuca, just behind us," murmurs Wan, standing next to me. "She's going to be Primary Consort for sure."

I look behind me. There's a very beautiful girl, her hair entirely jewel-free but filled with fresh flowers, her face serene and almost happy. I suppose she has been waiting for this moment for many years, certain of her future as an Imperial bride.

"Eyes front!" shouts the eunuch.

We stand still, an air of tension about us. The selection will come very soon, in only a few moments we will each know our fate.

Our fates seem to have been indefinitely postponed. We stand waiting for a ridiculously long time, until even the girls with the very best posture begin to slouch a little, their shoulders droop, while those of us with less composure shift from one foot to the other. Almost all of us are wearing cloud-climbing shoes, silken slippers precariously set upon high platforms, which require careful balance when walking. Standing still for a long time in them is uncomfortable. I risk another glance behind me to confirm what I expected: Fuca is still standing perfectly still, her head held high, her eyes looking only ahead. No wonder she's been pre-selected.

"Noble Consort Niuhuru, Primary Consort to His Imperial Majesty!" shouts the eunuch and we all straighten up.

The woman who enters the courtyard, surrounded by guards and attendants, must be about forty. She is very tall for a woman, she stands almost as tall as a few of her guards. She makes her way to a carved throne, which has been placed at one end of the courtyard, in front of our neatly-laid-out rows, then sits. Her attendants fuss about her for a few moments, adjusting the fall of her robes, angling an awning over her to keep the sun from touching her, offering fans, drinks and anything else she may be in need of before she irritably waves them away. Her face is set in a grimly determined expression and I wonder whether she dislikes the task of choosing exquisite young brides for her husband the Emperor, whether she is being eaten up with jealousy at this very moment.

By her side stands the Chief Eunuch, a very splendidly-dressed and imposing figure who arrived with her, currently consulting various folded papers so that he can give Lady Niuhuru advice on whom to select. These papers will give details of our families and fathers as well as any additional useful information: perhaps recent military prowess to be rewarded or noble connections to be taken account of. There is some discreet murmuring in Lady Niuhuru's ear before she nods and indicates three girls in rapid succession, each of whom falls to their knees and kowtows to her before the Chief Eunuch calls out their names and pronounces them concubines for the Emperor himself. There follows a few moments of murmured discussions, Lady Niuhuru shaking her head.

"There will be no further selection of ladies for the Emperor," announces the Chief Eunuch, looking a little disappointed, as do some of the girls who perhaps had their eyes on the Emperor.

A handful of girls are chosen as ladies-in-waiting. These look quite pleased: they will serve at court for a few years, catch the eye of a suitably high-placed husband if they can and be given a goodly sum of money with which to start married life.

"Her ladyship will now choose the Primary Consort and additional ladies for her son, Prince Bao of the First Rank."

Lady Niuhuru seems reluctant to begin the process of choosing her son's brides. She pauses and the Chief Eunuch leans to whisper in her ear. She looks up in my direction and for a horrible moment I think she is looking at me, before I realise that in fact she is looking at Fuca, standing in the row behind me. Lady Niuhuru nods.

"Lady Fuca! Chosen as Prince Bao's Primary Consort!"

I hear the rustle of silk from behind me as the newly-made Lady Fuca kowtows to her future mother-in-law. Wan gives a small nod, her prediction was correct.

There is another consultation. Another pause. Another nod.

"Lady Gao! Chosen as *gege*, concubine, to Prince Bao!"

"Lady Su! Chosen as *gege*, concubine, to Prince Bao!"

"She's not very high-ranking," murmurs Wan, who seems well-informed.

I watch the girl as she is led to one side. She is exquisitely beautiful. Whatever her family status, she has more than made up for it with her face and figure.

"Lady Zhemin! Chosen as *gege*, concubine, to Prince Bao!"

"She's related to Lady Fuca," whispers Wan.

I nod. It looks as though her family is being much favoured this year, being granted both a Primary Consort and a regular concubine.

A couple of other girls are chosen but they are standing right at the back and we cannot turn to see them.

Lady Niuhuru looks at our row and I hold my breath but her eyes rest on Wan instead. I can feel her whole body tense up next to me.

"Lady Wan! Chosen as *gege*, concubine, to Prince Bao!"

I want to turn and hug her but I cannot, so instead I stand very still and watch her as she is led away, beaming. I offer up a little prayer that she will be happier here than in her home if it made her so miserable, although I swallow when I think how young she is. How will she fare in such an exalted position, how will she cope with rivalries and petty jealousies?

I look back at Lady Niuhuru, who is shaking her head. I feel my shoulders relax. She has finished. The Emperor has a few new concubines, the court will welcome additional ladies-in-waiting and her son has not only a Primary Consort but a handful of additional concubines to begin his married life. The selection is over and in three years' time it will be Shu Fang's turn and goodness knows she wants to be chosen, the foolish girl. I smile a little at the thought of her. I might be married by then and she will be so excited at the thought of a wedding, it will be almost as good as being married herself, to be sister to a bride. I wait for Lady Niuhuru to leave so that we will all be dismissed, but the Chief Eunuch is whispering in her ear again. Lady Niuhuru looks over the rows and rows of girls still left over. I wonder whether the Chief Eunuch thinks there should be more ladies-in-waiting, for it is a great honour and a good opportunity for any girl and to choose so few might seem unfair for those families who hoped for advancement.

Lady Niuhuru's face suddenly brightens, as though she has had some good news. She lifts her hand and points a golden nail in my direction. I wait for a girl's name to be read out.

"Lady Ula Nara! Chosen as *gege*, concubine, to Prince Bao!"

For a moment I think another girl here must have the same name as me. I wait for her to move, to hear the rustle of her robes as she kneels. Then I see the expectant expression of the Chief Eunuch and realise that both he and Lady Niuhuru are looking directly at me. A great weight inside me drags me down. I feel my knees weakening, then the cold hard thud of cobblestones as I hit the floor without my will or knowledge. A huge pain spreads through me where my kneecaps have taken the blow of my body weight falling. I put out a hand to stop myself falling further. One hand on the cold cobbles, I look up in dawning horror at Lady Niuhuru and hear my voice, tiny in this large space, lost amongst the ranks of immobile girls towering over me.

"I do not wish to marry the Prince, my lady." Too late I see the Chief Eunuch begin to straighten up, his face shocked. But the words keep coming out of my mouth, I am unable to stop them. "I beg you to let me return to my – " and at least I do not say *my love* or even his name, *Niu Lang*, some last shred of self-preservation stops me but still I do not close my mouth " – to my family."

I hear muted gasps from the girls. Some cannot help themselves, they turn to gape at me, their mouths and eyes open, staring at me the better to tell this story when they return to their families, that there was a girl who was chosen, *chosen* and who refused, who told the Emperor's Primary Consort *to her face* that she did not wish to marry the Prince, her son.

Lady Niuhuru stares at me in the silence as though she can feel my fear, my dread of losing Niu Lang. She looks to the Chief Eunuch for help but his face is turning red with rage.

"How dare you question the Emperor's Primary Consort?" he screams at me, his voice echoing round the hard stone of the courtyard. "How dare you refuse the honour that has been bestowed upon you? You have been chosen and you will take your place among the Prince's ladies!" He makes a quick gesture and at once the guards snap to attention and Lady Niuhuru rises, still looking at me over her shoulder as she leaves, her face pale. The girls all sink to their knees as she departs. I hear myself moaning, a low sick sound as though I am an animal in pain, as if I am about to vomit. I place both hands on the floor and rock onto all fours, my head down, the moaning continuing, a thin dribble of saliva escaping my mouth and falling to the grey cobbles.

"Up," says a stern voice and my arm is gripped and yanked upright by a eunuch, only slightly less grandly dressed than the Chief Eunuch. "This way."

He has to drag me out of the courtyard. Behind me I hear the clatter of shoes and chattering voices breaking out as the dismissed girls are led back to the exit of the Forbidden City, no doubt only one topic of conversation between them. My name will be mud by the end of the day, my family will be shamed.

I stumble alongside the eunuch who is still gripping my arm tightly enough to hurt me, to a room where the chosen girls are waiting. No doubt they heard a commotion, but perhaps they did not understand what happened, for they look surprised to see me being forced into the room. At last the eunuch lets go of me, pushing me forward so that I totter towards the others. Wan hurries forward, her face full of pity.

"Ula Nara!" she whispers. "Are you a lady-in-waiting?"

I shake my head, unable to speak.

"Oh," she murmurs, embracing me and speaking into my ear. "Oh, I am so sorry."

"Silence!" shouts the eunuch, his demeanour evidently disturbed by the unexpected direction events have taken. He takes a moment to clear his throat and then bows, dignity restored.

"My ladies," he says. "You will be returned to your families to make your farewells, for all necessary preparations to be made and appropriate rituals carried out. You will return to the Forbidden City or the Prince's palace in Beijing in due course to take up your new roles within the Court. Officials will explain all protocols to your families. Please follow me, I will escort you to the gates where your parents will be waiting for you. They will be *honoured* by your appointments, I am sure," he finishes, looking hard at me.

The endless journey back through the Forbidden City seems like a dream to me. I manage to walk steadily only because Wan holds my hand in her tiny grasp, murmuring small sounds of comfort. I feel as though all my senses have been numbed, for I can barely hear her, can barely feel the heat of the sun on my skin. I walk because I do not know what else to do. I wonder why I am not crying, but when I put up a hand to my face I find it is wet.

Night Stars

THERE MUST BE CLOSE TO a thousand people waiting for the Imperial Daughters' Draft to be over and for the results to be announced. Most families are told their daughters have not been chosen and their responses vary from the shrugged resignation of those who did not expect such an honour, to those who look affronted at being overlooked. These daughters rejoin their families in short order and disperse swiftly from the gate, heading back across the empire, some facing long journeys home, which will take anything up to a month to complete.

Those chosen are greeted with smiles and amazement. Few girls have been chosen this year and so we are the elite among the mass of disappointment.

Wan squeezes my arm as she leaves me at the gate. "I will see you soon," she whispers. "We will strive for happiness, Ula Nara."

I nod at her kindness but I barely hear her well-meant sentiments. Instead I stand still, unable to walk forward without her little hand on my arm.

"Ula Nara!" Shu Fang is all but jumping up and down, trying to catch my attention. "We are here! Ula Nara!"

I do not move.

My mother makes her way through the crowd towards me, Shu Fang one step ahead of her, my father several steps behind. When Shu Fang reaches me and sees my face she steps back.

"Do you have to be a lady-in-waiting before you can be married?

But lots of girls do, it won't be that long…" She tails off, uncertain of how to proceed, unnerved by my silence, my falling tears.

My mother does not make Shu Fang's innocent mistake. Her face is grim. "Chosen for whom?" she asks.

"Prince Bao," I say and my voice is a croak.

For a moment I see my mother's expression struggle. Her daughter has been chosen as a bride for the heir to the throne, a man who will one day become Emperor, should all go well. And yet she can see my misery and she is fond of Niu Lang, we are all but betrothed. She embraces me and at last my silent tears turn to sobs, my face buried in her shoulder, desperately seeking a comfort that she cannot offer. When I open my eyes I can see my father standing behind her, his face solemn. He reaches out a hand and places it on mine but does not say anything. There is nothing to say.

Eventually, we can leave. My family have been told about the lavish gifts that will arrive from the Palace, a kind of reverse dowry, for families are not permitted to give dowries to Imperial brides, for fear of the Imperial Family then being indebted to them in any way. Besides this there will be appropriate marriage rituals, although they will be minor: I will be a concubine, not a Primary Consort, and my husband-to-be is still a prince, not an emperor. An auspicious date will be set for my arrival at the Prince's palace. I can only assume they mean auspicious for him, it cannot be possible for even the best astrologer to find a date that will be auspicious for me.

We travel home in silence. My mother tries to entice me to look on my future with a little less grief by using up all her limited knowledge of Prince Bao.

"He is the Emperor Yongzheng's only eligible son," she says. "They say this Emperor was only chosen to succeed because of how accomplished Prince Bao is, that his grandfather already had him in mind for the throne. He is a superior warrior, a gifted poet and calligrapher, they say he has a brilliant mind. If all is well he will be the Emperor one day."

Shu Fang wipes away my tears. "Why did they have to pick Ula Nara?"

"They can choose any girl they want," says my mother. "If she has been deemed suitable, she can be selected. There is no knowing why they choose any girl on the day itself."

My shoulders heave with renewed sobs.

"He is devoted to his mother and filial to his father," says my mother, trying a new tack. "That speaks well for him, doesn't it? I am sure he will be a kind husband to you."

I do not reply. In the end she falls silent, unable to think of anything to say that will comfort me.

When we arrive at our home I stay seated in the covered wagon in which we have travelled. I do not know how to get out and face Niu Lang, who will be waiting anxiously to know that all is well. I do not know how to look him in the eye and tell him that I cannot marry him, that I will instead be marrying a prince, that this month will barely be over before I will leave my home for good and we will never see one another again. I sit in the half-darkness of the wagon and try to formulate the words that will break the news gently to him. At last I think of something to say, a formal and correct sentence and I step down from the wagon but as I do I see Niu Lang waiting by our house and Shu Fang throwing herself into his arms, weeping.

"Niu Lang! Oh Niu Lang! Ula Nara has been chosen to marry the Prince! Oh, how will you both bear it?"

Niu Lang's arms catch her but over her head he looks at me and sees from my face that what she says is true. Gently, he sets her aside, leaving her to weep alone and then clutch at my mother. His eyes stay fixed on mine as he reaches me. He does not ask questions, he does not exclaim outrage or anger or denial. Instead he kneels at my feet and takes my hands.

"I will always be yours, Ula Nara," he says with a seriousness and a calmness that belies his years. "Know this."

I try to say something of equal importance, to swear my love for him, but I cannot find anything to say and so I only let my tears flow and clasp his hands.

My mother allows this for some moments before she clears her throat awkwardly. "Inside, now, Ula Nara," she says. "Niu Lang, my dear, you must leave us to rest. It has been a very tiring journey."

Niu Lang stands and looks down on me for a moment before he lets go of my hands and turns away, back to his house. I stand watching him until Shu Fang obeys my mother's whispered command and comes to pull me towards our house.

"It is very late," says my mother, although in fact it is barely dusk. "I think we should all be in bed." She shushes the servants' curious questions and harries everyone through the evening tasks until we are all in our beds. I lie in the darkness and try to think about everything that has happened and what my future will be like, but my tears have drained me of any ability to think. I drift into the darkness, glad not to think.

When I wake I think for a moment that in my fear of being chosen I have imagined the whole thing, that I conjured up the moment of horror as part of a nightmare. I look about the room to see what has changed, but all is how it used to be. I feel a slow smile creep across my face. I was wrong then, I dreamt all of it and now my family will laugh at me when I tell them. Niu Lang will look at me with his head on one side, grinning at my foolish fears. Then he will grow serious and say that such a thing would be impossible: why, we are meant for each other, nothing can come between us. I will laugh at my night-time fears and at having escaped the Draft. I will play in our garden with Shu Fang, I will walk hand-in-hand with Niu Lang to pick peaches and all will be well.

But when I move to sit up my arm hurts. I look down and see a dark bruise has appeared on the skin of my upper arm, just below the shoulder. I frown for a moment and then I remember the eunuch who yanked me to my feet, who forced me to walk into the room where all the other girls who had been selected were waiting. I feel something wet on my legs and look down to see tears already dripping into my lap.

My tears fall continuously without my knowing it. After a few days I almost grow accustomed to their presence. At first I wipe them away again and again but at last I leave them to fall. I wake and my pillow is wet, the front of my robe is marked with the salt stains of previous days and new-fallen tears. At first Shu Fang wipes them away, her own eyes brimming with sympathy, but after a while she, too, leaves them to fall.

My mother tries to think of ways out of the situation. "Do something," she castigates my father. "The girl will die of unhappiness if she goes on like this. She is barely eating as it is, she will be nothing but bones by the time she returns to Beijing. Tell the Palace she is sickly or half-witted. Tell them they have made a mistake, that she is not fit for the Prince. If they want to honour our family, let them take Shu Fang at the next Draft, she'd be delighted to be chosen."

My father does not even bother to respond to this. The Imperial Family does not stoop to ask the Banners which of their daughters is suitable for service, it chooses through its own methods, honed over generations. I have been judged and found suitable. I have been chosen. There is no way out.

"Scar me," I say to Niu Lang.

"What?"

"Scar me," I say. "I cannot be a suitable bride for the Prince if I am scarred. Take a knife and cut my face."

He shakes his head.

"You would not love me if I was scarred?" I ask.

"I would love you anyway," he says. "But I will not scar you."

"I will do it myself," I say.

I try. I sit for most of a day holding a knife. I place the cold blade against my cheek and I press it hard so that I can feel its sharpness, but I am too much of a coward to draw the blade down and feel my flesh give way.

"We could run away," says Niu Lang.

Even I know this is not an option. "They will find us and execute us both," I say. "I have been chosen. I am as good as the Prince's wife now. I will be accused of adultery and you will have seduced the wife of a prince."

Niu Lang traces the lines of my palm. "I will not marry, Ula Nara," he says.

"You will have to," I say, and more tears fall at the thought.

He shakes his head, serious. "I will become a monk," he says.

I stare at him. "A monk? Your family will not allow it."

"They cannot stop me," he says.

I hear Niu Lang's mother weeping with my mother. "A monk! He cannot become a monk!"

My mother calls me into the room. "Ula Nara. You cannot let Niu Lang ruin his life and his family's plans in this way. You must speak with him. When you are... gone, he must come to his senses. Tell him he must live his life fully, he must give up this nonsense of being a monk."

I nod.

"It is not for you to decide," says Niu Lang, in the darkness of our garden as we sit side by side on the swing.

"But your family will be so unhappy," I say.

"Do you want me to be married to some other girl?"

I want to say *no*, but I think of his mother's tears and I stay silent.

Niu Lang strokes my cheek. "My family is not your concern, Ula Nara. I will become a monk when you leave your family for the Palace. And whatever happens to you there, you will know that for all of our lifetimes, I will think of you with love and will not marry another. It is all I can give you. I would have given you so much more but this, at least, I can do for you."

"I can do nothing in return," I say.

"You can think of me," he says. "Every year at the Qixi Festival you will look into the heavens and you will see Zhinü and Niu Lang reunited in the stars. And you will know that I will be watching those same stars and thinking of you. Every year, Ula Nara, until we take our own places in the heavens and are reunited for good."

"I will not know where you are," I say, my voice cracking at the thought.

"I will be watching the stars alongside you," he says. "It will not matter where I am."

With an absurd bitterness of timing, the Qixi Festival must be celebrated the night before I leave. I wonder whether there are other girls weeping across the empire tonight, selected for Imperial marriage against their will, forced to abandon any romantic secrets they held in their hearts. Already the Palace dowry has arrived, wagonloads of goods of every kind, from furniture to silver to bolts of silk. My mother is torn. She would like to boast of the good fortune and honour that I am bringing to the family, would like to show her friends all the beautiful items that are being delivered. Yet her heart is troubled by my white face and endless tears as well as by Niu Lang's insistence on becoming a monk. So I hear her showing her friends all the expensive goods in half-whispers before she returns to embrace me and murmur words of comfort. My father, unable to deal with this domestic crisis, spends more and more time at the nearby barracks, carrying out unnecessary paperwork and inspections of troops.

The local girls, friends and family alike, are uncertain whether to include me in the rituals and celebrations. They are praying for husbands and one has already been chosen for me – or I for him – and also they are praying for happy marriages, which it appears I have been denied before it even begins, implying that the two heavenly lovers have not looked on me with kindness. Besides, as a half-married girl I ought really to be bidding the couple farewell alongside my own husband, something which is impossible since my future groom is in Beijing and my sweetheart is about to be lost to me forever. Shu Fang hesitates in my doorway, clutching examples of her dainty needlework.

"It's alright, Shu Fang," I say, weary of everyone tiptoeing around me. "You can go without me."

"I will burn incense for you at the temple," she says awkwardly. "Perhaps the Lovers will find a way to… to…"

"Thank you," I say, to make her go away. When she has gone I sit in silence until I hear something strike the window. Looking out I see Niu Lang below, a lantern in one hand, a large bundle of incense sticks in the other. Quickly I make my way into the garden, where I find him kneeling by the pond, lighting the incense by the dim light of the lantern.

"What are you doing?" I ask.

"Bidding farewell to the Lovers," he says. "As we said we would one day."

"We are not going to be married," I remind him, my voice bitter.

"We are as much married as they were," he says. "And we will remain so, as they did. Here." He hands me half the sticks of incense. I take the bundle and together we bow in each of the four directions before kneeling and kowtowing before the pond in which we can see the two Lovers' stars clearly reflected above us. When we plant our incense sticks firmly in the earth where they can continue to burn Niu Lang holds out his hand to me. We lie on our backs in the grass, still warm from the sun. The moon rises above us while we lie, hands clasped. We do not speak, only watch the stars above us and the moon's path across the sky, our breath rising and falling as one.

I wake cold and stiff, my robe wet with dew, the sun barely over the horizon. Niu Lang is gone, the stubs of burnt-out incense are all that are left of our night together. I make my way back to the house, creeping up the stairs so as not be found out of bed and wait to hear my mother's footsteps.

She comes soon enough, holding a pile of shimmering red silk in her arms. Shu Fang follows her, eyes brimming.

"It is time to dress," my mother says gently. For once she does not chatter but instead helps me into my wedding clothes in silence, before spending time twisting my hair into an elaborate arrangement pinned with silk flowers.

I descend the stairs to my father and we stand in front of one another.

"You bring honour on our family, Ula Nara," he says at last and his voice is gruff.

I do not answer. I do not know what to say. I only know that I will never see him again, nor any member of my family, and I cannot think what to say in such circumstances. My father embraces me, followed by my weeping mother, who lifts my red wedding veil over my head, plunging me into a gauzy red-tinted world. I am led outside, to where a red and gold palanquin awaits, surrounded by bearers and Imperial guards. Neighbours crowd about to watch me go. I look this way and that for Niu Lang but I cannot see him anywhere.

Shu Fang throws herself at me so hard that I stagger backwards. "Oh, Ula Nara! I will miss you! I will be all on my own!" She buries her face in my red silk and sobs.

I wrap my arms around her. "Where is Niu Lang?" I whisper into her tousled hair.

She gulps back her tears. "Gone," she whispers.

My mother is tugging at my arm.

"Gone where?" I hiss.

"To be a monk. He took his father's best horse."

I am pulled away from Shu Fang. I look over my shoulder and realise none of Niu Lang's family members, our closest neighbours and friends, are there to wave me off. I look back at Shu Fang, my eyes wide. There was something in me that had not believed Niu Lang, that had thought he had said such things only to soothe me, that he would eventually bend to his family's will and marry some suitable girl.

"I will miss you," says Shu Fang again, her little face white and miserable. As I am hurried into the palanquin I realise I will never see nor touch her again, that our last embrace was taken up with Niu Lang's whereabouts.

"I will miss you too," I say and hold out my arms to her. She steps forward but the bearers have already lifted me and I am moving away. I struggle with the veil over my head and the curtain at the window, fighting to catch a last glimpse of my family and of Shu Fang, whose voice I can still hear, calling after me, high and full of tears.

"Ula Nara! Do not forget me! Ula Nara!"

Tangled in my wedding veil, I sit back. I can no longer see behind me, all I see out of the small window is the shape of the guards surrounding me.

It takes me several moments before I realise that the small palanquin contains an object: a dome-topped container covered over with a dark cloth. Unpinning my veil and setting it to one side I hesitantly touch the cloth, then pull it away to reveal a birdcage, whose inhabitants squawk in surprise at the light suddenly reaching them. A pair of young magpies, huddled together for comfort, stare up at me as my tears begin to fall again.

The journey is long and the palanquin is stifling in the heat of the day. I am offered food and a rest somewhere at a nobleman's home part-way to Beijing but I refuse and the bearers and guards shrug and continue our swaying journey, no doubt anxious to complete their day's work and deliver me to my new home.

It is close to dusk when we come to the outskirts of Beijing and dark by the time we reach Prince Bao's palace, somewhere close to the Forbidden City. I do not know the city well, but when I look out of my tiny window I see bright lanterns everywhere in still-busy streets, hear the street-food vendors calling their wares. We pass through smaller streets lit by lanterns behind which stand girls in cheap but gaudy robes, softly calling their own kind of wares. I pull back into the darkness of my palanquin.

At last the steady marching slows and then stops. Greetings are exchanged between a sentry and my own guards. I hear the creak of heavy gates being swung open as I try to re-pin my wedding veil in place, although in the darkness I cannot see what I am doing and drop more than one pin. Once again the palanquin sways forwards and I hear the gates thud together as they close behind me.

Now the bearers increase their pace, trotting at speed through courtyards dimly lit with large lanterns. Here and there I glimpse the odd guard, but otherwise everything is eerily empty, my own palanquin and its escort the only thing in motion, the only thing creating any noise.

We come to an abrupt stop and I am set down. I wait, uncertain whether I should emerge or whether we have still some way to go.

A plump wrinkled hand appears, pushing aside the curtain, extended to me. Hesitantly, I take it and step out of the palanquin, my limbs cramping painfully after their lengthy confinement. I reach back and lift out the magpies in their cage. They flap and squawk at the movement and I set them on the ground before looking at the owner of the hand, an old woman, round and with a pleasant face, which creases into a smile. "Lady Ula Nara," she says. "Welcome to His Highness' palace. I am Dan Dan, your maid."

I nod. I wait for someone more senior to appear, but Dan Dan only stoops to pick up the magpies' cage, then walks away from me towards a half-open door from which light spills out. I look back at the guards but they are already marching off, the bearers following them with the now-empty palanquin bobbing away from me. I follow Dan Dan towards the door.

Inside I find I am in a large and pleasantly appointed living room. There is a table set for a meal for one, as well as couches placed here and there, little tables with board games and other trinkets placed on them. Several vases of fresh flowers as well as paintings and examples of calligraphy and poetry are displayed around the room.

Dan Dan sets the magpies' cage on an empty side table near a closed window and turns to me smiling.

"Shall I remove your veil?" she asks.

I hesitate. "Won't there be a – a ritual?" I ask. I wonder where my future husband the Prince is. I expected to meet him on my arrival here, to carry out some kind of ceremony. Back at home I and my family knelt before our family's altar and ancestral portraits and before certain items of importance brought from the Imperial Family. But I expected something additional: for the Prince to raise my veil, to kneel before his own ancestral portraits, to – to no doubt be taken to his bedchamber where I would turn my face away in the darkness, to think of Niu Lang even while being made another's wife without my consent.

Dan Dan shakes her head. "I will take you to the ancestral tablets tomorrow morning," she says. "And to the temple to pray, if you wish."

"Where are the others?" I ask.

"The ladies have been arriving all day," says Dan Dan. "Except for Lady Fuca. She was brought here almost immediately after selection, she has resided here for almost a month now."

Of course, I think. She was pre-selected, her dowry and any other official matters would already have been taken care of. Besides, as the Primary Consort she and the Prince would have had a more elaborate marriage ceremony. I was forgetting that I and the other ladies here are only concubines, not deemed worthy of anything more than a perfunctory ritual, our husband's presence not even required, our assent assumed. Slowly I remove my wedding veil and place it, unwanted and unnecessary, on the back of a chair.

Dan Dan bustles about, while I sit in silence at the table. She brings plates of food and I try to eat. The food is good but I have eaten so little of late that my stomach has shrunk, a few mouthfuls and I am already full. Dan Dan shakes her head when I say I am finished.

"I will need to fatten you up," she says cheerily and clears the table.

I rise and walk to where the magpies are now sleeping, huddled against one another. I stroke one of their silken wingtips through the bars of their cage, causing them to open their eyes in sudden consternation before returning to their loving embrace.

"You must be tired," says Dan Dan behind me. "I will make sure your birds are fed and watered."

I follow her to an equally well-appointed bedchamber. My bed at home was nothing as elaborate as this one, it is finer even than my parents'. Its heavy wooden frame is delicately carved, placed within an alcove and warmed by a *kang* stove beneath it. It is comfortably large enough for a couple, its heavy silken drapes embroidered with pomegranate trees and bats in a night sky, symbols of fertility, wishes for Imperial sons.

Dan Dan helps me to undress, my wedding finery gathered up to be taken away and stored, used only to journey here in solitude. She helps me into the bed as though I were a child and puts out the lanterns, leaving me in darkness.

I lie still and silent for a long time before I get out of the bed and make my way, hands outstretched, to where I recall the window was. I fumble with the shutters, struggling to open the unfamiliar catches, before sitting at the window seat and looking up at the stars. I wonder where Niu Lang is, whether his family have found him and brought him back or whether his father's best horse has taken him far enough away from home to evade their searches. I wonder whether he kissed my lips before he left me asleep in the garden and whether he is looking up at the Lovers' stars even now and thinking of me.

Rain on Water

"THE LADIES OF THE PALACE will take most meals together," Dan Dan advises me when I wake.

I shake my head. "I cannot," I say.

Dan Dan looks at me with a kindly pity. "It is normal to be nervous on your first day in your husband's household, my lady," she says. "But the Prince has given his orders and he cannot be disobeyed. Let me help you."

I wash and dress. Dan Dan opens one chest after another filled with robes that have been made for me. Dressed in a peach robe with delicate floral embroidery, my hair pinned with golden tassels and jade carved pins, I stand in the doorway of my rooms, uncertain and afraid.

Now that it is daylight I can see that the Prince's palace complex is large. It follows a fairly standard layout: Dan Dan indicates the direction of the main gates which give onto large courtyards and halls, housing temples and administrative rooms, receiving halls and other buildings relevant to the Prince's official and public life. Set back from this area, behind additional gates, mirroring the Inner Court of the Forbidden City, is a complex of small palaces and courtyards, each housing the Prince or one of his ladies, as well as some more communal buildings where we may eat, pray, or spend time together. These last are grouped around a large garden complete with a small lake filled with lotus flowers fed by a stream, as well as a little walkway through black twisted rocks.

"Brought here from the South," says Dan Dan as she leads me through them on our way to breakfast. "The Prince is very fond of gardens. He was brought up in the Yuan Ming Yuan."

"The Garden of Perfect Brightness? What is that?" I ask.

"It was the residence of his father the Emperor when he was just a boy," says Dan Dan as we walk around the perimeter of the water lily-filled pond. "Now it has been designated the Imperial Summer Palace. The Prince is having all manner of fine buildings and gardens developed within the grounds, some of them by the Jesuits in the Western style."

I have no idea what she is talking about and anyway my attention is focused on a hall straight ahead of us.

"The dining hall," says Dan Dan, seeing my eyes fixed on it. "Lady Fuca will be there already, she is an early riser. There may be some of the other ladies there too. You were the last to arrive, so this morning you will all be here."

I want to turn and run back to my own rooms, to hide there forever, but that is not a possibility. I take a deep breath and step through the doorway into the hall, Dan Dan following behind me.

"Ula Nara!"

"Wan," I say, sighing with relief when I see she is the only occupant aside from a few maids and eunuchs who are busy setting dishes on the table.

We embrace and she leads me to a place midway up the long table, to sit by her side. I see Dan Dan beam at us, no doubt pleased to see me smile for the first time since she has met me.

The table is lavishly full of dishes: not just the honeyed buns and rice porridge that my family would have served but steamed rolls, duck soup with yams, mushroom pastries, bamboo shoots, cooked lotus root and various other hot and cold dishes, as well as rice and pickles. There is watermelon juice to drink. The rest of the table is filled with beautifully presented dishes of fruits and nuts including walnuts and almonds, fresh peaches, dried dates and early pears. Wan gestures at the table.

"Enough for a banquet," she says, giggling.

Her demeanour here is different, it is as though a great weight has left her, turning her from a nervous child to a chattering smiling young girl. I cannot help smiling at her.

"Are you still unhappy?" she whispers.

"I will never be happy without Niu Lang," I say.

She nods and passes me a plate of pork and cabbage. "I pray you will find peace here, one day," she says.

I cannot speak of Niu Lang without crying and so I focus on Wan instead. "Have you met the Prince?" I ask.

She nods and smiles. "I arrived early yesterday," she says. "He walked with me in the garden. He is very kind, very gentle."

I nod. I am glad to hear good things of Prince Bao. I have enough unhappiness in my heart without hearing anything bad about him.

"Where are the other ladies?" I ask. "I was told Lady Fuca and the others would be here."

Wan nods. "My maid told me Lady Su is something of a late riser," she says. "But the others will be here soon." She frowns. "I am not sure where Lady Fuca is, I was told she was in the habit of rising early."

There is a slight commotion by the doorway and Lady Gao enters. I remember her from the Draft: not really a beauty, she has a calm, almost stolid demeanour about her. Behind her comes Lady Zhemin, a little flustered.

"I am sorry I am late," she begins. "I was feeding the ducks and lost track of time." Then she sees that only Wan and I are at the table. "Oh," she says. "I am Zhemin."

We all introduce ourselves and as we are doing so Lady Su arrives, her porcelain beauty untarnished by the journey here and the early hour. When I give my name I see the others' eyes flicker and know that they are remembering what happened when I was chosen, my name forever branded on their memory. I see them note my puffy eyes and am aware that they treat me gently, as though I may begin to cry at any moment. Since there is still no sign of Lady Fuca we settle round the table and eat. I cannot stomach much apart from fruit and nuts, but the watermelon juice is fresh and thirst-quenching.

"His Highness!" The eunuch making the announcement steps away from the door to allow first Prince Bao and then Lady Fuca to enter. Hastily, we all rise and step away from the table, then kneel to begin our kowtows to this man, our husband.

He waits until we have finished, then smiles radiantly. "Rise," he says. "I will join you at breakfast." He looks to his side at Lady Fuca. "Sit by me," he says.

They take their places side by side at the head of the table, although there is plenty of room for them to sit further apart. But I can see at once that there is already a closeness between the two of them. They allow their arms to touch and when he makes her laugh Fuca leans her head against his shoulder for a moment. He takes choice morsels from his plate and puts them into her mouth with his chopsticks, before remembering his manners and choosing select items for the rest of us, which however are passed to us on tiny plates by attentive servants, well-bred signs of favour but not of intimacy.

"I must leave you all," the Prince says after only a brief stay, during which he has eaten heartily, favouring dishes of game and noodles.

We rise and he nods his head to us all as we bow to him. "I will return soon," he promises, but his eyes are only on Fuca, who smiles and touches a late summer rose in her hair as though to acknowledge it as a gift from him.

"I suppose she has been here almost a month already, so they have had time to get to know each other," says Wan afterwards as we stroll around the little lake. "They look happy together," she adds a little wistfully.

I nod. It is clear to me already that the Prince is much taken with his Primary Consort. Nevertheless, he has other ladies and no doubt each of us will be called upon as a companion in due course. I feel my body tighten up at the thought of his hands on me, of his lips touching mine when mine have never even touched Niu Lang's. Part of me hopes he will be so besotted with Lady Fuca that he will simply forget about the rest of us altogether, perhaps forever.

We are called for, of course. First, to no-one's surprise, is beautiful Lady Su, who joins us at breakfast the next day blushing but all smiles when she sees the Prince. I don't feel that I know her well enough to ask any questions, but clearly both she and the Prince were pleased with the encounter. I wait for Lady Fuca to show signs of jealousy, but she does not, she seems happy enough and I think that probably she has been well-trained to expect this life, she will have been told that to show jealousy will not endear her to the Prince. And sure enough her gracefulness in this matter is rewarded, for several days go by before anyone else is called for, Lady Fuca returned to her place as favourite.

Lady Gao is called for and returns with her calm exterior unruffled. I cannot imagine that she is a very passionate bedfellow. Lady Zhemin looks a little flustered after her turn, but then she often does. When Wan is called I tremble for her but she returns more confident than before.

"He said I was very young," she confides. "He will not call for me until I am a little older. He says he will honour me in all other ways."

Reluctantly I give the Prince his dues. It was clear to most of us that Wan was very young to be married and he has not forced himself upon her still half-childish body. I have to concede that he is a kind husband. After that night he seems to treat Wan like a younger sister, bringing her the odd flower from the garden and teasing her a little when we eat together, showing her a friendly but passionless warmth.

Days go by and it is only Fuca who is called for. I know that the night she is not called for will be my own turn, for each lady has now been sent for except me.

The days pass so slowly I frequently think there must be some mistake and ask Dan Dan more than once if she is sure about the date. There is nothing to do here. At home there were visitors and we visited neighbours, went for walks, did errands, shopped, played in the garden. Here I feel I must act the part of a grown woman, for I am married now, and the Imperial Family, it seems, does not allow its women the kind of freedom most Manchu women enjoy. We do not leave the palace complex. Each day I wash and dress, then Dan Dan does my hair. I walk with Wan and the others in the garden, perhaps read or play a board game. I feed my magpies, whose wings have been clipped so that they cannot escape. They grow tame, eating from my hand and I have a larger enclosure built for them, an aviary in the garden courtyard outside my window, where I can see them flutter from perch to perch. I eat with the other ladies, sometimes the Prince attends as well, but mostly he does not.

I wonder whether he has been told something of my story, if he knows that I begged not to marry him or whether this information has been hidden from him. Either way, he has left me until last amongst his ladies and quite some time has passed since I arrived here, we are midway through autumn.

Outside there is a cold frost, the first of the year. I stand at the window watching the magpies, whose aviary has been moved to a more sheltered corner of the courtyard.

"The Prince has asked for you," says Dan Dan, bringing me a selection of robes, her round face beaming.

"Now?" I ask. "Isn't it breakfast time?"

"Not now," chuckles Dan Dan. "As a companion. Tonight. He sent a servant."

I feel a chill come over me. This, then, is the moment I have been dreading. It had to come some time.

It is the only day that has passed quickly here, breakfast seems to be over in moments. The Prince is there but I cannot bring myself to meet his eye and he leaves early, as usual.

I walk in the garden and feed the magpies, try and fail to read before asking Wan to join me in praying at the temple. Wan knows that I have been summoned and tries to take my mind off the fast-approaching nightfall. We pray at the Daoist temple, but all I can focus on are the monks. Does Niu Lang look like them now, I wonder? Is his head shaven and does he wear the dark blue tunic and leg wraps that they do? Does he spend his time at prayer and in practicing the martial arts he always loved? Wan takes me to her own rooms, offers me tea and sweets, plays a silly drinking game with me, hoping to lighten my mood and perhaps thinking that if I am a little tipsy I will not be so afraid or tense.

"I need to go now," I tell her, as dusk falls.

I am bathed and dressed, my hair filled with gold and jade, pulled so tightly onto a black lacquered board that I think I will get a headache. I cannot choose a robe, they all look the same to me in my jittery state, so Dan Dan selects one for me, a green that I think makes me look even paler than I already am. I do not care.

At the appointed hour she leads me to the Prince's own palace, larger than any of ours. It includes a receiving hall with a throne, adding to the formality of the place and reminding me of his supposed future. This man may be the Emperor one day: not just my husband but my ruler. A eunuch is waiting for me and Dan Dan leaves with an encouraging smile. I want to run after her but of course that is not possible. Instead I follow the eunuch.

We pass through a living room full of curious objects such as Western clocks, which make a ticking sound as I pass them: I have only ever seen one before but I count more than ten here. There are many delicate carvings on display, in everything from wood to jade. The walls are hung with scrolls of paintings and calligraphy, poetry. Clearly he is a man who admires beautiful things. I think of Lady Su and wonder whether she was chosen to add to his collection.

We reach the bedchamber, where the bed dominates most of the room. Even though it is set into an alcove as is usual it is, if possible, even larger than my own and hung with heavy drapes in a rich yellow, not quite the Imperial yellow reserved for the Emperor but certainly something which hints at it. There is little else in the room, focusing all my attention only on the bed. The Prince is nowhere to be seen.

"His Highness will be here shortly," says the eunuch, unfastening my robes. It feels awkward to stand alone in a room with a man, even if he is a eunuch, and allow him to undress me, but I stand still and let him dispose of all my clothes, leaving me entirely naked. I wonder whether he compares the Prince's ladies, since he has now seen each of us disrobed, whether he thinks that I am more womanly than Wan but less beautiful than Su, whether he feels any desire for us or whether all desire left him when he gave up his manhood to become a eunuch to the Imperial household. He does not seem very interested in me, once I am undressed he simply turns and leaves the room with no further instruction.

I shiver. I am not really cold, for the room is well heated, but I feel exposed, standing here naked and yet I am unsure whether I should climb into the bed or not. In the end I sit on the edge of it and pull one of the silken coverlets up a little to cover at least part of my body.

"Lady Ula Nara."

I stand up, still clutching the coverlet, to face the Prince. He smiles, apparently unbothered by the awkwardness of the setting: the two of us alone for the first time, he entirely clothed while I have been stripped naked. I try to offer a smile, although I doubt it looks convincing. I am trying so hard not to think of Niu Lang that he is all I can see before me. I wonder for a moment whether I should simply close my eyes and pretend he is here, accept the Prince's caresses as his and forget where I truly am.

"I hope you have been given everything you need," says the Prince.

"Yes," I say.

"Your magpies are delightful," he says. "A gift?"

"From my family," I lie.

He smiles. "A charming wedding gift," he says. "True love."

I nod. My lips are stretched out across my teeth but I am not sure I am smiling.

Finding me a poor conversationalist he begins to undress, his movements brisk and practical. I slowly return to my position on the edge of the bed.

"Be at ease," he says.

I make my way to the far side of the bed and cover myself entirely with the coverlets. The eunuch did not unbind my hair and the elaborate pinnings feel awkward if I lie on my side, so instead I lie on my back and look up at the ceiling. I hear the Prince reach the bedside and then the largest lantern goes dark, leaving the room in a dimmer light as he reaches out to touch me.

I try not to cry. But the tears start as soon as the Prince touches me and I cannot make them stop. It is not the pain, although there is a little pain. It is not his touch, for as far as I can tell he is gentle enough. He offers caresses and even a few words of tenderness, although since he barely knows me he might as well be speaking to any of his ladies, there is nothing meant only for my ears. He does not rush to take his pleasure but once he has done so, once it is all over, he strokes my cheek and finds the tears which he could not see in the dim light.

"Did I hurt you?" he asks.

I shake my head.

He rolls onto one arm, looking down at me where I lie, still and silent. I can just make out the shape of him in the darkness. "Is something wrong? Are you unhappy here?"

What answer could I give that would be acceptable? What can I say? There is nothing to say, so I say nothing. But this does not satisfy him.

"Speak to me, Ula Nara," he says. "Tell me what is wrong."

"There is nothing wrong," I whisper. "I am sorry, Highness."

"You may call me Bao," he says.

I nod.

"You must tell me what is wrong," he says. "I will make it right."

I want to laugh. Really? Will he send me away from here, back to Niu Lang, if I tell him that I have been taken away from my beloved, that I can never love anyone else?

"It is nothing, High – Bao," I say.

He tries again the next time I am summoned. My tears flow and he tries to find out what is the matter. And again. After those three times, I am no longer summoned. He treats me with every courtesy in public but he does not walk alone with me in the garden, as he does daily with Lady Fuca and sometimes makes time for Su or Gao, or even, more rarely, Zhemin and Wan. Each of us is called in dutiful turn to his bedchamber except for myself and Wan, whose body has yet to develop a womanly form. The Prince is tired of my tears, my silent refusal to name the source of my unhappiness. He does not wish to lie with a woman who weeps and weeps and yet cannot be comforted.

Winter comes and buries our tiny world in an unending whiteness.

Fuca, Wan, Zhemin and Su throw snowballs and giggle together, while Gao wades through the thick drifts in her high boots, her face solemn. I sometimes wonder if she, too, has a secret sorrow, but I do not have the energy to ask her, to create enough of a friendship to allow for such confessions. So we stand, the two of us, silent and apart from the others, watching a world we should be a part of yet cannot seem to join.

Our husband proves his virility as first one lady and then another lets it be known that she is with child. Zhemin almost disappears to her rooms, stricken with a constant nausea that means the kitchen can only prepare the plainest of cold food for her, hardly warming fare in the freezing late winter. I see her anxious face at the windows sometimes and wave to her but she only waves back and disappears again from sight. Su spends most of her time resting, for her pregnancy seems to weary her delicate beauty, she looks pale and tired. I visit her occasionally with Wan and we play board games together, but her rooms are kept at a temperature that I find stifling.

Only Fuca blooms. Her belly swells and her demeanour becomes ever more joyful. Her child will be born first and the Prince sets aside more and more time to spend with her, enchanted with her health and happiness. I see them sitting side by side on the garden swing as the weather turns towards spring, heads together, hands clasped. I hear their laughter and have to turn away. They remind me of what Niu Lang and I should have been. Instead, I have been chosen for a life I never wanted and I am not even successful at it: uncalled for, friendless except for Wan.

"You must try a little harder, my lady," says Dan Dan one day.

"What do you mean?" I ask her, stroking the male magpie who has come to eat from my hand. The female is nesting, I offer them little twigs and scraps of cloth and they diligently weave a home for their future eggs.

"You must try harder to be happy here," she says.

"How?" I ask.

"Make friends with the other ladies. Spend time with them. They will be your companions in this life for many years to come, there is no use in petty jealousies."

"I am not jealous of them," I say, although this is not quite true. I am jealous of them for finding some small happiness here. I am jealous of the love between Fuca and the Prince, so open and easy, far away from what I may ever attain.

"Then make friends," insists Dan Dan. "I have served the Imperial Family for many years, my lady. The happiest women are those who find friends amongst their companions, who seek some joy in their husband's company."

"I am no longer called for," I say.

"Begin with the ladies," says Dan Dan. "Make friends and find some happiness in your daily life. When the Prince sees your changed demeanour he will call for you again. He is good to his ladies, he is a man of virtue. He seeks harmony. He will gladly call for you again if he sees that you desire his company."

I do not desire his company, I think, but I nod and Dan Dan goes about her business, satisfied.

I force myself to spend more time with the other ladies but Gao is too solemn and silent for my liking. Zhemin and Su are about to birth their children, they are wrapped up in their own little worlds. I see them sitting together, chattering of babies and mothering. I cannot bring myself to join them for long. They sense my boredom and politely try to speak of other things but I know that they would rather return to their most-beloved topic and so I leave them to it. Wan, as ever, is a good friend, but I cannot spend every day with her.

"You should walk with the Prince," she suggests, seeing my isolation. "He is very kind. And he talks of many interesting things.

Have you seen his collection of clocks? He showed me how they work inside, all little cogs and wheels that turn. He let me wind one," she adds, like a child indulged by a loving father.

Dan Dan also encourages me, seeing how much time I spend alone. "The Prince might be a friend, at least?"

I tell myself that I do not need to love the Prince. I could be a pleasant companion to him. There is no need to be called to his bedchamber, he has enough women for that and more will be added over the years. I could simply be a woman with whom he can converse and share his interests. I have been well educated. I can read and write, recite poetry, I can play board games and paint a little. My calligraphy was praised by my tutors. Perhaps he would welcome such a friendship and I would not be untrue to Niu Lang, merely far away from him.

"Your collection of clocks is very fine," I begin, the next time I see him.

He looks my way and his face brightens for a moment but Fuca laughs.

"He is obsessed, Ula Nara! Do not talk to him of those clocks or you will never hear the end of it!"

At once his attention returns to her. "You do not understand their beauty," he says, teasingly. "Or perhaps you are simply jealous of the attention I give them?"

She giggles. "Are they more beautiful than I am?" she asks. "I think they must be, the amount of time you spend polishing them, dusting them, winding them. You are their servant!"

"I am your servant," he says, taking her hand and kissing it. "And none of them can match your beauty. You are without equal."

I look away from their faces, so bright with love and tenderness.

When Fuca retreats to her rooms and is delivered of a girl, I think that perhaps now Prince Bao will have more time for the rest of us while she is occupied elsewhere and besides, she has not given him a son. But he almost disappears entirely into her palace, visiting at all hours of the day and night to coo over his child. When both Zhemin and Su produce sons I set aside hope of a relationship of any kind with him. It is clear to me that I am superfluous to requirements. I cannot offer love, nor children, nor even hero worship as Wan seems to. I have been chosen for no reason, he would barely notice my absence were I to disappear or die, yet I have given up the man I love at the command of his mother, Lady Niuhuru.

I see his mother again for the first time since I was chosen, when we visit the court. Once more we enter the Forbidden City, this time not as candidates but as the chosen few, concubines to a man who will one day become an emperor. Everywhere we turn people bow to us, the eunuchs are excessively servile, maids scurry to do our bidding. We are dressed in our finest robes, our hair is bejewelled, we are the future of this court and the older concubines look at us with something approaching fear. The Emperor is still a man in the prime of life, of course, but on the day he dies, they will be banished to the back palaces, crumbling draughty places while we take their exquisite palaces and make them our own.

The Emperor sits in his carved throne, high above us. His Primary Consort, the Prince's mother Niuhuru, sits by his side.

"Why is she not the Empress?" I ask Wan, who always seems well-informed on court politics.

"She asked not to be named Empress," says Wan, her eyes wide at the very thought. "There was rivalry amongst the ladies and she did not wish to be the source of it."

"But she is still the Primary Consort," I say. "She is treated as an empress and she must carry out all the duties of the role. Why not take the title?"

Wan shrugs and shakes her head. It is an odd thing to do. Every lady of an emperor dreams of being made an empress, it is the pinnacle of achievement, superseded only by being a living dowager empress, mother to an emperor. The current Emperor's mother died within a short time of him taking the throne, so she did not even live long enough to fully enjoy the role.

We kowtow, the little group of us, Fuca at the front, leading the way, her every move perfectly formed, the epitome of grace. Prince Bao looks on, beaming, as his children's names are read out before the court, each lady who has birthed a child blushing with rightful pride. Those of us who have not yet produced a child lower our eyes, for no-one will care much for us until we have done so.

The Yongzheng Emperor looks weary, his face is pale and although he pauses in his work to celebrate his son's offspring and to greet each of us kindly, still a eunuch hovers by his side, holding a sheaf of papers.

"You must excuse me," says the Emperor. "I have much work to do."

We all kowtow again and he nods, distracted. I watch him as he takes up a writing brush dipped in the vermillion ink reserved for the Emperor alone and, frowning, looks through the folded papers he is being handed, writes a few notes here and there, passes them on to another eunuch and reaches out for yet more papers.

"He looks tired," I say quietly to Wan.

She nods. "He works very hard," she says. "They say he stays up late at night and then rises early again, he barely sleeps four hours each night. He drinks an elixir of longevity every day, for he says the empire will need much work for many years to come. He wishes to stamp out corruption, reform the taxes and ensure better provision for the very poor, such as orphans."

He sounds more like an diligent administrator than the Son of Heaven. "And his ladies?"

Wan shrugs. "He is not particularly interested. They are called for very seldom. He is a very dutiful man."

I look at the small gathering of older concubines and nod. Certainly he has very few ladies for an emperor. His father was known for having dozens of them. I wonder whether his taste does not lean that way, although from what Wan has told me of him it sounds as though he is simply too wrapped up in his work. Judging by the Prince's current behaviour I suspect he will be more like his grandfather than his father. I wonder what it will be like to have more and more ladies added to our numbers over the years. I shake my head a little. What do I care? It is not as if I will be jealous of them. I do not love the Prince. If there are plenty of concubines then I will continue not to be called for, which will be a relief to me.

"Lady Ula Nara."

I turn and find myself face to face with Niuhuru, the Prince's mother. I begin to kneel but she reaches out to stop me. Her face is very pale and up close her eyes are an odd grey colour that I have never seen before. As I recalled, she is considerably taller than I am, I have to look up to her.

"I hope that…" she begins and then clears her throat. "Are you well?" she begins again.

I know she is remembering the moment when she chose me, when I begged her to reconsider, her hesitation when she looked at the Chief Eunuch and was swayed to let her decision stand, when she looked over her shoulder to see me on all fours on the cobbles of the courtyard, my weeping as she chose my fate for me against my will. I look at her. I should assure her that I am well, that I have been much honoured by her choice of me for her son, that I am very happy here.

I cannot shape the words. I gaze into her grey eyes and say

nothing. I watch as she waits for the reassurance she so badly wants and then the dawning realisation that I am not going to speak, that the damage she did to my life was greater than can be forgotten so lightly, so glibly.

At last she swallows. The silence between us is growing too long, it will be remarked upon. "I wish you happiness in your marriage to the Prince," she manages, as though she were some lowly courtier seeking to ingratiate herself. I only bow my head. I cannot find it in me to forgive this woman, who allowed protocol to override mercy and now wishes to be forgiven for it. There is a cold splinter trapped in my heart and she is the one who put it there.

Summer comes. The heat in Beijing is stifling. I think that it is almost a year since I was chosen and I wonder where Niu Lang is now. I wonder how he spends his days: whether in sadness or whether his life, of meditation and prayers, of constant and arduous physical training in martial arts, has brought a peacefulness to his life without me that I cannot seem to find without him.

"Tomorrow we will visit the Garden of Perfect Brightness," announces the Prince at breakfast. "We must leave very early to have time to walk around all of it, so that you can see how beautiful it is and how many great works are being undertaken there."

The sun has barely risen when we set off. I realise that, with the exception of the Forbidden City, only a short distance away, this is the first time I have left the Prince's palace since I was brought here. My world has grown smaller than I could ever have imagined.

To speed up our journey we are carried in mule-drawn wagons, something like merchants would travel in, but these have been equipped with as much luxury as possible, we are seated on thick cushions while silken drapes protect us from the gaze of any common passers-by, the wagon is surrounded by an escort of guards. The Prince rides ahead of us.

Fuca, as ever, is all bubbling happiness. "I am so excited to see the Garden," she says. "The Prince loves it so much. He has great plans for it."

I think that no doubt she knows all about his plans, for they spend so much time together, he shares all his thoughts with her. For all that she was chosen for her family's noble background, for her good breeding and elegance, somehow the heavens smiled on her match to the Prince, they genuinely love one another. I think with bitterness that I, too, could have had such a marriage if Lady Niuhuru had not chosen me for her son. I, too, could have listened to Niu Lang's plans for the future and shared in his enthusiasm for projects come to fruition. We would have planned our lives together, we would have been happy. I would have given him not one but many children and he would have cooed over them even as the Prince does, delighting in their every tiny gesture.

The other ladies babble together and I turn my face away, my excitement at being out now soured, looking through a tiny gap between the drapes into the world beyond, a world from which I am closed away.

The Yuan Ming Yuan, the Garden of Perfect Brightness, is more beautiful than I expected. My spirits lift a little as we walk along tiny pathways on the edges of large lakes filled with water lilies, over which iridescent dragonflies skim. The Garden is not some small country estate, it is a vast area, criss-crossed with water everywhere, from tiny streams one can step over, to canals and up to the largest lake of all, the Sea of Blessings.

"I grew up here," Prince Bao is saying, his face lit up with joy in his surroundings. "It was such a happy place to be a child. My own children must play here often."

I feel something in me soften towards him. I think of the Prince as a child, playing here by the lake's edge and can see why he loves this place. No doubt he is a good-hearted man. I do not love him, but that is hardly his fault, even as he does not care for me because I was meant for another and cannot help but show it. We should never have come together, each of us already had their own true love: he, Lady Fuca, I, Niu Lang. But he is happy because his true love is by his side, whilst mine has been lost to me forever.

"And now the Western Palaces," Bao announces. "You will be amazed."

I do not like the Western Palaces. The whole area designated for them is in turmoil. The tranquil beauty of the rest of the Garden is shattered here. Heavy squat buildings made of white stone tower over us, their facades over-carved with motifs that mean nothing to me and the whole lacking the delicacy of our own buildings. They are like hulking stone giants, lowering down on us puny mortals. Their whiteness reminds me of death and mourning robes. A few of the buildings are complete, others are half-built, sweating men toiling over their construction, dust everywhere. Piles of materials, felled trees and half-dug trenches threaten to harm us if we do not step carefully. Absurdly, Prince Bao leaps into a trench and tries his hand at the backbreaking work of digging, his silk robes growing stained with sweat and damp earth. Fuca and the others cheer him on, giggling at his efforts, but I stand back. He is like a child showing off to his mother, expecting applause for some foolish parody of a grown man's labour. At last he climbs out, grinning as though he has done something worthy of praise, then summons us to come closer and hear how the plans are progressing from his chosen architect, a Jesuit priest named Lang Shining, although the Prince addresses him as Giuseppe, apparently his original name. He is dressed as a scholar might be here, in long black robes and a tall black hat, all of which have become covered in dust and mud in a way that would be most unbecoming of any scholar. His face and forearms are sunburnt to a deep walnut, his eyes are a rich brown and he has a dark curly beard. He must be in his forties, a similar age to the Emperor and indeed the Prince talks to him as a child might a beloved father, with an eager expectation of being humoured mixed with respectful awe at his abilities.

"He is building a maze," he informs us, then turns back to Giuseppe with a laugh. "Will people really get lost in it?"

The Jesuit smiles, humouring him. "For a little while."

"Make it harder!" says the Prince and the other ladies all laugh. He turns to Fuca. "Giuseppe is building a maze in which you will get utterly lost," he says. "I will have to come and rescue you. You will be wandering there until it is dark!"

She smiles up at him and touches his arm. "I know you would rescue me before dark fell," she says confidently. "You would not leave me to wander alone and afraid."

He covers her hand with his and offers her a tender smile. "I would run to your side at once," he assures her and they gaze at one another. Some of the other ladies give forced giggles, no doubt each of them wishing the Prince would jest like this with them. I look away, wondering for how many years I will have to watch a loving relationship at close quarters whilst being barred from one myself.

At last we leave the works. The Prince promises that we will return soon, for another inspection. He plucks yellow flowers from a bush as we pass it and spends a few moments clumsily pinning it into Fuca's hair while she laughs at his efforts. "The maze should have Imperial yellow flowers planted all about it," he calls back to the Jesuit, who bows as we depart the Garden and return to our tiny world.

The Qixi Festival comes and goes. I see some of the unmarried maids giggling together, taking their little embroidery samples to the temple.

As darkness falls I feel an eagerness grow in me. Tonight Niu Lang and I will gaze at the stars together and we will be united in spirit. I should not be celebrating this festival any more, for it is only for unmarried girls, but I cannot feel that I am truly married to the Prince. So in secret I have been stitching a little sample of my embroidery: two magpies entwined, like the ice carving Niu Lang made for me. I cannot take it to a temple of course, but I go early in the morning to the part of our lake that tapers off into a stream, which leaves the palace complex. I drop it into the slow-moving current, thinking that in this way I have made an offering and perhaps the Lovers will accept it as proof of my undying love for my own beloved.

The night is warm and as soon as the first stars can be seen I make my way into my own little courtyard garden. I look up at the vast dark sky and the tiny sparkles of each star. When I make out the Lovers' stars I wait a few moments but feel only emptiness. Niu Lang promised me that on this night we would be together in spirit but I feel nothing. What had I expected? That we would magically be together? That I would hear the fluttering of my magpies' wings, turn and see him standing by my side, come to his beloved, as his namesake the Cowherd once did in a land of fairytales? The stars glow in the dark night sky and I stand alone, whatever romantic notions I had for my life fading. The cold realisation sweeps over me that I will never see Niu Lang again, neither in spirit nor in body. I will live out my life in this enclosed world without love or friendship. I cannot even be a well-bred companion to the Prince, for he loves elsewhere and has already discarded me as a bedfellow. I will never be released from this place, from this marriage, except by Prince Bao's death or my own. I wonder which will come first.

"Are you well, Ula Nara?" It is Fuca.

"I am well," I reply stiffly, wondering why she has sought me out.

She is quiet for a moment, gazing at the stars before she speaks again. "I would like you to be happy here," she says at last.

"Why?" I ask, before I can stop myself. "You are happy here, why do you care if I am?"

She nods, as if what I am saying has confirmed something for her. "I care because I am Bao's Primary Consort," she says gently. "It is not my purpose simply to seek my own happiness in marriage. It is my purpose to care for all of His Highness' ladies, for the rest of my life. I am to choose his brides, to ensure they settle well into this life, strange as it may be. It is my role to set them a good example."

"You should have had a son then," I say spitefully. I cannot bear to hear Fuca, who has everything I could wish for, tell me that she wants me to be happy.

She is quiet again. "I pray one day I will be fortunate enough to bear a son," she says at last, with no hint of anger or hurt at my insult. "Meanwhile my daughter is a blessing to myself and the Prince." She does not remind me that I have not borne any children at all. "If you ever wish me to help you in any way, Ula Nara, I will willingly do so," she says, and then she walks away, towards her own palace.

I swallow. I have been unforgivably rude to the Prince's Primary Consort, a future Empress. I should be afraid. But there is a little bit of me that took pleasure in speaking hurtful words, in lashing out at Fuca's eternally sunny disposition. I find myself, sometimes, thinking of what else I could have said to hurt her, to make her as unhappy I am.

The Lovers' Festival has passed. Barely ten days later, the Festival of Hungry Ghosts is upon us. There is food laid out all over the palace complex for the ghosts who will walk among us when night falls, searching for food and worship to assuage their hunger. There are huge halls laid out with long tables covered with food and smoking incense, at which nobody sits, for these places are reserved for the dead. On this day the gates of the underworld open up and ghosts come wandering into our world. There are those who are our own ancestors, whom we honour by burning models of what they may be in need of in the other world: paper houses and money, horses and servants. There is food that they may eat. But there are other ghosts, unknown to us, unvenerated by their families, who are hungry and yet can never be filled. Afraid of the misfortune they might bring upon a family, food is also left for these wandering souls, hoping to appease their never-ending hunger. Every temple displays vast platters of food and even the maids and eunuchs place little offerings of food to add to the sacrifices. The temples' altars are heavy with offerings of food and incense, paper in vast quantities is burnt, folded and painted into the shapes of horses, money, food, houses, ploughs, palanquins and more, all of which will come to life in the afterworld and be at the service of those who came before us.

I wake that night to the clattering of guards running in our courtyard, a scream in the darkness from Fuca. I jump out of my bed and hurry to the window, where I see her form in lantern-lit shadows, hair loose and dishevelled, robes still being put on by servants who cluster around her before she is hurried into a palanquin, whose bearers run out of our courtyard at full tilt.

"They say the Prince is very ill and Fuca has been sent for," murmurs Dan Dan by my side.

I watch the palanquin as it rocks unsteadily away at top speed with Fuca inside it, the only one of us summoned, each of us reminded again of our worth to the Prince by this choice. Outside I can see Wan is already speaking with the guard. Everyone tells everything to Wan, her delicate features and wide eyes inviting confidences so that she is always the best informed of all of us. I make my way to her, as do my fellow concubines.

"They think Bao has been poisoned," Wan says, tears brimming in her eyes. "They say he was at a banquet in the Forbidden City and they believe his own brother Hongshi sat beside him and slipped poison into a dish that he ate from. They say his tongue has turned black. His mother and the Emperor are in attendance with the Court Physician."

The other girls gasp and chatter. I wonder what will happen to me if the Prince dies and I am widowed. Will I be handed a white silk scarf and encouraged to *follow-in-death*, as the Manchu women of old would have done? Probably not. These days it is more usual to become a 'chaste widow': to never remarry and instead live a life devoted to the memory of my deceased husband. But there is a part of me that wonders whether I might be permitted to remarry after all. I know that a few women are. I am childless, young. I am not an emperor's concubine. I am not even the Prince's Primary Consort. I might be sent back to my family. I might marry Niu Lang after all. My hands are shaking.

"Let us all sit together and comfort one another," says Wan, after Zhemin has had a fit of hysterical crying and it has taken three maids to calm her down again.

Reluctantly, I follow the others into the dining hall, where the maids light the lanterns, then bring hot tea and little dishes of sweets and nuts, of dried and fresh fruit, as though any of us would wish to eat in the middle of the night while our destinies hang in the balance.

We sit, mostly in silence, only broken by Zhemin still sniffling to herself. The lanterns burn on and on as the long dark night proceeds to a watery dawn and finally the arrival of a messenger who comes to tell us that all is well, the Prince will recover. Zhemin breaks into hysterical weeping again, unable to manage her emotions one way or another.

"I will go to the temple to give thanks," says Wan and Su follows her. Gao looks at me.

"I am going to bed," I say, although when I stand I feel my knees give way and have to clutch at the table to stop myself falling.

Fourteen days after the Festival of Hungry Ghosts, lanterns must be lit to guide the spirits home, for fear that any should stay here in our world. Each of us places tiny lanterns in the little stream that feeds our lake and then watch as they bob in the darkness. Each light that goes out is a spirit returning home. I sit by the lake long after all the flames have gone out, the darkness all around me a strange comfort. I cannot see my surroundings, can imagine that I am somewhere else, perhaps in a household of my own, with Niu Lang somewhere nearby.

The poisoning of the future heir cannot go unpunished and we are all summoned to the Forbidden City to watch the wrath of an empire fall on Hongshi, older brother but discarded heir. For once Yongzheng does not look like a weary scribe, he looks like an Emperor, his thin body encased in the heavy Imperial yellow silk that marks the Son of Heaven. Niuhuru, at his side, is white-faced and grim-mouthed. Hongshi is nowhere to be seen but his mother, Lady Qi, stands before the thrones, her hands clenching and unclenching.

"The son of this miserable woman is sent to the Cold Palace, he has been banished from the Forbidden City," begins Yongzheng and Lady Qi falls to her knees. "This unworthy son's name has been stricken from the *yudie*, jade plate."

Lady Qi wails.

I swallow. Hongshi's name has been erased from the Imperial Genealogical Record. He will no longer be listed as the Emperor's son. This is what a court can do to those who fail to comply with its rules and expectations, who dare to challenge it.

"We can only hope," continues Yongzheng, "that this dishonour will lead him to take the only possible action expected of a man."

Lady Qi screams and sinks to her knees.

I look at Wan, whose slight frame is shaking at the spectacle. I take her hand to try and comfort her. I wonder whether it would have been us, standing here, asked to take our lives, if the Prince had died.

Now Niuhuru speaks. "Lady Qi will be removed from her palace and will join previous ladies of the court in the back palaces."

Lady Qi crawls towards the throne, her voice ragged with sobs. "I ask for mercy. For my undeserving son and for myself, his unworthy mother."

"No mercy will be granted," says Yongzheng. He rises to his feet as Lady Qi's arms are grasped by the guards, who drag her screaming from the room.

The room empties quickly once the Emperor leaves but I linger by a large embroidered screen, half-hiding myself so that I will not be expected to visit the Prince in his sickroom, as the other ladies are about to do: what would he want to see me for? I do not want to cluster with the courtiers and hear more whispering gossip, I have seen and heard enough for one day. I feel sick to my stomach.

I trace the design of the screen for a few moments, feeling the silk beneath my fingertips, a pattern of delicate blossom against a mountain vista. At last I take a deep breath and compose myself. I will return to the Prince's household.

But there is a whispering going on in the huge empty room, the murmur of voices. I look out from the screen and see Niuhuru standing alone with the Jesuit Lang Shining, or Giuseppe as the Prince called him, although I cannot pronounce it.

I frown. Niuhuru's hand is on the Jesuit's sleeve as though they were close friends, their eyes are fixed on one another as she speaks.

"I cannot live like this," she says. "I cannot, Giuseppe."

"Come to the Garden of Perfect Brightness," he says, as though he has the right to invite her anywhere.

Behind me a maid appears, whom I wave away, losing track of what else the Jesuit has said to Niuhuru. When I look at them again her eyes are filled with tears and his hand is placed over hers, their bodies so close they could kiss with the slightest movement forwards. For one moment I think they will actually do so, before she steps back and hurries away, almost running, as though to stay one moment longer is to risk a terrible temptation. I stare. Have I just caught a glimpse of a forbidden relationship between the Emperor's Primary Consort and a Jesuit? It cannot be and yet the way they looked at each other was full of love and longing, full of fear of being seen. I cannot believe it.

The Jesuit is standing looking down at the floor, his face grave. I step out from behind the screen and approach him.

"You are a great comfort to Lady Niuhuru," I say.

He turns, startled. He had not seen me, believed himself to be alone. His eyes flicker towards the doorway where Niuhuru has just left, perhaps wondering what I have seen between them. My eyes widen. I am right. His eyes, his reaction, have told me everything, as though he had fallen on his knees and confessed it. But he is too good a courtier not to know how to smooth over this moment.

"Lady Ula Nara," he says, bowing. "You must be relieved that the Prince is making a recovery."

I want to laugh. Surely the gossiping maids have made half the court aware by now that the Prince has no interest in me. "Lady Fuca is by his side," I say.

"Of course," he agrees, a little flustered at my lack of courtly politeness. "Although I am sure he would find the care of any of his ladies a comfort at this time."

I will not allow this to go unchallenged, for him to keep repeating untrue statements while he tries to cover up what I have just witnessed. "His Highness only has eyes for Lady Fuca," I say bluntly.

He forces a smile. "Considering what has just happened, it is best to put aside rivalries if possible," he says. "We must take love where we find it and be content with what we find."

I look down at his sleeve, where a few moments ago Niuhuru's hand and his own were touching. "Take love where we find it," I echo. Does he think he can fool me, that he can take away what I have seen? Or is he confessing to me, allowing me to know some of the pain he feels in loving a woman who is absolutely forbidden to him? For a moment I think of Niu Lang and wonder, will I still feel this pain when I, too, am forty?

"I will leave you now, your ladyship," the Jesuit says and bows, then walks away swiftly, his body tense as though he can feel my gaze on him, can feel the knowledge in my eyes following him.

And so my life in the Prince's household continues. He makes a full recovery and life goes on as it did before, we women daily bejewelled and coiffed for the benefit of a man whom we do not even see each day, a man who loves only one and merely lusts for a few others, the rest of us already discarded before we have even reached our full maturity. Wan fills out a little and is summoned to the Prince's bedchamber once or twice but then seems to be as little desired as Gao and I, although she does not seem to care. Wan and the Prince seem to have achieved what I have failed at: they are friends. He sends her little gifts including a puppy, walks and talks with her, teases her as though she were a beloved younger sister while she makes fun of him in a way few of us would dare and this seems to content both of them.

"Don't you want more?" I ask her once, exasperated by her eternally sunny disposition.

"You left a happy family and a sweetheart to be here," she reminds me, her face solemn for once. "I left a home where I was beaten and worse. Here I am safe and cared for, with friends and a man who will protect me from any harm. I have been set free."

I nod, although I want to tell her that her notion of what life could offer has been stunted by her miserable beginnings. But I am unhappy enough, I do not wish to take away her contentment.

The early autumn arrives. My magpies are so tame I sometimes let them out of their aviary and they will go for brief flights before returning to me, to sit nearby and wait to be fed tidbits. I walk in the garden, watching golden gingko leaves twist in the air as they fall, the red swirling bodies of the fish rising for food in the pond at the sight of me. There is a beauty to the natural world that gives me comfort and I think of the Garden of Perfect Brightness, wondering whether we will be able to visit it again soon. Perhaps, when one day Bao is made Emperor, we will all live there every summer. The thought brings me some small happiness.

Up ahead I hear laughter and rounding the corner I catch sight of the Prince and Fuca. She is pressed up against the trunk of a red-leafed maple tree, its leaves entwined in her tumbling hair, which has escaped its gold and jade pins to fall down to her waist. The Prince's face is bowed to her neck, then lower to the top of one breast, half exposed through her unbuttoned silk robe. He is covering her with kisses and caresses, her face tilted up to the sky, eyes closed in delight.

I should turn away. I should hurry back through the twisting black rocks to another part of the garden or to my own rooms, should look away from their moment of intimacy and yet I cannot. I watch them, one hand on the cold black rock, the other clenched by my side. I watch their caresses and hear their whispers, I see their desire grow and in the end, shameless and choked with my own unmet desire, I watch their coupling, the wild intensity of it followed by the softness of their embrace, their secret murmurs as they leave the garden dishevelled and sated. I watch and know that this, what I have seen, has been taken from me without my knowledge, without my consent, that this happiness has been lost to me without even knowing it could exist.

The cold days draw closer. One night the heavy thud of running men in armour comes again to our quiet world and brings the announcement that we did not expect to hear for many years. The Yongzheng Emperor has died, overworked by his own diligence. The golden box hidden behind the throne in the Palace of Heavenly Purity is opened with much ceremony to reveal the name that all the world already knew would be there. Prince Bao is named the Qianlong Emperor and we, his women, are called to the Forbidden City.

Rain falls on the dark water of the lake in our garden as we leave, the Lovers' tears falling from Heaven.

Rosewood

THE FORBIDDEN CITY IS FOGGED with incense, the choking fragrant clouds billowing everywhere we turn as the weather grows colder. We wear white mourning robes for the Yongzheng Emperor, our pale faces disappearing into collars of thick white fur, our black hair unbound in grief and startling in contrast, whipped about our faces by the winter's winds.

If I thought I was lonely before, now I know the true meaning of the word. Where once we women all lived together and there was at least some company whether you wished for it or not, now we are isolated even from each other. Our palanquins clustered together one last time as we travelled through the vast stretches of the Outer Court on that first day when we entered the Forbidden City as the new Emperor's ladies, before one after another disappeared into a different gateway. Each of us has been assigned to a grand palace of our own, our meals will be taken alone unless we are called on to attend a formal banquet.

I walked from room to room inside my new palace, spaces which dwarfed my previous accommodation. The rooms were strangely empty, stripped bare of all but a few necessary items of furniture.

"The palace has only just been vacated and the furnishings returned to storage," the eunuch accompanying me said. "You must order whatever you wish in the way of decoration and furniture from the Imperial storerooms, it will be sent at once."

I wonder who the woman was that I dislodged. A previous

concubine of the Yongzheng Emperor, now relegated to a back palace, her status gone in the dying breath of her husband. I noted, too, that whoever she was, her furnishings were not really her own, even if she chose them and lived with them for many years. They belong to the empire and they were taken away when she was no longer highly-ranked enough to have them about her.

Now I may choose furnishings to surround myself with, from the items befitting my rank as newly-made Consort to the Emperor, while Fuca chooses from the more exalted storage rooms and furnishings which only an empress may command the use of.

Alone in my hastily re-decorated palace I stand with a rosewood *ruyi* in my hands, the ceremonial sceptre I was given as each lady stepped forward to be acknowledged by the new Emperor, our husband, Qianlong. His old name is now taboo, we must not speak his childhood name nor his princely title. Each of us was given a new title, a *ruyi* to clasp, a list of entitlements read out: taels of silver, bolts of silk, servants. Our entitlements did not include friendship, love, nor even the sating of suppressed desire. Only material goods, with which I am now surrounded in abundance.

"Your ladyship?"

I lay down the *ruyi* and turn to the eunuch who is managing the arrangement of each new household. "Yes?"

"Your new chief attendants."

A wizened old maid, gnarled hands and a hunched bony frame, as old as Dan Dan but less pleasant in demeanour, bowing.

"My name is Ping, ladyship."

"Ping is a very experienced maid, ladyship. She has served in the Forbidden City all her life," the eunuch assures me.

I wonder why Ping did not take her freedom when it was granted, leave while she was still young, why a woman would choose to remain here as a maid, unmarried and childless, forever serving the whim of one pampered court lady after another. I nod to her and look to the man who is to become my senior eunuch, head of my household. A tall man, broad of shoulder, he has a masculine air about him, unlike the other eunuchs, most of whom are fairly short and tend towards a soft plumpness.

"Feng, ladyship," he says, bowing.

"Feng is not *perfectly pure*, your ladyship," says the other eunuch a little worriedly as he sees me looking Feng up and down. "If this concerns you, you have only to say."

Most eunuchs, I know, are castrated at a young age, before they are grown to men, making them *perfectly pure*. But some men choose to become eunuchs at a later age, once grown to their full manhood, and these, having known life as a man, cannot be classed as such.

I shrug. "He may stay."

The eunuch bows. "You will have other servants attached to your palace, of course," he assures me. "But Feng will be the head of your household and Ping will be your chief maid."

I nod. I do not much care who serves me.

The Forbidden City swallows us up, our small group vanished into the endless courtyards and palaces, pomp and ceremony. All of us have multiple court robes made ready, we are obliged to carry out endless rituals to promise prosperity and happiness, fertility and good harvests for the empire, now that a new Emperor has been crowned. My days seem endlessly to be spent in temples, praying for harvests or rain, sun or good crops. When I return to my rooms I hold the rosewood *ruyi* in my hands and wonder: is this what I gave up love for? For the title of Consort to an emperor and a carved rosewood sceptre? For the bowing of the courtiers as I pass them and heavy robes of silk in a yellow shade not *too* close to the Imperial yellow that Fuca may now wear as Empress?

We sit for the coronation portraits, each of us women dressed alike, our hair and make-up the same. As court painter, the Jesuit is commissioned for this most important work and he labours for many hours while we sit in perfect silence, our posture upright, our lower lips stained vermillion. When the portrait is complete, a long scroll featuring Qianlong and his ladies, it is hard to tell one of us apart from another: not so much an artistic failure on the Jesuit's part, but the result of our transformation into Imperial ladies: the same hair, the same robes, the same makeup. We are modelled on those who came before. Those who come after us will be modelled on our own image, one Imperial woman turning into another down the generations, all of us the same.

Ping knows her work, I cannot fault her service, but she has a taste for telling stories of the history of the Forbidden City that I find both frightening and compulsive listening. Once the night call has gone out, warning that all men must leave the Forbidden City on pain of death, Ping will begin her tales. She does not light enough lanterns in my rooms, even when I ask for more, so that the shadows are deeper than they need to be and her tales can creep about in them.

"Did you know how the Forbidden City was built?" she asks me on my first night.

"The Ming Dynasty's Emperor Yongle ordered it built," I say, thinking back to my history lessons.

"Yes," she says. "It took fifteen years and he press-ganged more than a million men to create it. It has over a thousand buildings and nine thousand, nine hundred and ninety-nine rooms, one less than the rooms of Heaven."

"It is very grand," I say. "Although it does not feel very homely, even here in the Inner Court."

"How could it?" she asks with relish. "Tens of thousands of

labourers died building it. Their vengeful spirits must be locked into every room of the Forbidden City."

I shiver a little and her eyes gleam. "Oh, the labourers are nothing," she says. "Did you not know about the concubines?"

"What concubines?" I ask.

"Yongle had hundreds of Korean girls brought to the Forbidden City as his concubines, for he admired their beauty. But one of the concubines had an affair with a eunuch and when she was discovered she took her own life."

"How sad," I say, hoping Ping will stop talking.

"Oh, that was only the beginning," she says with satisfaction. "When the Yongle Emperor found out about the affair he had every Korean concubine slaughtered, their bodies sliced up into pieces."

"I am going to bed," I say.

But on the following night Ping is ready with the next part of the story. "Only one Korean concubine survived," she says. "A Lady Cui, who was a favourite and had been ill during the massacre. She returned to see the bodies of her fellow concubines lying in pools of blood, their limbs hacked off."

I swallow.

"And it seemed Heaven was displeased, for the Forbidden City was struck with lightning and set on fire. Many, many men and women burnt to death."

"And Lady Cui?"

"Ah, she survived. But the Emperor fell ill and died, cursed by the Immortals."

"He was justly punished," I say, a little relieved by the triumph of good over evil in this story.

"He was," says Ping, her wrinkled face shadowy in the darkness of the corner of my room. "But Lady Cui was still not safe. His will insisted that his remaining ladies should never lie with another man."

I think of the women and their relief at having outlived a cruel husband. "Perhaps they were willing to live a quiet life, after all they had seen," I say.

"They were not given the choice," says Ping. "Lady Cui and fifteen other concubines were taken to a quiet hall in the Inner Court and given white silk scarves."

I stare at her in horror.

"They were obliged to take their own lives," says Ping.

She will not stop, even when I ask her to talk of something else. Every night she tells me other stories: of ghostly dogs who run through the tiny paths between the palaces of the Inner Court, of a woman wearing white mourning clothes who weeps and walks but does not reply to those who approach her and fades away as the sun rises. She talks of concubines who loved one another and were discovered and punished, beheaded for daring to find some small measure of happiness here. She tells tales of maids beaten to death for trivial misdemeanours, of desperately poor men who sought to feed their families by entering Imperial service as eunuchs and whose castrations went wrong, leaving them to die in agony and their children to starve to death. It seems she has a different story for every dark night and even though I do not want to hear these stories, still they draw me, so that I listen every time she tells them and then startle at shadows, shiver in fear under my covers, dare not look out of the windows into the darkness of the night, afraid of what I may see there. The Forbidden City, already hard and cold, becomes a place of ghosts to me, of horrors lurking in every one of its nine thousand nine hundred and ninety-nine rooms, with otherworldly beings stalking both the tiny pathways of the Inner Court and the vast open courtyards beyond. I sleep badly and wake often from half-remembered dreams in which I take the place of all these past miserable people who once lived here and now are gone.

I cry out in the dark from a dream in which an unseen person hands me a white silk scarf and I know, from the deep sense of dread I feel, what is expected of me. Awake, I whimper to myself, wishing I had insisted on a lantern to be kept burning all night, too afraid to step out of my bed and light one myself, lest some shadowed half-being should reach out its ghostly hands and touch me.

"Ladyship?"

"Feng," I say, with relief, seeing him framed in the doorway, a lantern in his hand.

"Is anything wrong?"

"I had a bad dream," I say, trying to sound unafraid. "It was nothing."

"I will sleep by your door every night, if you command it," he says.

I want to say no, for I feel like a foolish child, but the dream was too full of dread for me to easily dismiss it and his voice is comforting. "Yes," I say at last. "If it does not disturb you," I add, my voice trailing away.

"It is my honour," he says.

I hear him pad away and then return shortly with a bedroll, which he lays out across the threshold of my closed door. He lies down and covers himself with a blanket before blowing out the lantern. I lie still and take comfort in the sound of his breathing, even when it slows and I know he is asleep, the thought of another living person in my room soothing me until I drift into sleep myself. True to his word, from then on Feng sleeps every night in my room and I am grateful for it. Ping's stories still make me afraid, but at least I know that I have only to cry out and Feng will be awake and at hand.

The Imperial Daughters' Draft comes around again and I wait to see the new faces who will join us. Qianlong is a different man to his father. There are plenty of women chosen this time: official concubines but also many young ladies-in-waiting, for Qianlong wants a bright and lively court, one full of beauty and splendour. An anxious-looking young girl named Qing arrives and tries to befriend me, asking me whether we ladies spend much time together, but I shrug her away. It is only when the ceremony is over and I find myself weeping in my rooms that night that I realise that somewhere in my heart I had hoped Shu Fang would be chosen. This was her year, her chance to be selected and she has not been: she has been returned to our family, to marry whomever she pleases. I think of what it would have been like if she had joined me here. She would have brought her foolish cheerful ways with her, her lightness and romantic notions. She would have made me laugh, would have been my ally in this world of rivalries and constant striving for greater power. Her heart would not have turned bitter here, it was too full of joy. I realise that I will never see her again, will never hear her laugh or shriek my name and I sob and sob as though I will never stop, curled up in my lonely bed in my too-large rooms.

"Ladyship? Is it another dream?"

I shake my head although Feng can barely see me. "I – I miss my sister," I gulp.

In the darkness I see his shadowy figure move towards me, he sits on the side of my bed and gently pats my heaving shoulders. "Tell me about her," he says.

I talk for a long time, an incoherent jumbled mix of our lives together as children and Shu Fang's character, her silly ways. The time we got lost and how cross our father was with us, the way she laughed, a kitten we had and somewhere in all of it there is Niu Lang too, the headstrong boy from next door who was always getting into trouble. How we followed his lead but then hid when trouble came and how he never told on us. The snowball fights and taunts and then the day when something changed, how we passed in a single moment from childish friends to something else which we could not even name, only felt it grow within us, taking form until we acknowledged it fully and by then it was already too late. I fall asleep still talking and when I wake Feng is asleep also, lying by my side, one hand still on my shoulder. At first I pull away, shocked, but then I watch him sleep for a few minutes, thinking of how he patted me throughout my garbled outpouring, never speaking but only listening. I lie back down beside him and pretend to awaken only after he quietly leaves the room and returns to open my shutters, accompanied by maids with hot water, ready to dress me for the day ahead. He does not speak of the night before and neither do I. But soon after that night I wake up with a start, afraid of a dark dream in which Ping's face is too close to me, her wrinkled face turning into something from one of her horror stories and at once Feng is close to me, his hand on my shoulder again, bringing me instant comfort. We do not speak that following day, no agreement is made, but when I retire that night Feng blows out all the lanterns as usual, but instead of retreating to his bedroll I feel his weight on my bed and his hand on my shoulder and that night I sleep better than I have ever done in the Forbidden City. From then on, he sleeps every night in my bed and I feel as though Ping's dark shadows have retreated one step further away.

My days are still lonely, though. Thinking back to Dan Dan I wonder whether she was not in fact right, that I will not survive this life without some friends in this place. So I seek out the women I first came here with, hoping for a friendship I did not cultivate at the time, but find I am too late. Zhemin died just before Qianlong was made Emperor. Su has grown jealous of the new women who have joined our ranks. Although she has given the Emperor two sons and a daughter I am known for not being a favourite and perhaps she feels a friendship with me would tarnish her in some way, so she does not welcome my half-hearted overtures. Gao has retreated from court life, she has taken up a liking for praying and her solemn demeanour now appears almost dour as she makes her way from one temple to another. I am not sure what she prays for, but I cannot find it in myself to become close enough to her to find out. There was a Lady Jin amongst our early numbers but she is busying herself being moved up the rankings as fast as she can and so does not wish anything to do with me. The new women who arrive hope for advancement, they hope to supersede those of us whom they see as already established, they hope the Emperor will want newer, younger women in his bedchamber.

But Qianlong still favours his Empress. Fuca is his true love, he smiles when he sees her, he always has a tender word for her. She has already borne him two sons and there is no doubt that he considers them his first choice as heirs, much to the disappointment of the other women here. Fuca is called often to his rooms, the rest of his ladies are always a second choice as bedfellows. I, of course, am not sent for at all and so cannot even hope for a child one day. The only person in the Forbidden City whom I might still consider a friend is Wan. I visit with her sometimes, although I find her ever-sunny demeanour more grating than anything else as time goes by. How can anyone, no matter what their family background was, find happiness in this place? Wan seems to have a knack for making friends, she is always with one lady or another, always smiling. She likes to fill her hair with flowers and jewels, she has a eunuch whose skills at hairdressing are beyond compare and she sports one elaborate style after another, outdoing even the Empress. Fuca prefers a simpler effect, using only fresh flowers or tiny creations woven from coloured straw, even though the jewellers of the Forbidden City are at her command.

"I don't know how you can spend your whole life just decorating your empty head with flowers and trinkets," I slur to Wan during a drinking game we have been playing too long. "Who is it for? Qianlong treats you like a baby sister. You'll never have a man's real love, you'll just sit here playing stupid games until you're old and wrinkled. You'll die without ever having been loved. Without ever feeling desire." I watch her cheeks flush. The ladies-in-waiting we are playing with look away in embarrassment and I know, even in my drunken state, that I have gone too far. "I am going now," I say and make my way back to my palace, where I vomit and then sleep, waking with a bitter taste in my mouth that has nothing to do with the contents of my stomach. I send flowers, fruits and a note of apology to Wan the next day, which she readily accepts, but after that I visit her less and less, preferring to avoid losing the one person who might feel some kindness towards me, even if that means barely seeing her.

The Western Palaces are complete. Qianlong is delighted. He insists on a special outing, accompanied by his mother and half the court. It is, apparently, a surprise for his mother, and for the rest of us. We make our way there in a never-ending procession of palanquins, surrounded by guards, and servants. When we reach the Garden of Perfect Brightness, he sends most of the group around to the Western Gate, whilst we enter through the Grand Palace Gate in the southern part of the complex. We almost tiptoe through a small passageway, before emerging onto the pathway by the lake. And suddenly a cacophony of noise explodes around us, and most of the ladies squeal with surprise. For the whole pathway is lined with tiny stalls, manned by eunuchs, who are dressed as common street vendors, pretending to sell their wares. There are singers and musicians, who have broken into song, which, combined with the shouts of the eunuchs, makes for an unbearable level of noise all around us. The Empress Dowager's face is a mask of barely concealed horror at what her old home has become. No longer is it a quiet retreat, full of flowers and lakes, wildlife and tranquillity. Now it is like a gigantic play, as though we are living inside a theatre. Eunuchs throw handfuls of gingko leaves from the trees above us, painted so that they look like butterflies. They flutter all around us as they fall to the ground and are trampled on. The real butterflies have been frightened away by the noise. All around is clamour and colour, little scenes which we are to observe or even take part in.

Fuca is ready to play her part. She goes from stall to stall, pretending to haggle for items that are hers for the asking.

"Husband!" she cries, giggling, drawing Qianlong's attention to her. "I am being disgracefully taken advantage of! This stallholder is charging me three times what I should pay for a bowl of noodles. You must help me!"

At once he is by her side, laughing, making an outraged face at the eunuch and demanding that he lower the price at once. The eunuch plays along, dropping the price only one tiny bit at a time, until at last, of course, the Emperor is successful and the delicate bowl of exquisitely presented noodles is offered to the Empress.

"They are delicious," she says smiling up at the Emperor. "And now, I must buy a fan."

"There is a stall with fans," he replies, delighted with her enthusiasm. "Let me show you."

The other women, seeing what is required of them, hurry to each stall and pretend to make little purchases, giggling and chattering amongst themselves, each glancing over her shoulder to see if she can draw the Emperor's attention to her. I stand still and watch them, unable to find in myself the spirit of the game being played. Besides, I can see the Empress Dowager's face and she is not happy. She forces a too-bright smile on her face every time her son looks at her, but she is not happy. At last she grasps Qianlong's arm and suggests that we make our way to the Western Palaces. Of course, the Emperor is delighted with this idea and we make our way along tiny paths over canals and streams, to the squat stone buildings from far away, Qianlong's pride and joy. Here we must admire the maze, now complete, and each of us is encouraged to enter it and become lost.

"We must have a festival here," the Emperor declares. His eyes shine with the idea he has in mind. "I will sit in the central pavilion and each of you ladies must try to find your way to me."

"Delightful," says Niuhuru, one hand on a carved flower in the grey stone that makes up the maze's walls. She does not sound delighted.

"And it must be by night, of course," he goes on. "Every lady will be given a little lantern. Think how charming it will look, in the darkness, to see little bobbing lights as they make their way through the maze."

"And is there to be a prize," asks Fuca, clasping his hand in hers. "Perhaps for the lady who reaches you first?" She looks up at him, suggestively, conspiratorially, and I have to look away.

"Of course," he says, his voice low and intended only for her hearing.

We are installed in our respective palaces within the Garden, according to our rank. I see that Niuhuru would prefer to stay in her old palace, a pretty little thing, surrounded by flowers, with an old wisteria trained across it. But apparently this is no longer good enough for her, and she is hustled away, to a larger and grander palace further down the lakeside, her face showing only loss beneath her smiles. I wonder if she knows that I alone can see what she truly feels, having spent enough time smiling to cover my own pain.

"Tell me how you came to serve here," I say to Feng in the darkness one night.

"I had – have a wife," he begins. "We had four children, more

89

than I could feed working as a farmer, there were poor crops for three years and I could not stand by and see them starve. I thought I might find work in the city, so I came to Beijing but there are so many people wanting work here and I could not send back enough money to my wife. I heard of a man who had recently become a eunuch even though he had a family, he was able to enter service in the Forbidden City and his family were fed and clothed well because of it, his eldest son was even able to study a little, so that he might better himself."

I turn towards him and put my hand on his shoulder as he has done on mine all these past nights, and wait.

He draws a ragged breath, tight in his chest as though he has never spoken these words before. "I found the knifers who do the cutting, swore that I would go through with it and borrowed six taels of silver to pay for their work. I got drunk the night before, so drunk. I went to a whorehouse and lay with three women, one after the other and with every woman I cried out my wife's name. In the morning the knifer gave me more spirits to drink, I could barely walk by the time he told me to lie down. He tied me down, so that I could not fight him and bound me up – there – tightly so that I would not bleed away my life, then he gave me a tea to stun me and poured hot pepper tea on my member to numb the pain." He half-snorts at the idea. "The pain was like nothing I had ever felt. I screamed and screamed and cried out that I had changed my mind but it was too late by then, it was done."

His body shudders and when he speaks again it is in half sobs. "They fit a metal plug to ensure that the hole where one may urinate does not close up, then you must walk about the room for three hours, which they must support you to do, for your legs will not hold you up. Then I lay in that room for three days, neither drinking nor urinating. There were times when I did not know where I was and I was afraid that I would die, but on the third day they pulled out the metal plug and I urinated. After that they dismissed me and said I would survive."

I find myself with my arms about him, his arms about me, in a close embrace. I feel pity such as I have never felt before, even my own woes seem insignificant. Tears are running down my face. "And so you came here?"

"After a time. There are princes of the Imperial Family who must find, train and present eight eunuchs a year to the Imperial household and I was lucky to find one who treated me well enough. Once I was in service I could send back money to my village. Now I know that my children and wife are fed and clothed because of my sacrifice."

"What did your wife say?" I ask.

He is silent for a few moments. "She does not know," he says at last. "I could not tell her, could not find the words. She has letters written to me from time to time, asking when I will come and visit them and I cannot reply. She knows I found work but she does not know what I do, what I am now, it would break her heart. She loved me." He is silent again. "I loved her," he says, his voice very low. "I love her still."

And somehow in the darkness our embrace grows tighter and his lips touch the bare skin of my neck and instead of withdrawing I seek out his lips with mine and our bodies press tightly together, as a desperate heat grows between us and our mouths grow violent with the need to find tenderness. I do not know when I fall asleep but I wake bruised and with dark circles under my eyes and do not speak much that day, only wait till night descends again and Feng comes back to my bed.

The nights that follow do not bring love, nor release. They bring an endless hunger that cannot be sated, a bleak lust that neither of us can give up nor gain true pleasure from. Our coupling, if it can be called that, continues, unnamed, unspoken of, silent and sullen, brutal and addictive. We do not speak of it, we only turn to it because we have nothing else, because what we truly want and desire is so far away from us, so far beyond possibility, that this wretched shadow of it must suffice. I think of Niu Lang and wonder if this is a betrayal but it does not feel like it, it is so far from what I felt for him, what I still feel for him, that it does not seem to be wrong on my part. It feels like part of my sadness, part of my longing for him.

A bitterness begins to grow in me, not just the endless sadness that I had almost grown used to but something darker. I find myself watching Fuca more and more, following in her footsteps at court rituals as though by imitating her I might find happiness myself. I watch the way she walks and model my steps on hers, raise my hand as she does, turn my head with her same movement. Back in my rooms, I mimic how she moves before a mirror so that I can better mould myself into her likeness: the way she bows at the temples during rituals, how she takes her place on the throne at Qianlong's side. I bend to greet an imaginary beloved son, smile at an imaginary loving Emperor. Feng catches me at it but does not comment, only watches me in silence as I imitate the only woman I know who has everything her heart desires. I think that others will comment when I bow as she does, turn as she does, mimic her in every way but this court is too wrapped up in its own business, its own secrets and rivalries and whispers, it does not see an out of favour concubine who moves like the Empress.

I go further. I order great tomes of history from the Imperial libraries. I learn all the history of the Qing dynasty, the Ming before them and further back. I learn the histories of the Manchus, the Mongolians, the Han Chinese. I study Confucius and his sayings, I study the teachings of Buddha and the Dao Way. I make it my business to know the correct court etiquette for every occasion. I learn the rituals for every ceremony that the Empress must attend, I follow her to each ceremony and watch what she does, the words she must speak, the movements she must make. I commit hundreds of poems to memory. My days are spent in study more suited to a scholar, on secret observation more suited to a spy. There is nothing else to do here for a woman who is not in favour.

I stand before a mirror, light imaginary incense, bow to the four directions, kowtow. I stand, speak the words of the ceremony for praising the silkworms that are the Empress' sole preserve, it is her task to exalt them for everything they do for our empire.

Feng watches me. "She may die one day," he says, his voice low.

The words hang in the silence between us.

I hear through whispers and alleyways that a concubine has been found with the eunuch. Not one of us, but a concubine from the previous Emperor, one of Yongzheng's women. These past concubines live in the palaces at the back of the Forbidden City. Not that they are palaces in the way ours are. These buildings are battered by time, weathered by snow, sun and rain. The women who live in them share rooms, they do not have the luxury of space that we do. They huddle in these back palaces, forgotten by the court, made nobodies in the dying breaths of an emperor. Most are as old as the Emperor was, which is to say not very old. Some are very young. Chosen for service in the Imperial bedchamber only a year before his death, these girls have not yet reached their twentieth year, and yet their lives are already over. They have not had to *follow-in-death*, as they might have done in the past, but still, their lives are over. Now, it seems, one of the youngest has been found with a eunuch, their naked bodies intertwined, so that there could be no doubt, no dismissal of accusations. The eunuch has been beheaded at once, and now we wait to find out the fate of the concubine. It seems her punishment has been left in the hands of the Empress Dowager. Niuhuru. I think of her, her tall frame, her strange grey eyes, of the look on her face when she chose me for service and watched my life crumble. She showed no pity then, only guilt afterwards. Now she must rule over what will happen to a concubine who dared to dishonour the memory of a man she barely knew.

Word comes. The concubine has been visited by the Empress Dowager, and something passed between them. A white silk scarf. Now we wait. One day, two days, three days and it is done. The concubine, whatever her name was, is no more. I think of Ping's stories of the Korean concubine who lived through a massacre of her peers and then was forced to take her own life. I think of this concubine, following the women from long ago, taking one step and then another onto a wooden stool, her cloud-climbing shoes lifting her high enough for the white silk scarf to do its duty. The sudden moment when the scarf jerked and the concubine was no more. I had thought that Ping's stories were part myths, that perhaps the events she related were not as bad as she made out. Perhaps there were fewer girls, perhaps there were more reasons. Yet here is this concubine, in my lifetime, in this same palace as those who went before, and it is all true. This is what can happen to a woman of the court, to a concubine like myself, if we step out of line. If we offend the man whom we call husband, even though he barely knows us, as we barely know him, still we can be found guilty of dishonouring him. And if we do, this is the fate that awaits us.

"Her name was – " begins Feng.

"Be quiet!" I say quickly. "I do not wish to hear her name."

"You said you wanted to know about her," says Feng.

"I wanted to know what happened to her," I say. "I do not want to know her name." I cannot explain why to Feng. Perhaps it is that I wish for the girl, the concubine, to remain unknown to me, to remain only one of Ping's stories, told in the flickering half-light of darkness. I do not wish her to be a real person, a concubine like me, who turned to a eunuch, as I have turned to Feng. I do not want to think of Feng, beheaded, while I dangle from a white silk scarf. I do not say this. "She is not important," I say.

Feng nods and turns away. Perhaps he understands. Perhaps he, too, does not want to think of such things, knowing he stands too close to them for comfort.

I think of Niuhuru and wonder how she managed to give the order to the concubine. Did she tell her baldly to her face? Did she look down on her from a golden throne and ignore her request for mercy? Was there nothing in her, not one moment of doubt, of horror in what she was asking? If I hated her before, now I hate her more.

More women arrive that summer, including the rarity of a Mongolian girl, tall and pink-cheeked, with fierce eyes and a long-legged clumsy stride, a far cry from the elegant glide practiced by most court ladies. Named Ying, she takes an inexplicable liking to the hapless Qing, who has remained as little favoured as I. I see them walking together in the Garden of Perfect Brightness, hear them laugh and wonder how friendships seem so easily made when they have constantly eluded me. I stroke the silken feathers of my magpies, grateful for their friendliness, their loyalty in returning to my hand when they could leave this place forever, flutter into the bright blue sky and never be seen again.

The Qixi Festival comes round and once again I step out of my rooms when darkness falls and search the sky for the Lovers' stars. They shine bright above me while I strive to feel Niu Lang close to me and fail, as I have always failed. The bitterness that rises up inside me cannot be suppressed, it grows greater all the time as I feed it with my misery. The love I gave up is for nothing. I am one of many, one of so many that I cannot even be picked out from the crowd, a crowd which will only grow larger as the years go by, as the Imperial Daughters'

Draft delivers ever more innocent girls into the dark splendour of the Forbidden City. I have lost a great love and received nothing in return.

I will be paid, I whisper to myself as I stand in the blackness of the night and feel my bare feet grow cold on the stone paving of my palace courtyard. *I will not be one of many. No matter what it takes, I will be chosen from the crowd, the sacrifice I made will be recognised. What I gave up is worth a great price, and it has not been paid.*

I will be paid.

Black Sandalwood

THE FIRST TIME I HAVE a maid beaten it is for something serious: she has been caught stealing, a jade comb was found hidden in her sleeping roll. She will be dismissed, of course, but first she must be beaten.

"You do not need to watch," says Feng, but I do, I watch from a window as she is beaten in the courtyard, Feng's arm coming down again and again and her yelps give me some satisfaction, there is something in her sobs as she is led away that gives me peace, as though it were I sobbing, as though she has taken some of my own pain away.

When Ping tells me months later that another maid must be punished for something less important, some foolish slip which has led to a vase being broken, I tell her that I will beat the girl myself.

"No need," says Ping, looking surprised. "Feng or I will do it."

"No," I say too quickly. "I will do it."

I hesitate before my arm comes down for the first time but once I begin I feel again the strange release, a greater release than my nights with Feng. I bring my arm down over and over and in the end Ping has to pull me away, I have beaten the girl so hard her skin has broken and she is bleeding.

After that I seek out chances to punish. My maids and eunuchs grow fearful of me, for I become known for the severity of the beatings I give on the most minor of pretexts. When my own household grows so cautious, so well behaved that there can be no reason for beating them, I go further afield. I look out for misdemeanours wherever I go, sometimes I will loiter near another woman's palace and catch her maids gossiping or the eunuchs being lazy and report them, watch their beatings from a distance and find a twisted pleasure in them. I listen for secrets whispered in dark corners and find those who have transgressed: stealing, adultery, treasonous plans, all of these somehow fill a gnawing need in me. I draw away from Feng and our dark touches, I allow them now only when I have sated this other need and he learns this, seeks out misdemeanours that he can bring back to me to claim the reward of my skin against his.

He brings me word that Lady Wang, a young concubine, slapped a maid's face. This is forbidden. A woman's face is her fortune, even if she is a maid.

"Who knows about this?" I ask.

Feng shakes his head. "Nobody. Wang and the maid. They were alone in the room at the time."

"Who told you?"

"The maid came to me."

I nod. Feng has developed a reputation of his own, as a eunuch who will handsomely reward any rumours or secrets brought his way.

"Bring the maid here," I say.

I make the maid tell me every detail of what happened, every detail of Lady Wang's bedchamber, which I have never been in. Then I dismiss her and turn to Feng.

"Send for the Chief Eunuch," I say.

I tell the Chief Eunuch that I was present in Lady Wang's bedchamber ("we are great friends," I affirm) and that I was witness to the maid being slapped across the face. Lady Wang, called on to explain herself, stands aghast at my testimony against her. She says I am lying, but I am able to give details of her bedchamber and of the incident that tally perfectly with her maid's account. Lady Wang ends up demoted by a rank and that night Feng and I do not sleep until dawn.

I see other women and even courtiers begin to draw away from me. They fear my interest in them, the way my eyes gleam when I see something that should not be seen, hear something that should not have been said out loud nor even whispered. When I find out that a lady-in-waiting has grown too close to the court perfumier, when a little love note is found and he is whipped while she is dismissed in disgrace I watch it all, my heart beating hard. I know what would happen were Feng and I found out and even the thought of it brings me to a shuddering release greater than I have ever known. I search for greater and still greater misdemeanours, I watch every woman at court trying to find her at fault, trying to find a way in which I can bring her down, to taste a disgrace as bitter as my sadness. There are days when I stare in my mirror and wonder what I am doing, what I am becoming, but I cannot stop, I feel driven to continue.

Feng and I grow closer in our quest. He will whisper to me of what he has heard among the servants, I hiss to him of women who I believe have transgressed, what will happen to them if I can only find proof, he presses against me and describes whippings that have already taken place, those that are yet to come, of beheadings and exiles, of stocks and chains and death by a thousand cuts and in the darkness I dig my golden nail shields into his skin and feel the pain of his teeth on me and somehow in this pain there is a dark joy.

One morning I wake to deep snow. The Forbidden City has disappeared: the golden roof tiles turned to white as though I am no longer here but somewhere else, in another time and place. I think of Niu Lang's ice sculptures and wonder if I could make one, if I could form the snow into shapes from my past. The strange blue light that snow casts seems to change my surroundings and for once, just for once, I feel as though its light might penetrate this darkening life of mine, if it might turn me from the path I have begun to follow. I think that if I walk through the silent City, through the clean white snow, that I may return to my palace a different person, all my fears and bitterness swept away.

As I hurry to dress Feng presses his hands hard against the silk of my half-undone robe but I cannot be with him when my thoughts are filled with Niu Lang. "No," I say and he stands back, bound to obey. But his eyes are dark on me as I finish dressing and I know, can feel, that if he could, if I were not who I am, if he possessed his lost manhood, I would find myself forced to his pleasure against my will.

"My furs," I say to a maid and she brings them.

"Where are you going?" asks Feng.

"Out," I say.

He moves to accompany me but I shake my head. I cannot have him with me, cannot have our dark ways follow me into the clean whiteness.

The Inner Court is very quiet. The deep snow crunches under my boots, the bitter cold makes me shudder, but there is something exhilarating about the silence and cold. No servants and Imperial guards, no rivals, no Qianlong: it is as though everything that makes me miserable has been taken away, leaving behind only happy memories of long ago. I try to create a sculpture from the snow and it comes out badly, my memories of Shu Fang are fading into something generic and the sculpture before me could be any girl-child, but I smile as I stroke the little face I have shaped and for a moment I think I can hear my laughter and that of Niu Lang, Shu Fang's yelps as we played snowballs together in our garden.

But now I realise the laughter is not in my memory. Somewhere up ahead of me, through the gates into the Outer Court, come more yelps and laughter. I wonder whether some of the Imperial children have been allowed out to play, though it seems unlikely their guardians would allow the risk of any of them catching a chill. I walk more quickly, almost falling over a hidden step, then slow as I look through the gate into the courtyard beyond.

Concubines Qing and Ying are playing together in the snow. Ying is a good shot, almost every snowball she throws hits Qing, who is so overcome with giggles that she can barely stand up straight, let alone make and throw snowballs back.

In that moment I want to ask to play alongside them, to be part of their friendship, to forget all that has happened so far and only enjoy what is here and now. I think of making a snowball and throwing it at them, of laughing when they turn, preparing to duck when Ying – for it will surely be Ying – throws one back at me. She will probably hit me, her aim is excellent. And I will yelp and laugh and there will be something between us, a lightness that signals something that could be: a new start, a fresh beginning in this fresh snow, a way to change the direction my life is taking, to move away from a path that leads only into darkness.

But as I watch, Qing falls and Ying helps her up. Qing clings to her desperately, trying to steady her slipping feet on the icy paving and Ying's eyes are filled with such tenderness that the darkness wells up in me again. There is something between them, it would take a fool not to see it. All at once, I am the one outside again. They are nothing but another pair of hearts closed to me, open only to one another.

"What good friends you are," I say and my voice is so low, so bitter, that it frightens even me.

They turn, Qing still clinging to Ying for balance. Slowly they let go of one another and Qing speaks, her voice shaky.

"Lady Ula Nara," she says. "Are you well?"

I cannot help myself. I want to see their eyes when they know their secret is discovered, the fear I will make grow there. "I was told the two of you were friendly," I say. "I did not know you were *such* good friends."

Qing's eyes do not change in the way that I crave, she only looks scared and confused. But Ying's face changes. Her hand moves away from where she was still touching Qing's elbow, her eyes grow cold and sullen with recognition of what I am insinuating.

And the old game has its hooks in me again, the dirty pleasure of other people's secrets and fears fulfilling me for a moment. I feel a cruel smile grow on my face. Qing may be an innocent for now but Ying knows what I am thinking and she is fearful of my knowledge, of my power over her. "I'll take that silence as agreement, shall I?" I say and suddenly the pure whiteness of the snow everywhere is gone. I am back in the Forbidden City, the snow has hidden it from me only for a moment before revealing it again, its claws outstretched, ready to twist the hearts and minds of those who live here. I turn back, unable to meet Qing's wide-eyed gaze, Ying's protective anger. I walk fast through the snow, taking no pleasure in it. When I return to my rooms I am barely out of my furs before I press myself against Feng and he presses back against me, our hands frantic, each of us trying to get from the other something neither of us can give.

The promotion ceremonies are always boring, one stupid woman after another glowing at the thought of being moved one step closer to the Emperor without realising that his heart is already filled. They dream of success: of their name chip turned over and over on the silver tray, of ever grander titles and robes, of somehow securing Qianlong's favour. But today there is a stir of interest as the promotions are announced: a lady-in-waiting is made concubine, an uncommon event. Not chosen for the Imperial bedchamber during the Draft, somehow she has caught Qianlong's eye in the crowd and is now to join our ranks.

"Lady Ling is promoted from lady-in-waiting, she is made Concubine," announces the Chief Eunuch.

"Only so that the Emperor may lie with her and satisfy a passing lust," whispers Feng.

I nod. She is a nobody.

"Lady Ling is promoted from Concubine, she is made Imperial Concubine!"

"Twice in one year?" I hiss to Feng.

"Whore," he mutters. "She will have made herself useful in the bedchamber."

I look her over more carefully. No woman has been promoted so quickly in all the time I have been here. She is Han Chinese in origin, although honorary Manchu status has been bestowed on her family. She is only young, not even twenty, but she carries herself with an easy confidence, as though she knows herself valued. This second promotion has come as no surprise to her, it has been murmured to her already by Qianlong, whispered against her bare skin. She walks past me as the ceremony comes to an end. Her movements are languorous, she walks like a woman who knows the Emperor watches her. There is an easy plumpness to her body, not fat but a roundedness that comes from eating well and fearing no harm. She does not have about her the tight slenderness of many of the women here, whose nerves are shredded from fears and rivalries, from jealousy and pettiness. She has risen above such things, knowing the path she has chosen is successful, fearing no-one.

"Whore," I agree. It is an easy name to bestow, an easy dismissal. In the darkness that night we whisper to one another, is this what Ling does for the Emperor? This? She is a whore, she is clawing her way up the rankings of the concubines through filthy tricks, by doing *this* and *this* and *this*. We grow to hate her but there is nothing we can find that can be said against her in public, no way to wound the Emperor's second most favourite woman.

I follow Ling. I know that I follow her with a frown on my face, that my brow furrows every time I see her. I watch the way she walks, so different from Fuca, who glides elegantly, as an empress should. Ling does not glide. She sways. Even in the long shapeless robes we wear, an observer can be left in no doubt as to where Ling's hips are, as they sway back and forth, back and forth. She walks like a woman who is being watched and who knows that it is her walk, her body, that will have her called, again and again, to the Imperial bedchamber. Ling is no fool. She plays her own game, and she is winning. All these years, concubine after concubine has tried and failed to rise above the rest to become a favourite. All these years the Emperor has loved his Empress above all others. The rest of his women have been called to the bedchamber but without much favour. There is no pattern. But here comes Ling, called again and again, promoted twice in one year from a lady-in-waiting into a Concubine and then again to an Imperial Concubine, an unheard of rise in favour. She is not about to become Empress, for Fuca still lives, but certainly Fuca is not being called to the bedchamber quite as regularly as she once was. Ling's face has an air of calm to it, of security in the knowledge that she has been seen, has been chosen from the ranks of women available, and raised up above them. Whatever she does when she is alone with the Emperor, whatever she promises with her swaying walk, she knows that it works and she continues on her chosen path. The rest of us can only wonder at what might take place in the Imperial bedchamber between the two of them and wonder why none of us have succeeded in doing the same.

I receive word that my mother has died. I think of Shu Fang, how she will weep and weep, of my father and how he will manage without my mother's constant chatter, which he used to roll his eyes at, but which he will miss now it is gone. I wonder if she managed to control her pride at knowing I was named Consort to an Emperor, since she knew I was unhappy. I think of her fondness for Niu Lang and I weep.

It is time for the Festival of Hungry Ghosts. Feng and Ping busy themselves with an altar in my own courtyard, heaping it with both real food and paper offerings. I make my way there and burn what is to be burnt, bow and kneel, my eyes growing red with the clouds of incense surrounding me.

"There are ghosts who are good, our venerated ancestors," says Ping as darkness falls. "But there are those who remain forever hungry. A hungry ghost searches for what cannot be offered, for revenge or love, ever searching, never finding. It grows wasted, its belly always empty, its eyes always searching for what it cannot find. Such ghosts are not easily appeased."

"I am going to bed," I say, cutting her off.

Feng and I lie in the darkness, wrapped in a tight embrace, while outside ghosts walk the Forbidden City, welcomed for this one night only, invited back to our world to eat and drink their fill, to feel the warmth of our veneration and respect, to satiate and keep them at bay for one more year. I wonder if my mother walks close by me tonight, if she eats from the food I have offered, dresses in the paper clothing I have burnt, if her constant chattering annoys the other ghosts as much as it ever annoyed my father. I wonder, if I stepped into the darkness, if I would feel her arms about me one last time, but I am too afraid of Ping's stories of what else might lurk outside in the darkness.

Fourteen days later comes the time to light paper lanterns and float them on the waterways of the Forbidden City, each tiny light a flickering guide for any lost spirits to follow back to their own world, for fear that they should remain trapped in this one. As each light is extinguished, a ghost returns from whence it came and leaves us safe. I watch with my household as our tiny boats set sail, as Feng and Ping and the other servants' tiny candles burn out and go dark. Only mine shines on, even as the little boat turns out of sight we see its flame still burning.

"A hungry ghost still walks among us," declares Ping. "It has not returned to the other world."

The other servants murmur.

"Be quiet, you stupid old woman," I say. "You have spoken once too often."

I beat Ping myself, red weals rising on her wrinkled back, her knees giving way beneath her before I stop. I walk away from her and none of the servants dare step forward to raise her up. She lies there for some time and when she dies a month later, I turn my face away at the news and never speak her name again. A new maid rises to prominence among my servants but she knows better than to talk when she does not have to. My palace grows silent, the servants do not speak above a whisper for fear of being heard.

The court grows sombre. Lady Fuca's older son has died. He should have been heir to the throne and now that task will fall to his younger brother, her second son. Fuca's face when she has to appear at rituals and official events is white with grief. Qianlong treats her very gently, all of the court must tiptoe around her sadness.

I search for sorrow in my heart for the little prince and there is nothing there. I wonder how low I have sunk that I cannot mourn a dead child and yet there is still nothing, only a dull anger. Why should I feel sorry for Fuca? She still has Qianlong's heart. She still has another son, one whom we all know will be heir one day. The boy was under the care of another concubine, about whom nobody worries, even though she was more the boy's mother than Fuca. No one thinks of her grief for a child she has raised since he was born. Such is the way of the court. Such is the way of this world in which I live.

"You are to be promoted," says Feng.

"What?"

"You will be made a Noble Consort at the next promotion ceremony."

"Why?" I have not given the Emperor a son, have not given him pleasure. There is no reason for me to be promoted.

Feng shrugs. "I think they're afraid of you."

It's a possibility. I know full well that no-one at court is fond of me. Lady Wan perhaps may still speak my name with pity, but she has always been absurdly kind in her evaluations of people. Everyone else is afraid of me, shifts away from me if I stand too close, falls silent when I approach. No-one seeks me out, they would rather I were not here. Perhaps those who decide such things believe that I am overly ambitious and think that by promoting me to a higher rank they may soften me, take away whatever it is that makes me unhappy, for there are those who still tell the story of when I was chosen and begged Niuhuru not to take me.

The *ruyi* I receive at my promotion is made of black sandalwood inlaid with rubies. The wood is an odd choice of setting for the rubies, for it is so dark that the rubies do not shine pink or crimson but rather a dull red, like dried blood, their lustre lost without light shining through them. I place it on a silver stand beside the carved rosewood and stand looking at them for some time, unsure that this new piece is any better than the first, for all the gems embedded in it. Its darkness echoes the darkness inside me and does not promise change.

Green Jade

THEY PROMOTE ME AGAIN, AS though the title of Imperial Noble Consort, just one rank lower than Empress, is an offering to placate an evil spirit. There are whispers that Niuhuru herself asked for me to be promoted, desperate to atone for the past. The *ruyi* I receive this time is a weighty green jade, ornately carved by a master craftsman. I stand in my rooms after the ceremony, twisting it in my hands. It is grander by far than the rosewood, grander than the black sandalwood. I wonder whether it is enough, whether its weight can equal the weight in my heart, balance it in the scales of my life. I set it on the new, larger, more elaborate silver holder that has been sent to my rooms. I look at the three sceptres sitting side by side and swallow. It is not enough. I think of that flickering flame that would not go out, the hungry ghost still roaming the Forbidden City, wanting *enough* and never finding it. Nothing would be enough except to sit by Qianlong's side as Empress and that is not something that I can make happen: it lies in the hands of the Immortals and my whole life has been lived under their injustice. Why would they relent their cruelty now?

The dark days of winter come and with them a great fear. Smallpox. The word is on everyone's lips and there are stories everywhere: a maid, a eunuch, one of the dressmakers, not names that bother anyone. But then a new name is spoken. Fuca's second son, heir to the throne, has died.

The court falls silent. Qianlong disappears from view, as does Fuca, both wrapped in sadness. Fuca has no other sons and she is thirty-six now: it is unlikely she will bear more sons in any hurry. Suddenly, those concubines with sons spot an opportunity. They stand a little taller, they dress a little better, they make sure to mention their sons at every possible opportunity. The younger concubines, still at the peak of their fertility, hope to be blessed with children, for now there is a chance to be noticed, to vie for promotion based not just on beauty or desirability but on the ability to birth a healthy son.

I am unlikely ever to bear Qianlong a son, so this means nothing to me. It only means that my path to the top will be made harder, for there are women who can beat me by playing a game I do not have the pieces for.

Now Qianlong decides we must somehow cheer Fuca, take her mind off what has happened.

"The astrologers say there may be evil influences in her charts," says Feng, returning with gossip. "She is not to stay in the Forbidden City."

"It's too cold for the Garden of Perfect Brightness," I say. "Or the hunting grounds. Wrong time of year."

But Qianlong has in mind Shandong, in the south-east. We are to visit Mount Tai and the birthplace of Confucius.

"Well, that would make any grieving mother happy again, I'm sure," I say to Feng. "Did she agree to this?"

He shrugs, directing the packing of my clothes. For some reason I am one of the ladies chosen to go on the trip, along with Qing and Ying, Ling and some others.

"The Chief Eunuch told us that we are there to make merriment, to lift the spirits of the Empress," I say. "I'm sure what she wants is all of us with her," I add. "To be constantly reminded that there are plenty of ladies just snapping at her heels to fill Qianlong's bed at night and provide a son and heir. They must be mad, arranging this journey."

Spring has not even come when we leave the Forbidden City behind us. As I expected, the travel is long and tedious. We must move constantly from one resting place to the next, one unfamiliar set of rooms after another while bowing nobles and local officials try to ingratiate themselves with us when we stay in their palaces. They know nothing of court politics, they cannot tell a beloved concubine from one who has not been called on for years and so they creep and bow and flatter, hoping for favour. I ignore them all.

Qing and Ying, set free from their usual routines, feeling part of a privileged group for once, flower on this journey. They chatter and laugh, they play silly drinking games and spend time feeding fish in ornamental ponds and other such nonsense. I find myself watching them all the time. Ying knows what she is about, that much is clear, the way she looks at Qing is plain enough for any idiot to see it. Qing is more of an innocent, I am not sure she has yet put a name to what she feels for Ying, but it is there, in the shining eyes and sudden giggles, it is one word away from love, one glance, one kiss away from passion.

I cannot bear it. It twists my stomach when I see them together. I find myself taunting them, even in front of the other ladies, who draw back when they see me, pretend not to listen but hear every word I say and remember it next time they look at the two of them.

I commission Feng to find me a pillow book for Qing, one filled only with images of women together, for he says such things exist. Sure enough, when I provide the silver, I find in my hand a pillow book that suits my needs. I give it to Qing and watch her pull away from Ying the day after, holding herself stiff and apart and there is something base in me that is glad to see that shine gone from her eyes.

The tour is the bore that I knew it would be. Everything revolves around Fuca's wellbeing. Qianlong is with her all day, their heads pressed tenderly together, his voice low when he speaks to her, the rest of us are only there to make up the numbers. He is a hypocrite anyway, for as much as he spends time with Fuca by day, by night it is often Ling who is sent for. I see her setting off for his rooms time and again, returning late, her ruffled hair loose, her robes thrown on any which way. She looks relaxed when she returns, her skin rosy, her body loose-limbed with sated desire. I do not know if she sees my face at the window, but if she does, she shows no sign of seeing me. She only returns to her own room and spends each day in cheerful chatter with other ladies or leisurely dressing, certain of Qianlong's eyes on her that coming evening.

Feng is gleaming with a secret.

"Fuca is ill," he says.

"What with?"

He shrugs. "A chill, they said."

The last few days have been cold again, after a first glimpse of spring we seem to have retreated back to winter. "Is she at dinner?"

"No."

I brighten a little. I am the second ranked woman here. This means that I will sit close to Qianlong, which does not happen often. It is a chance to outdo Ling, to show her that she is still not winning this game. "Get out the other robe, then," I say. "The purple, not the blue."

I ensure that I am at my finest and make my way to the meal. There I take my place by the Emperor. I turn my face away from Ling, but not before I see the look of pity she gives me. I will not be pitied by a woman barely over her twenty-first year only because she is a slut in the bedchamber. She has yet to reach my own rank and if I had my way, she never would. Where I have put on my best robes and dressed my hair with care, Ling is in a robe better suited to an informal dinner with a friend, her hair loosely pinned. I think for a brief moment how easy it would be to undo her hair, how quickly it would tumble from its pins and spread over a pillow. No doubt this is exactly what Ling would like the Emperor to be thinking when he looks at her hair.

The other women chatter amongst themselves, making little effort to entertain the Emperor, since they can see for themselves that I intend to keep his attention on myself. Qing and Ying sit with their heads together, murmuring to one another in low voices that no one else can overhear. The servants scurry around us, busy bringing plates of food, while musicians play for us. But there is a doleful air in the room, a sense of something missing. I try to talk to Qianlong, but his face is grave and he does not respond much, only eating his way through the many plates offered, as though it were a task he must perform and one he would rather get over with as quickly as possible. I wonder why he did not just have his food taken to his own rooms, instead of insisting on a formal dinner surrounded by his women. Perhaps he does not wish to be left alone with his thoughts, since despite his efforts to cheer the Empress, he, too, has lost a child of late, one whom he had expected to favour as his future heir. He all but grunts when I speak to him of the day's various scenic visits we have all been forced to undertake.

"Is Lady Fuca well?" I ask at last and his eyes immediately focus on me.

"I am concerned for her," he says, frowning. "The physician said it is only a chill but it has been very cold today and in her present state of mind…"

I nod, as though I care about Fuca. "I will pray for her," I say perfunctorily and he smiles and pats my hand.

"Thank you, Ula Nara," he says. "That is a comfort to me."

The rest of the dinner proceeds without much further conversation.

Ling catches Qianlong's eye and we are promptly all dismissed, she no doubt making her way to his bedchamber again, since Fuca is not available.

Morning comes and Fuca is still ill, we are left to our own devices. I follow Qing and Ying, but lose them in the gardens and get turned away by Qing's over-officious eunuch. In the end I sit alone and watch the sun move through the sky, my mind empty, bored.

Another day passes and another and still we are stuck waiting for Fuca to recover. The physicians bustle back and forth, her servants will only say she is still unwell, but by the third day they are beginning to look afraid.

"Find out what is happening," I tell Feng. "Something is not right."

Local visits and banquets are suddenly cancelled. A message is sent to each of us to pray for Her Majesty's good health.

"She is very ill," says Feng. "The Emperor has decided we are to go back to Beijing."

"We left Beijing for the good of her health," I say.

He shrugs. "The Emperor is getting worried."

Our chests are packed up and we leave the fawning local nobles and officials behind, boarding the Imperial barge.

"Why aren't we moving?" I ask Feng, after darkness has fallen and still nothing has happened. The room I am in is stifling. The gentle rocking of the boat is making me feel nauseous. I wave away the snacks and drinks I am offered, afraid I will be sick.

He shrugs. No one knows anything. No one is saying anything.

"I am going to sleep," I tell him. "Do not wake me. With any luck when I wake up we will be on our way back to Beijing."

I try to sleep but the nausea I feel makes me twist and turn. From outside comes the low but endless and unmistakeable sound of monks chanting for Fuca's health. I wish they would be quiet and allow us to depart. If she wants to go back to Beijing, then we should go. The monks can chant in a temple for her good health. I try to plug my ears but nothing works. Then the door opens and I see Feng silhouetted in the light.

"I told you not to wake me," I hiss, forgetting that I have anyway not been asleep.

"Fuca is dead," he says.

Vomit spills out of me, a bitter yellow bile I have suppressed too long, staining my silken covers.

My hair hangs loose, jewellery and flowers are set aside. White robes arrive from the Imperial storerooms, our usual bright colours abandoned in mourning. The men of the court cut their queues. It makes them look like half-shaven monks.

In his grief, Qianlong gives absurd orders. We return by boat along the canal and when we reach Beijing thousands of men are called upon to line the streets with leaves to form a slippery surface. Then they are ordered to pull the whole barge up to the Forbidden City, so that Fuca's body should not be disturbed as they bring her home. The Palace of Eternal Spring, her residence, becomes a mausoleum for her body. Every member of the court visits, bowing to her stiff body, lying in state while Qianlong kneels by her side, weeping.

I stand by him, looking down on Fuca's empty face and his shuddering shoulders. I feel nothing for Fuca, but as soon as I think of Niu Lang dying, tears spring to my eyes. It seems I do have a heart left, after all. I kneel next to Qianlong and perform my kowtow. When I raise my face Qianlong is looking at me. He sees the tears in my eyes and takes my hand in his, nodding to me as though to recognise the grief we are sharing. I let him hold my hand and when he lets me go I leave.

Qianlong is now a target. Every woman in the court with even a shred of hope for securing the title of Empress has him in her sights. But he is oblivious to us all. His eyes are red-rimmed from tears, his face is white. He spends every day in the temples, praying for Fuca, his white robes a stark contrast to the orange-clad monks who surround him. Meanwhile the court whispers. It does not take long for them to decide who is in contention as the next empress. I know that two names are spoken. Mine. And Ling's.

"Ling," says Feng.

I look up at him, eyes narrowed. "Say her name again and I'll have you whipped," I snarl.

"He likes her," he says bluntly. "He doesn't like you. He loved Fuca, now that she's gone he'll have to find someone else to love. It would help if he liked the woman to start with."

"He doesn't have to love his empress," I object.

"Don't you know him at all?" asks Feng, exasperated. "He's a romantic. He chose Fuca's children as his heirs without even seeing how they would turn out. He was touched by her making him that stupid leather pouch like the old Manchus had to celebrate his heritage: he went on about it for months. He wants a woman he can love."

"I'm the highest-ranked woman at court," I say.

Feng shrugs. "He can promote Ling or anyone else to whatever rank he likes," he reminds me. "He doesn't need to pick the highest ranked woman. You have to do better than that."

I look down.

"What have you got?" asks Feng. "You have to come up with something. He doesn't love you and your rank counts for nothing."

"I am a Manchu," I say.

"So? Half the other women here are Manchu."

"Ling isn't. She's Han Chinese."

"Oh, so you do realise she is the most likely to be chosen," he says. "Her family have been made honorary Manchus."

"That's good enough for a concubine," I say. "Is it good enough for an empress?"

"I wouldn't risk it on that," says Feng. "Find something else."

We are silent for a while.

"What does he need from an empress?" asks Feng. "You can't offer love, he can get sons from any woman here, so what does an empress have that the rest of the bitches don't have?"

I think of walking one step behind Fuca for all these years, her grace and elegance, her faultless knowledge of every ritual and ceremony to carry out for the good of the empire. I think of the days and years I have spent studying so that I might equal her in this knowledge. "A partner," I say. "The rituals and ceremonies, they have to be carried out by an empress. They have to be flawless. An empress is not just a pretty face and a companion for the bedchamber, that's what the concubines are for. An empress is something more."

Feng considers this. "Better," he says doubtfully. "But is it enough?"

I lower my head. "Probably not."

"What have you got, Ula Nara?" he asks. "Think harder."

I think of the secrets I know, the whispers and rumours of the court, what I have seen and heard over the past few years. Most of them concern minor ladies-in-waiting or concubines, those with no power.

"You need someone with power on your side," Feng reminds me when I do not speak. "Someone who owes you something."

Slowly, I raise my head and meet his gaze.

"You have something," he says. "What is it?"

Niuhuru is always uncomfortable in my presence. When I am shown into her rooms she stands up, as though for a more senior-ranked woman. Her odd grey eyes flicker over my face.

"Are you well, Ula Nara?" she asks.

I don't engage in niceties. "I want to be made Empress," I say.

She blinks, then swallows. "I did not know you felt so strongly about my son," she says.

"I don't," I say.

Her personal maid Yan watches me from a corner of the room, her face very still. I would dismiss her but even I cannot dismiss the maid of the Empress Dowager.

Niuhuru swallows again. "Why do you wish to be Empress?" she asks.

"In compensation for all I lost when I was chosen by you," I say.

Her face grows paler, one hand flutters to her chest. Perhaps she cannot believe I would be so honest, but I do not care what she thinks. I have one chance to achieve what I believe I am owed and this is the only way I can make it happen.

"Qianlong does not wish for a new empress to be appointed," she says. "He says that it would dishonour Fuca's memory."

"Every court needs an empress," I say. "There is always an empress."

"I am sure in due course, when he has finished grieving…" she begins, but then trails off.

"Then he will choose another woman," I say. "He will choose Ling for whatever filthy tricks she performs in his bedchamber."

Niuhuru looks shocked, but I don't care. Now is not the time for politeness.   "Or he will fall for some new girl and have the romantic notion of making her Empress at once, of raising up a nobody to the very pinnacle of the court, like some sort of fairytale. I cannot wait for him to finish grieving. I need you to appoint a new empress now. You are his mother, you have the power to do so."

"And what reasons will I give for choosing you?" she tries.

"I am a Manchu," I say. "I am the highest-ranked woman at court. And you will find that I am well versed in court etiquette. I have walked one pace behind Fuca for long enough. I know all that should be done and how to do it. I will not disgrace you."

She looks away for a moment and then back at me. "And will this satisfy you?" she asks and her voice has a pleading note to it. "Will it make you happy, Ula Nara?" She wants me to smile and say that yes, if she does this all will be forgiven, that I will be happy and she can let go of the burden she carries every time she sees me.

"I do not know," I say and then I play my last, desperate, move, the only move I have left. "Does the Jesuit make you happy?"

There is a tiny gasp from Yan and Niuhuru's eyes widen before her face closes up entirely. For a moment I think I have lost the game, that my final move was too much, that she will hit out and send the board flying, the pieces scattered at my feet. But she only says, "It is time for you to go now," and turns away, leaving me alone in the room with Yan, who does not stand to show me out as she should do, only watches me in silence as I leave.

I wait for an announcement. The whole court waits. I hear the whispers, I know they watch Ling and I to see who will win this secret silent battle.

But Qianlong has the whole court gripped in fear. His grief is greater than any of us could have foretold, he cannot think of anything but Fuca and whether she is being adequately mourned. He has a list of over fifty names drawn up, officials and nobles whom he feels have not been sufficiently grief-stricken by Fuca's death. He has the Han Chinese ones demoted by two grades and the Manchu ones executed. The court tiptoes around him, shocked by his transformation from benevolent monarch to vengeful overlord.

"Cut my hair," I say to Feng.

"What?"

"Cut it off," I tell him.

"Why?"

"Mourning for Fuca," I say.

"You don't need to," he objects. "You would only need to if it was Qianlong or his mother."

"She outranked me," I say.

"She outranked everyone," says Feng. "Having your hair unbound and undecorated is sufficient."

"Qianlong is losing his mind over this," I tell him. "I need to be seen to be mourning her more than anyone else."

I watch the long locks of my black hair fall to the ground.

"Make it look rough," I say. "As though I have done it myself in desperation while grieving."

"Madness," says Feng.

I shake my head. It feels oddly light. "He will like it," I say.

He does. I see him note my hair the next time he sees me and the way he nods, as though satisfied. A few other concubines do the same, although it is too late now, they will only be seen to be copying me, sycophants with no sense of originality, of true sorrow.

My hair cut, I begin the next stage of my plan. I approach the Chief Eunuch and remind him that, as I am the most highly-ranked of Qianlong's woman, and as there is no empress, he, the Chief Eunuch, must be finding certain ceremonies very difficult to arrange. I will stand in for the role, I tell him.

"There are a great many rituals, my lady," he says doubtfully. "You may not wish for such a burden."

"It is no burden to help the Emperor at this time," I say. "I studied the late Empress Fuca for many years, I am well able to perform her duties. And you may brief me if needed."

He is right, of course. The rituals and ceremonies are tedious in the extreme. Mostly they consist in wearing the correct robes, being taken to certain temples on certain days at certain times and then ostentatiously praying. I pray for the empire, interceding with the Immortals. I pray for rain, sun, good crops, healthy livestock, strong backs and hands of the peasants. Sometimes I feel like a farmer. I hold vast bundles of smouldering incense sticks and learn not to choke in the trailing clouds of perfumed smoke that surround me as I bow to the four directions, kneel and pray. I was right, though. I have stood one step behind Fuca all these years and I know what to do. I do not falter, I do not stumble. I remember all the right words and gestures. The Chief Eunuch visibly relaxes as one ceremony after another proceeds with elegance and correct ritual. At least I can be relied on while the Emperor has lost his mind. He bows more deeply to me, treats me as though I were already Empress, whispers in Niuhuru's ear that all is taken care of, that Lady Ula Nara has proven more than worthy to be promoted.

"Ling has been called as the Emperor's companion tonight," says Feng.

I feel my stomach drop. Qianlong has not called for anyone since Fuca died. But now, it seems, his grief has lessened sufficiently that he has remembered more carnal desires which have not been assuaged for some time. And of course it would be Ling who is called, Ling with her confident smile and her swaying walk, her quick glance at him which always results in the rest of us being dismissed. What does she do with him? What games does she play, what skills of the bedchamber does she offer?

"You have lost," says Feng. "The time was before now, while he forgot which of his women he enjoyed the company of."

I think of Niuhuru's eyes widening when I spoke of the Jesuit. "I may still win," I say, but I am afraid. What if I have gone too far this time? How could a concubine accuse the Dowager Empress of any misdemeanour, let alone what I have threatened her about, and be believed? And if she decides to brazen it out, she may then decide to eliminate me as a threat altogether. I think of what she might find out about me. "I am cold," I tell Feng. "Fetch me a jacket."

His eyes tell me he knows full well that it is not the weather making me cold but he fetches me a padded jacket anyway and I huddle into it, but feel no warmer.

Ling is called for again. When I hear of it, I slam my hand down on a table in anger.

"But another girl was called," says Feng, standing in the doorway, watching my reaction to this news.

I frown. "You said Ling."

He nods, his dark eyes gleaming with something he knows. "*And* another girl."

"On the same night?"

He nods.

I think of the album I gave to Qing, the images of more than one woman with a man and my eyes flicker. "Report back to me tomorrow night. And every night."

Ling is summoned every night. But every night some other woman is also summoned. And those chosen do not crow over their popularity as they usually would, they do not hold their heads high and look with disdain at those of us not yet summoned. Instead they go about their days with lowered eyes and are silent. Only Ling smiles. Her smile grows even broader after the previously utterly unfavoured Qing and Ying are summoned on the same night.

"Three women?" I ask Feng, to be certain. "He had three women in his chambers at the same time?"

Feng grins. "Ling is no better than a brothel keeper," he says. "She is tantalising the Emperor with all the goods of the court but keeping his seed for herself."

"Don't be so vulgar," I say, but there is something in me that wants to hear more, my breath comes a little faster. This is akin to the nights that Feng and I spend together, our whispered descriptions of what others do. "They won't be called again, they're two of the most unpopular women he has."

But I am wrong. Now only three women are called to the Imperial bedchamber. Ling, Qing and Ying. Over and over again. "Why them?" I ask Feng. "Why are they suddenly in favour? He never cared for their company before. And the two of them only have eyes for one another, any fool can see it even if they can't."

Feng's eyes meet mine. "Oh, but I think they can," he says. "I think their eyes have been opened and now the two of them are enjoying each other's company. And the Emperor is enjoying their pleasure."

"And Ling?"

"Ling will get what she needs, never fear," says Feng.

"Empress?" I ask.

Feng shakes his head. "You only think of what you want, Ula Nara," he says. "You need a better imagination."

Feng shakes me awake, his hand rough on my shoulders.

"What?" I ask.

"There is to be an announcement," he says. "You are summoned to the throne room."

"I?"

"You and all the women of the court," says Feng.

There is a tension in the throne room. First Ying and then Qing are promoted. I look from one to the other of them but their faces are like stone, they do not look in the least pleased with these promotions, they seem more unhappy than anything else, which I cannot understand. They surely cannot harbour romantic feelings for Qianlong, knowing how they feel about one another. But they do not even seem to acknowledge one another, they pass one another rigidly, their bodies stiffly held apart. I frown. What has happened between them? Certainly they have been rewarded for their part in Ling's scheming. She must have got what she wanted from them.

Ling catches my eye. I glare at her and am about to look away but she smiles, as though she is a friend to me, then drops her hand to her belly where I see an unmistakcable curve. I feel a great wave of rage sweep through me and with it comes a cold understanding. The bitch is with child. She has used Qing and Ying to titillate Qianlong, shown him something forbidden, something new. She has used every woman at court as living pictures from a pillow book while drawing the Imperial seed into her own body to achieve the ultimate success: a child for the Emperor. I can feel my hands curl into fists, can feel my back muscles clench so tightly that my whole body is shaking.

But no-one is watching me. The Empress Dowager is on her feet and all the attention is on her.

"My son's loyal and wise first Empress has left us bereft at her passing," she announces, her voice loud in the vast room. "He is, naturally, full of grief at this loss. But a court without an empress is not a proper court and therefore I have chosen a new empress for my son."

Her eyes have been looking about the room but now they settle on me. I meet her gaze and know what is coming. She hopes to repay me with this, she believes that in taking this step she will give me back the happiness she took away when she chose me for her son. She hopes that my lips will stay closed on what I have seen, on the spark between herself and the Jesuit, a love so deeply forbidden it cannot even be hinted at.

The court is alive with anticipation. Every eye is on Niuhuru. I look at Qianlong but he is looking straight ahead. Probably he is thinking of Fuca, resenting his mother's intrusion on his endless mourning for her.

"Lady Ula Nara will be the successor to the first Empress," announces Niuhuru and I look towards Ling. Her eyes drop, she chews her lip as she thinks about what this means for her. She had better have a son in her belly, for if she does not then her gamble has been for nothing. The court rustles as everyone turns to look at me.

My long-overdue payment is about to be made. The hungry ghost inside me is waiting to be fed.

Gold

I MAKE LING PAY FOR HER rank-creeping, for the bedroom games she played with Qianlong in her efforts to be his favourite. I take Lady Ying as a 'companion,' have her moved close to my palace, as though I actually want the sulky-faced girl anywhere near me. I know that she would like to refuse but in the end she says nothing, only does as I command. She attends me in silence, her face white with misery. I see her cry silently for her lost love Qing and I think, *you do not know what it is to lose a true love*. After all, Qing is still nearby, if Ying had any guts at all she would walk barely three hundred paces to Qing's palace and declare what she feels, speak the name of this forbidden love and see what Qing has to say in return. But she does not, she is a coward under the outer show of bravado she likes to put on.

I see Qing creep to Ying's new palace under cover of darkness, her fluttering head eunuch accompanying her. I see them watch as Ying weeps and I take pleasure in the way they scurry away as soon as I step out of the shadows and stand guard over Ying's miserable crouched figure.

The ceremony to make me Empress is absurdly long but I am used to such rituals by now, I do not move, do not shift awkwardly on my cloud-climbing shoes. The stiff silk robe in Imperial yellow to which I am finally entitled hangs heavy and motionless around my frame. On my head is the Phoenix crown that Fuca once wore: excavated from the Imperial storerooms and brought to my own palace this morning. A heavy gold central headdress of pearls and gems, topped with three phoenixes created from blue kingfisher feathers finished with dangling ropes of pearls on either side. Its weight reassures me that this moment has finally come, that I am made Empress, that what I have worked for has come to pass. My payment is due.

Qianlong looks down at me from his throne, his mother's anxious face beside him. He does not look happy, but he is playing his part as required. Now he holds out the *ruyi* sceptre with which I will promoted. I reach out and take it from him. Intricate gold filigree studded with precious gems and characters, it is heavier than I imagined. I wait for the last part of the ceremony to be completed: the Chief Eunuch will announce my new title and then I will take my place in the empty throne by Qianlong's side, will turn to face the court as the highest-ranked of his ladies. I will meet Ling's gaze and relish her failure.

"Lady Ula Nara is promoted from Imperial Noble Consort. She is henceforth to be known as the Qianlong Emperor's Step Empress."

I should step forward, the empty throne is now mine, it waits only for me. I can hear the rustle behind me as the court kneels, ready to kowtow to me, ready to wish me ten thousand years. But I am unable to move. *Step* Empress? What is this title Qianlong has given me? No such title has ever been given to an empress, even one following a previous holder of the position. Each woman to take on the role has been known as Empress. No more, no less. With this title Qianlong is signalling, forever, that I am second choice, that his heart still lies with Fuca. I look to Niuhuru but she does not meet my gaze. I look at Qianlong but he only looks back at me and now everyone is waiting.

I take one step and then another. I have not spent all these years emulating Fuca for nothing. My every move is perfection, elegance personified. I reach the carved throne at Qianlong's side, turn, sit.

Sitting in Fuca's throne, I feel the weight of the gold *ruyi* in my hands, the Imperial yellow silk against my skin, the Phoenix crown weighing down my head. The court kowtows. I look down at the ranks of courtiers, see pregnant Ling on her knees to me and already I know: the payment I have received is not enough to feed the hungry ghost who lives inside me.

It will never be enough.

Ling has a son. Feng brings me the news.

"Bitch," I curse. "How does that woman always outrank me?"

"You are Empress," he reminds me.

"Step Empress. To an Emperor who spends his time sniffing after that bitch as though she were on heat," I snarl. "Watch how fast she is called back to the bedchamber to perform whatever services she has to offer and whelp another child. Watch how fast he promotes her for giving him a son."

Feng nods. "She has already given her son to Qing to bring up," he says.

"Oh, a reward for services rendered?" I sneer.

Feng shrugs. "Qing and Ying are living in the same palace," he says. "Do you want to report them?"

I shake my head. I know they are under Ling's protection now, she would speak up for them, not in the court but in Qianlong's ear, reminding him of the desire he felt in watching them together. His pleasure has cast a protective spell over them, to break it would only bring down his displeasure on my head. He dislikes me enough already, it would not take much to dislike me further.

Feng no longer sleeps beside me. As Empress, I am too surrounded by guards, by servants. There would be talk. I cannot risk whispers. Once, after the promotion, he tries to touch me when we are alone, his desire suppressed for many months, but I push him away, afraid of being found out and afraid of my own desire for him, angry that even now that I am Empress it is not enough to satisfy my desire to be held, to be touched.

He leaves the room without speaking and the next morning I hear a maid screaming. When I follow the sound, I see for one moment, for one terrible moment, for one endless moment, Feng's body twisting in mid-air, his face turned away, his dark hair loose as it was on my pillows. I turn and run screaming away before his body turns to face me, for I cannot bear to see his face grown discoloured, the white silk scarf wrapped round his neck.

I mourn him in silence and secrecy. Perhaps what was between us was wrong, twisted and dark, forbidden, but it was all that either of us had to cling to here. I send money to his family, making sure that his role at the Palace should not be mentioned by the messenger, although I wonder if his wife knew, if she realised the sacrifice he had made for her and for his children and grieved for it, for what they had both lost.

I dream of him endlessly. Dreams in which I give him the silk scarf myself, dreams where he offers it to me, asking me to join him beyond this life. I dream of our nights together, our bodies pressed tightly together and then hear him choking and realise I am holding the white silk, slowly strangling him, my hands gripping so tightly that he cannot prise them open. I wake over and over again with a start, gasping as though I am suffocating. I cannot tell my servants what is wrong when they hear me scream and come running, I have to send them away and be left alone in the dark to dream again.

The summons had to come.

"When are Your Majesty's monthly courses?" enquires the Court Physician.

"Why do you need to know?" I ask.

"His Majesty has requested that his household be informed of when Your Majesty will be most fertile," he says.

Reluctantly, I give him the information. Sure enough, as the days approach when I am most likely to conceive a child, I am given warning that I will be called on as Qianlong's companion, something that has not taken place for more than a decade. I note with bitterness that Ling's courses are not remarked upon: she is called whenever Qianlong desires her, which is often, without worrying about whether or not she will birth a child. Of course she is nine years younger than I. At thirty-two, the chances of my having a first child now seem remote. She is only twenty-three and has already born an Imperial son, she has many more years ahead of her in which to birth still more.

Our encounter goes exactly as I expect it to. I am rigid with nerves and Qianlong is dutiful. He greets me with all courtesy and indicates the bed. Once I have awkwardly made my way onto it he joins me.

"Are you comfortable?" is all he asks and I nod stiffly. My body is laid on silk, my arms and legs have enough space around them. The fact that I feel cold despite the warmth of the *kang* under the bed and that I am almost shaking with tension is irrelevant. He does what he must do and I am dismissed with a nod of his head, a eunuch appearing so quickly to take me away that I think they must have been forewarned. I am called for each night for three nights and then no more until the next month. As soon as the Court Physician hears that I am suffering with nausea, Qianlong ceases to call for me. I am the Empress, I am with child. All is as it should be. I see him only at the rituals and ceremonies that we complete together: in temples and the great receiving halls. As soon as I am too large to comfortably carry them out, I am excused all such tasks. Some other keen concubine will leap forward, beg for the chance to be seen and praised.

We are transferred to the Garden of Perfect Brightness for the summer and find ourselves without Qianlong, for he is much occupied with his generals, poring over maps in their ongoing battles to try and conquer the vast territory of Altishahr, to the West. With him gone, it feels as though the women of the court relax. There is no-one to impress, no-one to score points against as a rival. I walk through the gardens and see Qing and Ying walking ahead of me, their bodies close. Qing carries a bundle in her arms and I realise that it is Ling's son, whom she gave to Qing to raise. I hear their laughter and Qing's cooing to the child, see them come to their own palace and Qing's head eunuch waiting for them, stretching his arms out for the child as though it were his own, a beaming smile on his face. Most of the eunuchs are like this with children, they fuss over them as though they were their own mothers. I walk past them and Ying turns to look at me. She bows her head, as she must, but there is no love or loyalty in her gaze, only a defiant fear.

I sit alone in my rooms, my belly swelling, and weep again for Feng. Perhaps he would have softened at the idea of a child, since he missed his own children so greatly. Perhaps he would have been kind to a baby and we would have been something like a family together, would have felt something like the closeness that Qing and Ying have managed to create from nothing. Perhaps our darkness would have been lightened by a child. Perhaps mine will be.

Whether it might have been or not, I will not find out. I howl with the pain of birthing my son Yongji, the midwives hovering about me, concerned at my advanced age in birthing my first child. They think either I or the child will die, I hear them whispering it.

"Shut your mouths or I will see to it you never speak again," I scream at them and watch them draw back in fear. After that, they tend to me in silence broken only by my own screams and by the wailing of my healthy son as he enters this world.

I hold him in amazement. He is so tiny, so perfect. He is like a miniature copy of Qianlong and it is the first time I feel true tenderness towards him, seeing his image replicated here in my arms, so small, so trusting in my ability to love him, to mother him. I feel a great welling up of love and have to stop myself from snatching Yongji back from the wetnurse. My own breasts cry out to feed him, they swell up with milk and each time he cries they leak, staining the bindings my maids wrap about me, regardless of how many layers they wind around. I dandle him on my lap and smile at him when he awakens, touch his tiny hand and laugh as he makes a fist around my one finger. Qianlong visits us and beams at the sight of him, sends me flowers and jewels, his demeanour towards me somewhat softened at this proof of my further suitability to take on the role of Empress.

"Your Majesty will wish to choose the concubine who will raise the child, of course," says the Chief Eunuch. "I have taken the liberty of drawing up a list of suitable candidates."

I feel sick. "No," I say quickly. "I can raise him myself."

The Chief Eunuch's brows come together and I feel the room swirl about me, knowing that yet again I have come up against one of the rules of court that must be obeyed. I look at the list I am being offered and choose a name almost at random.

"But I must see him every day," I insist.

The chosen concubine kowtows and promises that of course, of course, she swears to bring the child up as her own, he will have every care...

I watch her leave my presence holding Yongji and wonder how many times a heart can be broken.

I see Yongji on the first day as promised, on the second day also, but then the Chief Eunuch returns me to my duties as Empress and first one day and then another goes by when I cannot see him because I must complete the right rituals, be present at the right ceremonies. I must sit by Qianlong's side and when at last I am free of my duties, then the baby is asleep or he is feeding, he is unsettled and must be kept quiet. If I think of him I weep, even in situations where to weep is unacceptable, and so eventually I try not to think of him. I pretend there has been no child, for to think of him is so painful I cannot bear it. I send word to the concubine that she does not need to worry herself, she must take every care of him but I will see my son only when it is convenient. This comes to mean hardly ever and meanwhile I am summoned back to the Emperor's bedchamber. One heir by the Empress is not enough, it seems, it would be most auspicious to have more and so I must lie still and wait for the day when the Court Physician pronounces me with child again.

There is a daughter the following year. It seems I am fertile after all, despite my advancing age. Who knows how many children Qianlong could have had by me if he had continued to call on me, all these past years. This time I turn my face away from the tiny dark head, I do not brush the little cheek, for I know what is coming. Another concubine kowtows at the vast honour of being given the Empress' child to raise, even if it is a girl. I have my breasts bound so tightly I can barely breath and the child is quickly taken away, so that I need never hear her cry out for her mother.

I do not hear her cry for me before she dies, either, when she is only two years old. I barely knew her. The hapless concubine who had the care of her kneels and weeps, begs my forgiveness and I turn my face away, say nothing. This woman was more the child's mother than I ever was, I think, and yet she is forced to beg my forgiveness for the loss and grief she has suffered in my place.

A year after my daughter dies I produce a second son, who again dies within two years. Another sobbing concubine shakes with fear as she kneels to tell me what has happened. I look down on her from my throne, my face blank, silence the only thing that stops my tears from flowing.

"I have a ritual to attend," I say, rising, as though her news is irrelevant to me, an inconvenient interruption.

In the temple I speak words without knowing what I am saying. I keep my eyes on the nuns. Their heads shaved, their faces devoid of emotion as they chant the sacred texts, offering incense, their eyes closed in peaceful prayer. I try to keep my face like theirs, still and remote, not of this world.

Qianlong no longer calls for me. Apparently my surviving son Yongji grows well, he has taken his place among his living siblings to be educated as befits an Imperial prince.

I come across the Imperial children one day by accident as they learn archery in the Garden of Perfect Brightness. At my approach, they all stop what they are doing and make their obeisances, from the elegance of the older children to the clumsy attempts of the youngest.

"Come forward, Yongji," says the tutor, gesturing to one boy to step forward. "You must greet your mother, her Majesty the Empress."

I swallow. If I had been asked to choose Yongji from the group I would have struggled, I might even have failed. Now he stands before me, very upright, his bright eyes on me.

"Mother," he says, bowing deeply.

I think of the concubine who raises him and wonder what he calls her, if he calls me Mother. What name does he give to the woman who strokes his hair before he goes to sleep, what word does he cry out when he is afraid at night and wants her by his side?

He is waiting for me to say something. I do not know what to say. I know nothing of children, only what I remember from my own childhood. I do not know what Yongji likes to do best, what games he plays, whether he has been given a pet, if he chose a dog or a cat, perhaps a little cricket or a slow-plodding tortoise. I try to smile.

"Yongji," I say, aware of how often I have whispered his name through tears, how few times I have spoken it aloud. "Are you well?"

"Yes, Mother," he says politely.

I do not know what else to ask. I look to his tutor. "Does he do well at his studies?" I ask, as formal as though this were the Imperial Examinations rather than a mother asking how her son does.

The tutor bows. "He is an excellent archer," he says. "A true Manchu. Soon he will be learning to draw a bow on horseback, as his ancestors did."

I nod. I have barely heard what he said. I look back at Yongji, who waits expectantly for me to say something else. "You must obey your tutor in all matters," I say, as though he has been chastised, as though I have been informed that he is lagging in his studies.

He bows. "Yes, Mother."

"I must go now," I say, although in truth I have nowhere to go, nobody to see. Everyone bows again and I walk away. When I have gone a few steps I look back, thinking, hoping, that perhaps Yongji will still be watching me, but he has already turned back to the targets, eager for his turn.

Ling has a child every summer without fail for three years, her first son growing under the watchful eyes of Qing and Ying, who love him as their own. Any chance I might have had to find motherly love has been taken from me.

The summer that Ling provides the Emperor with another son the child's birth is celebrated with fireworks and glory, festivities and feasting.

"What news?"

The maid hovers. She does not want to say what I have asked her to tell.

"Well?"

"Lady Ling is delivered of a son, Your Majesty."

"You must think I'm a fool not to know that," I say. "There were fireworks all of last night. I could not sleep. I asked you to find out details."

"Yes, Majesty."

"Well?"

"He has been given to Lady Ying to raise, Majesty."

Slowly, I nod. Ling is still rewarding Qing and Ying for the services they performed in the Emperor's bedchamber, several years gone by now. Whatever they did, however they pleased him, it was Ling who benefitted, and she has not forgotten their service. Qing plays mother to Ling's first son, and now the family unit that Qing and Ying created together has been enhanced by this new addition, another princeling to raise, more favour shown to them by the Emperor's favourite.

"And?"

The maid hesitates.

"*And?*"

"And... Lady Ling has been made... Imperial Noble Consort."

And here is proof, if proof were needed, that Qianlong does indeed have a favourite, and she is Lady Ling. This title that has been given to her, this promotion, now ranks her as second only to the Empress, to me. It is only the rules of hierarchy that prevents him creating a second Empress. But there can be only one Empress, and I am still alive, therefore Ling is barred from the position he no doubt would have gifted to her, had he been able to. Had he had the chance to finish grieving for Lady Fuca, he would have chosen his Empress with more care. It would have been Ling sitting in the throne by his side, not I. He was bludgeoned into choosing me, by his mother, by court expectations, by years, decades, centuries of dynasties. And now Ling is ranked second only to me, ready to become Empress should anything befall me.

I become watchful, afraid, jumping at shadows. I fear assassins with knives in the dark, I fear poison in my food. I check the silver strips that are placed in every dish at my mealtimes, check them myself for any sign of staining, of darkening, of poison leaking out and making itself known in the shining surfaces of the tiny strips that are meant to protect me. My eunuch taster must taste everything before I put it in my mouth, sometimes more than once before I am satisfied. I cannot eat while the food is still hot, for perhaps the poison will not take effect for some time, and so my taster eats long before I do, and by the time I eat my food is cold and congealed on the plates. It loses its appeal, and so I find myself eating less and less. I pick at my food and swallow each morsel as though it may kill me. More servants must sleep in my rooms to protect me, until what ought to be my private bedchamber becomes a dormitory. None of my servants dare speak to me about my behaviour, but I see them look to one another as dish after dish is returned to the kitchens, as they wait for their chance to eat my leftovers and watch the food grow cold and stale. They exchange glances when they dress me, when they wash me, as I grow thinner. Sometimes I look down at my long bony hands, made longer still by the golden nail shields I wear, studded with gems, unable to hide the pallor of my skin, stretched out over bones. My robes must all be remade, for they hang on me, baggy and loose. I sit by the Emperor's side, heavy in my court silks and my jewels, high above the other women on my gilded throne, knowing that the man I sit beside would rather it was another woman beside him.

I am desperate to find a way out of this life, a freedom from what I feel, from what I have felt all these years. To be released from the grief of losing a distant love, to let the pain go and instead to feel nothing, to feel calm and free. To forget the child taken from me and made another's, to forget the two children lost to this world. To step away from the darkness inside me and the constrictions and horrors of the world around me, and instead live a life of simplicity and purity.

During another endless ceremony I notice the nuns again and suddenly I think that perhaps I could follow a new path. Perhaps I have come to it too late, unlike Niu Lang, who knew at once what steps to take to avoid the pain of our lost lives, but at least I have come to it now. I could become a nun. I think that the Emperor will not refuse me this, for there can be no shame in it. For an empress to choose a life of spiritual growth and piety cannot be an embarrassment to him. If he lets me go, I can become a nun and he may choose whomever he wishes to join him on the golden thrones. No doubt it will be Ling who sits by his side, but I find, much to my surprise, that I do not care. Let her have her time as Empress. Let her find out for herself that it is not the glorious role she thinks it is, as all the women here think it is. They look at the Imperial yellow silk that makes up my robes, they see all the jewels of the warehouses in my hair, and they imagine that to sit by the Emperor's side, bedecked in these treasures, must lead to happiness. As did I. But I have found that I was wrong, and now I have seen for myself a possible solution, the path I should have chosen long ago, if I had been as brave as Niu Lang was. I think that his choice to become a monk when the life he had planned was denied to him was a strong choice, a pure choice. He will not have grown bitter and dark in his thoughts and deeds, as I have. He will have found freedom over the years, will have meditated on our love and blessed it, will have let it go peacefully from his heart and risen above the pain. He will think of me sometimes, perhaps, and smile, he will wish me good things in the life destiny chose for me. He will have been taught acceptance by his religious masters, perhaps struggling at first but eventually coming to a place of harmony that cannot be disturbed by the petty concerns of daily life. I wonder if I, too, could make such a choice, could learn another way. I think of what it would be like to shed my silken robes and shave my head, to wear the simple robes of a nun and spend my days in prayer and contemplation. How slowly, over time, I would feel the pain of these past years leave me and instead find an inner peace, a way to accept what has been and let it go without judgement, to feel a lightness of being I have not known since I came to this place.

I request an audience alone with Qianlong and am shown into his private study. I kowtow.

"I have a boon to ask."

"Ask," he says, his tone benevolent, not looking up from his work, as though he will grant whatever I name without even thinking about it.

"I wish to become a nun," I say.

"What?" he asks, looking up from his papers, his attention suddenly on me.

"I wish to renounce my title as Step Empress and become a nun," I say. "I will leave the Forbidden City and go to a nunnery somewhere remote, I will pray for the good of the empire. I wish to take up a holy life."

"No," he says. I wait for him to ask why I do not wish to be Empress, but he does not ask this.

"There are plenty of other women who would be happy to take my place," I say. "Lady Ling, for example," I add, swallowing my pride to name his personal favourite, hoping that the thought of offering her such public favour will sway him.

"No," he says. "It would not be seemly. People would talk, they would suggest you are unhappy as Empress and that would be inauspicious."

"You can say that I have retired because of grief for my children," I suggest.

"No," he says. "And anyway, you have a living son."

I think of Lady Fuca, dying of a broken heart after losing two children, how tender he was with her. How I, too, have lost two children, but have not been shown the same tenderness. I stay on my knees.

"I beg you to let me go," I say and my voice shakes. "I will not cause trouble. No-one can object to an empress being devout. My sacrifice in becoming a nun can only bring favour to the Imperial Family."

"No," he says.

"But I – " I begin.

"No," he says. "This conversation is at an end, Ula Nara. Your request is refused." He is very calm. He does not need to raise his voice or be angry or upset at my request, he is the Emperor, he can simply refuse and know that his word must be obeyed. I leave the room in silence and he does not watch me go.

I try to accept the emptiness of my gilded life. I carry out all my official duties, the meaningless bowing and praying, the movements and costumes required for each occasion. I no longer have to listen to Ping's horror stories, I do not engage in the dark yearning of the nights with Feng. My three children are gone, one way or another. Every woman and servant at court fears me, including the Empress Dowager. Ling will never be Empress while I still live, even if one day her sons make a bid for the throne it will mean little to me, for my living son hardly seems my own.

I had not known such emptiness could exist, such deep loneliness even beyond yearning for a lost love. I wonder how many years it is possible to live like this, a hollow shell giving the appearance of life, like one of Qianlong's beloved Western clocks, exquisitely decorated, ticking and ringing, made up of only cogs and wheels inside, endlessly turning for the amusement of their master.

I ransack the Imperial storerooms to which only I, as Empress, have access. I can have anything I want sent to my rooms and so I plunder their contents. I fill up my rooms with exquisite furniture and priceless ornaments: vases, precious calligraphy, board games, fans, trinkets, jade carvings. My rooms do not have the sparsely luxurious air that Qianlong likes to cultivate about him, they grow crammed and heavy with wealth. I wear only Imperial court robes, not the more informal robes the other women wear, choosing colours to suit their moods or needs, instead I wear only the coveted Imperial yellow. I have the jewels to which I am entitled brought to me and I wear them all. I spend my days weighed down with jewellery, from ropes of pearls and gemstones to heavy jade pendants, headdresses which shiver with gold filigree strands and pearls, or wholly made up of the tiny, exquisitely gleaming, and highly prized kingfisher feathers. I do not know how many tiny darting kingfishers have been killed and plucked to create my hairpieces. I do not care. I know that behind my back the court compares me unfavourably to Lady Fuca's style of dress, how she preferred freshly-plucked flowers or little creations made from plaited straw, how Qianlong himself would place wild flowers in her hair, how she wore only simple robes unless called on to perform a formal ritual. I do not care. The Imperial storerooms are at my command day and night and there is not a jewel I might command that I have not worn. Anything and everything that is mine by right of my position, I take. When I dress each morning a third of my own bodyweight is added to my frame in the form of heavily embroidered robes, cloud-climbing shoes so high no other concubine can wear them, the crowns and jewels that adorn me. The weight is a comfort to me, it is like a burden I must bear each day, but one which can be supported physically rather than in my heart and mind. I wonder whether perhaps I have found a way to continue this life, balancing the emptiness within with the weight of clothes and jewels and rituals on the outside. Perhaps this is the best I can hope for, to keep this balance, to feel as little as possible, to act as a hollow adorned shell of a woman.

But news comes that disturbs my delicate balance. Altishahr, the Muslim territory bordering China to the West, has finally fallen, Qianlong's armies have won a battle that has been going on for decades. Renamed *Xinjiang,* New Territory, it is added to the empire, vastly expanding its size. Prisoners of war and huge quantities of jade, in which the new territory is rich, are brought to the capital. There is whispering among the ladies of the court. A new woman is to join our ranks, not through the Daughters' Draft but from this new territory. A noble family of the area turned traitor on their own people and joined us as allies. Now they are rewarded with access to Qianlong's very own bedchamber, for their daughter will become a concubine.

Qianlong is already half in love before she even arrives, he talks of nothing else but his New Territory and the woman who is to be sent here, he applies himself to studying her language so he can speak with her. He wants to revel in this glory. I can imagine that the idea of lying with a woman from this conquest fills him with desire, as though he will conquer the land over and over again each time she is brought to his bedchamber. I can see that even Ling, confident in her many healthy children, is a little anxious at the idea of this new arrival. She has new robes made, her children are drawn to Qianlong's attention more than usual, she even has the Jesuit paint her portrait with her little son, a permanent reminder of her ability to breed Imperial heirs.

I arrive in the vast receiving hall, dressed in Imperial yellow, my head weighed down with the kingfisher-feather and pearl Phoenix crown. The Chief Eunuch looks distressed at the sight of me.

"Your Majesty," he says, bowing very low.

"Is something wrong?" I ask.

He bows again, uncertain of what to say. The Chief Eunuch was chosen for his ability to know what to say and do in all circumstances, even how to deliver bad news to senior members of the Imperial Family. "His Majesty…"

"Yes?" I say. I look up at Qianlong and his mother, already seated. Qianlong is looking through papers. My empty throne awaits.

"His Majesty has asked that you stand with the other ladies today."

I don't ask why. I am not stupid. Qianlong is excited about this new arrival, this woman who stands as a much-anticipated symbol of a new conquest. He does not want to be reminded that he has an Empress already, he wants to believe this new woman promises a new romance about to blossom. I feel some of the emptiness that I have so carefully cultivated slip, emotion rising up in me. I try to crush it back down. I make my way forwards and find a place to stand, knowing that the other women have read this slight correctly, they are too well-versed in court etiquette not to notice that I am stood amongst them rather than being seated above them.

Wan arrives and smiles brightly at me. She is caked in too much makeup, as though to keep her status as Qianlong's youngest bride, even though she is by now forty-three and there are women here who could be her grandchildren. I have heard that she is now entirely bald, through some illness, though her eunuchs are experts in wig-making and dressing and therefore her hair is as silkily black and elegantly over-dressed as it ever was.

"I hope the new lady will speak Mandarin," breathes Wan. "I have tried to learn a few words of her own language but really, I cannot make it out at all. The Emperor has learnt it with no trouble at all, it seems! He is so learned. A true scholar."

I don't answer her. I have already arranged for a translator of the new woman's language to stand by my side, so that I will not be left out of any conversation she may have, so that I will have a ready-made spy to observe this new arrival's progress. I am watching Qing and Ying who have arrived together, as usual. They do not even hide their relationship, they go everywhere together. Ling is already here, well-dressed and smiling at the Emperor, who for once is not taking much notice of her, instead looking over papers while his mother sits by him, looking tired.

Behind me I can hear rustling and whispers, but what I am really listening to is the steady thump of feet from outside, the bearers of a palanquin running towards us. And then there is silence. The Chief Eunuch leaves Qianlong's side and makes his way out towards the doors where the woman will be waiting for his signal to make her entrance. There is an absurdly long pause. No doubt the Chief Eunuch has in mind some auspicious moment which must be exact, as though it will make any difference at all whether Qianlong sees her now or in several moments' time, as though it will somehow change their destinies.

Now one woman after another turns and although I want to keep my back turned I cannot. I turn to look at her.

She looks very odd to my eyes. She is dressed all in red, as befits a bride, but rather than our long, loose-fitting robes she wears a skirt of many layers that comes out from a tight waist. She has little shoes with high heels and a billowed-sleeved shirt with a waistcoat over the top, again fitted tightly to her form. The whole outfit hugely accentuates the curves of her body in a way that looks positively immodest. Her hair is long and black like ours but it is woven into many tiny plaits that fall to her waist, while on her head is a little embroidered cap.

She looks terrified.

Her own translator, a eunuch, is gesturing to her to move forwards, but she shakes her head, touches his sleeve as though to make him come with her. He shakes his head in turn and by now the Emperor has noticed her. He stands and comes towards her. She ought to kowtow, of course, but she hesitates as though she has not been told what to do.

"Welcome to court," says Qianlong in her own tongue, hastily translated in a whisper by the man at my side.

She looks astonished. He looks delighted at having made such a good first impression. Qianlong always did like to be praised, to be admired, I think wearily.

"I speak all the languages of my empire," he says. "I have been learning yours in preparation for meeting you."

She doesn't reply, only looks awkward. I think of the ceremonies when new women arrive following a Daughters' Draft, how polished each girl is, how they have been drilled for days, perhaps months, on how to behave at court, how to respond to pleasantries from the Emperor. This girl has all the polish of a peasant.

Qianlong, meanwhile, is looking her over. "Your clothes are not court dress," he remarks. He does not sound annoyed, only curious. He cannot visit his new dominion, so this girl is a symbol of it, something he can explore. He likes her odd appearance, I can tell, it shows he has conquered a truly far off and exotic land, not just some minor annex to China.

She blushes. "They're – they are the traditional clothes of... Xinjiang, Your Majesty. I thought it would please you to see them."

He smiles at once. "Of course. Turn around."

She turns awkwardly on the spot, like a piece of livestock for sale.

"Charming," says Qianlong, looking at her hair. "All those little plaits."

"There'll just be two tomorrow, Your Majesty," she says.

He frowns. "Why?"

Her cheeks grow scarlet. "I will be m-married," she says. "Married women wear only two plaits."

"Then I will look forward to seeing you with only two plaits," says Qianlong suggestively.

The courtiers titter. We women do not.

She looks as though she would like to leave, but Qianlong is not done with her yet. "One more thing."

She waits.

"I have been told that you have a special attribute."

She looks at him.

"I have heard that your body emits a natural fragrance."

She looks down.

"Is it true?"

"I've been told so, Your Majesty." It comes out as little more than a whisper.

He smiles. "Come closer."

She steps forward, still leaving a considerable gap between them.

"Closer than that," he says. "I am not a hunting dog, to scent you from so far away!"

The courtiers titter politely again. I can see Ling's face stiffening. If the Emperor wishes to flirt with a new lady, must we all be forced to bear witness?

She comes one step closer to him and he leans forward. He inhales loudly, putting on an amusing show for the courtiers, but clearly her perfume is of quality, for he closes his eyes for a moment. "It is your own scent? Not a perfume?"

"Yes, Your Majesty."

"Remarkable. It reminds me of lotus flowers."

Of course it is not her own scent, I think. *It is some perfume from*

145

her own land that half the women there wear and he does not know any better.

There is a whispered consultation between the Chief Eunuch and Qianlong before the new arrival's court name, status and privileges are read out.

"We welcome the noblewoman of Xinjiang, now made an Honoured Lady and given the court name of Lady He."

He has named her after a lotus flower in honour of her supposed natural fragrance. Absurd. At least her rank is not high, she is sixth-ranked, she will have to work hard before she reaches the heights of Ling, who is looking relieved. But clearly the girl has no idea that she must now take on a new name for the rest of her life, she looks confused and her interpreter-eunuch has to murmur explanations before pushing her forward to perform a kowtow, which she stumbles over. As she stands, Qianlong holds out a *ruyi* carved from a dark wood inlaid with white jade panels. She takes it, looking mystified. Again I find myself wondering about how ill-informed she is over courtly customs.

The Emperor reaches out and traces the carved characters with his forefinger. "It says that all the world is now at peace," he says, smiling. "Now that Xinjiang is part of our empire's family and Lady He has joined the ladies of the court, the world is at peace."

The court applauds. The palms of my hands touch one another, though they make little noise.

A few more proclamations are made, covering additional gifts given to her family. Her father and brothers are to live in a newly-created Muslim quarter of Beijing, situated just outside the walls of the Forbidden City. The newly-named Lady He does not look happy about this. I wonder if she, like Wan, was ill-treated by her family. If she was, she can take comfort in the fact that she will never see them again.

Eventually, she is led away to her new palace and I return to mine. But I have a restless night. The deliberate lack of feeling I have tried to cultivate of late has been disturbed by this new arrival. Watching Qianlong flirt with her brought back a rush of unhappy memories of how he used to be with Fuca. And something about Lady He bothers me, there is something not right about her. I try to tell myself that she is from another country and culture, that she is unlikely to behave as I would expect her to, but still it is almost dawn before I sleep. The next day I am bad-tempered with the servants. They in turn grow skittish with nerves, remembering the bad old days when I would watch and wait for misdemeanours so that I could lash out with punishments out of all proportion to their faults. They prefer the numbness I have cultivated of late.

Now that the army has returned from Xinjiang, glorious from success in battle, rich with jade, gold and prisoners of war, there must be a large celebration, a parade. Slowly, I dress myself, and am carried in my palanquin to the seating that has been arranged, high above the Meridian Gate. The whole court is gathered, ready to celebrate the conquest, the enlargement of the empire.

I make my way to my allotted seat by the Emperor's side, I feel a little breathless and dizzy, for the seating is steeply raked.

"Ula Nara," says the Empress Dowager, bowing her head to me. It is I who should bow to her, but she is like this with me, anxious to please, able to see for herself that becoming Empress has done nothing for my happiness. I ignore her.

"Your Majesty," I say to the Emperor. He nods, as though to a common courtier, his attention wholly taken up with the procession below and the casket on which his hand rests. It is supposed to contain the left ears of two rebels, a gory trophy. I shift my attention to the people below, the prisoners of war. A few women, mostly men, dressed in the style we have seen on Lady He, little hats perched on their heads, the women with billowing skirts, all of them with colourful waistcoats. I look for Lady He in the crowd and spot her, looking back at me. Her face is anxious, her eyes flicker to me and then back to the procession, she looks as though she may cry. Perhaps she does not wish to see her countrymen as spoils of war, although she must be a fool not to realise that she is a prisoner of war herself, a trophy, although prettier than the ones in the Emperor's casket.

The Emperor has gone so far as to write a poem commemorating this celebration, as he likes to do for important events, thinking himself something of a poet.

> "The casketed Khodja's heads are brought from desert caves;
> The devoted Sultan knocks at the Palace gates…
> By Western lakes, the might of Qing Eternal is decided,
> At the Meridian Gate our triumph is thrice proclaimed.
> From this day forth, we no longer stay this military course.
> My people, sharing joyful plenitude, now shall take their rest."

There is applause. Lady He wipes away tears. I shift in my throne. Now that this is over, I hope that the Emperor will stop with his incessant talk of conquest. Although, from what I have been told, he has yet to conquer his new concubine.

Now that the procession is completed the court begins to disperse. I rise to leave. But the Empress Dowager, seated on the other side of the Emperor, has other plans. I see her speaking to a servant and realise she is about to summon Lady He. I wait, my head turned away, my ears straining to hear.

"You cried," Niuhuru says to Lady He, without any opening niceties. "When the prisoners of war were displayed."

I can barely hear the reply when Lady He answers, it emerges as half whisper. "Yes, Your Majesty."

"Why?"

"I – I am a little homesick, Your Majesty," she stutters.

Niuhuru is silent for a moment. Perhaps she is thinking of the day she chose me, wondering whether this concubine also has a secret love, a secret heartache. She speaks a little more kindly. "All the ladies are at first," she says. "You will grow accustomed to your new life and the world within these walls. Each lady finds her own way to be happy." She pauses and I know without looking that her eyes flickered towards me. "Or not."

"Yes, Your Majesty," Lady He replies, her voice soft.

The Dowager must make some gesture of dismissal. I watch as Lady He makes her way down the steeply raked seating to her palanquin. She stumbles as she enters it and is saved from falling only by the quick wits of her eunuch. There is something about the way she looks around quickly, as though afraid that her stumble is somehow reprehensible, a fault for which she can be chastised, that makes me curious, it echoes how she behaved when she arrived here and stirs something in me from the days when Feng and I whispered and watched together.

I ask for news of her, give little coins here and there, to receive reports of her days, of how she spends her time, of how the Emperor treats her. Oddly, it seems that the Emperor has forgotten her. He has not yet summoned her to his bedchamber, nor even visited her. I cannot understand why. His conquest of her homeland certainly stirred something within him, for he looked younger, stronger and happier than I had seen him in a long time. Surely, Lady He would stir such feelings in him also.

The news I have of her is not very interesting. She likes animals, it seems, for first she adopts a kitten, followed by caged birds that are hung in her garden and the walkways of her palace, as well as in her living rooms. She fills the pond in her garden with fish, and appears to enjoy feeding them. The little dogs that almost all the eunuchs seem to keep are allowed to roam about her palace and treated as though they were her own pets. Her palace quickly becomes known as a noisy place, full of the sounds of animals. Still the Emperor does not visit her. At last the second-hand information is not enough for me.

I send word that she is to come to my palace and meet with me. No doubt her eunuchs, if they are loyal to her, will warn her against me, will tell her of the secrets I have hunted down and the punishments I have ensured were meted out when they were discovered.

I can hear the sound of her palanquin's bearers, trotting into my courtyard. She will think my own garden different to hers, for I only allow white flowers in my garden, the colour of mourning, loss and grief. I hear footsteps coming towards me. I am not sure what makes me do it, perhaps a memory of waiting and watching with Feng, but at the last moment I hide behind a giant black and gold screen and wait for her to enter what appears to be an empty room. From where I stand, I cannot be seen, yet I can observe her.

The eunuch showing her into the room knows better than to comment on my absence. Instead, he indicates a chair by the window. She sits looking about her, a worried frown on her face. She gives a little nod to a maid who brings her tea and a small dish of sweets, but she does not touch them, only peers out of the window at my garden, as though she expects to see me there. She shifts in her seat, uncomfortable with the silence surrounding her and my absence.

I continue to watch her. A part of me thinks that I should show myself now, that I should step out from the screen and speak with her. Still, there is something about her that seems strange. I am not sure what it is, she does not remind me of the other concubines, something about the way she sits or the way she moves, seems wrong. Then again, of course, she is not one of us. Perhaps women in her country do things differently, behave differently. Still I watch.

She stands, as though unwilling to wait longer. I wonder if she will leave, or continue to wait for me. She walks about the room, pausing to look at the stand on which my four *ruyi* are displayed. The rosewood, the black sandalwood inlaid with rubies, the green jade, which perhaps reminds her of home. She pauses over the fourth, the one I received when I was made Empress, its intricate gold filigree weighed down with precious gems, characters for greatness spelled out across it. Whether she can read them or not, I do not know. She sits down again and sighs to herself.

What she does next confirms the strangeness I felt in her. First, she dips a finger into the cold tea and sniffs her finger as though expecting to smell something on it, perhaps poison if she mistrusts me. Her uncouth behaviour surprises me. Now she taps her feet, growing ever more restless as she waits for me. Just as I am about to speak, to reveal myself, she looks down her nose, making her almost cross eyed, and blows a spit bubble, something I have not seen someone do since I was a child, and saw ragged urchins in the street blowing them to amuse themselves. I am so shocked that I speak from behind the screen without even stepping out.

"Is this how they raise the daughters of Xinjiang's noble families? Or just you?"

She jumps to her feet, spit dribbling down her chin. She looks about her and wipes her chin with a shaking hand. She looks towards the door and takes a few quick steps to it, touches it but it is fully closed.

"Behind you."

She turns quickly but I am still hidden. Her breath comes loudly, she is panting with fear. She looks about her and suddenly her eyes fix on the screen, on the tiny gap between the panels, where she can see the glint of my eyes. I step out, move forwards, come close to her. She gasps at the sight of me.

"Answer me." She tries to take a step backwards, but there isn't much space between her and the door.

"W – what?"

"Are all the daughters of the noble houses of Xinjiang allowed to blow bubbles from spittle, or just you? Or are there no nobles in your cur-ridden land? Have we been sent nothing but a street rat, a flea-infested stray from the back alleys, a prisoner of war masquerading as a woman fit for an emperor's court?"

Her eyes widen with horror, rather than narrowing with outrage, as though what I am saying is true, rather than deliberately insulting. "Your – Your Majesty – I – I didn't know you were…"

"Clearly not," I say. I glance at the tea and sweets. "You have not partaken of the refreshments I offered you."

"N – no," she says her voice barely above a whisper.

"Why not?" I move slightly to one side, allowing her, if she wishes, to go back to her seat. Awkwardly, she does so, and stands looking down on the cold tea and sweets. I follow her. "Drink. Eat."

"I – I would rather…" Her voice trails off. Slowly, she reaches down without looking away from me and touches the small bowl of tea. She lifts it, her hand shaking so that a little tea spills over the side, but she does not react to it. She brings the bowl to her mouth and takes a little sip, then suddenly gulps it all down, with sounds more befitting to an old woman without teeth than a court lady. The tea finished, she sets the little bowl down.

I will not let her go so easily. "Eat," I say. I do not take my eyes off her.

She eats all of the sweets, one after another, choking a little, one hand over her mouth. When she has finished she stares at me, her eyes wide and terrified, like an animal waiting for the kill. I step one pace forwards, put my face so close to hers that she is blurred.

"Welcome to the Forbidden City, concubine," I say.

But she still stands there, as though unable to believe that she is free to go, that she could have left this room at any time, what could I have done to stop her? For a moment neither of us moves, until finally I speak again.

"Return to your rooms," I say at last.

She backs away, as though I am about to follow her, feels behind her for the door, then turns and runs. I hear her footsteps in the garden, turn to see her almost fall into her palanquin, see her shout something that I cannot hear to her bearers, who look up, startled, then quickly lift her and begin to run.

And she is gone. My garden is empty, full only of the white flowers and twisted black rocks that make up its sole ornamentation. I feel dizzy, afraid, as though it were she who threatened me, as though it were she who made me eat and drink, while insulting me. I have to lean against the wall for a moment, until my breath returns to normal. After that I stay away from her for as long as possible. I am not sure what I have seen in her, but it is something strange and because I cannot name it, I must bide my time.

Finally the Emperor visits her, but only briefly. Then he sees her again, and again. But she is not called to his bedchamber. It takes me a while before I understand what he's doing. He is courting her. The man who could summon her by turning over a bamboo chip on a silver tray to indicate her name to his servants, is courting her. As though she were some new romance, as though he were a young man falling in love for the first time, rather than an emperor, with dozens of women at his disposal. It is sickening; it makes me angry, that he should play this game, and worse, that she should believe it. I think of Feng, of how he described the Emperor as a romantic, a man who wishes to pretend that he must court his ladies, that they truly love him for himself and not because they must. No doubt this is why he does not love me, why he can barely abide me. It is because he knows full well that I do not love him, that I will not play his game of courtship and romance. That I know who and what I am, and who and what he is, and I cannot be persuaded otherwise.

Summer comes and we move to the Garden of Perfect Brightness, where the Emperor has Lady He installed in one of his beloved Western Palaces, as though the Western referred to her own homeland, rather than a place across the seas that she has never visited. He even gives her a second palace, in which she may pray, sometimes watching her as she does so, as though her prayers are some sort of exotic and charming behaviour singular to herself.

Hunting season comes. My furs are unpacked from perfumed storage chests and then repacked for the journey. As ever, the whole court must attend what is, effectively, the Emperor's private hobby. Certainly none of us ladies are interested in the hunt, for we do not take part, we are there only to marvel at Qianlong's prowess and applaud such prize kills as a tiger or a bear. We are expected to listen once again to the story of how a bear nearly killed him as a child, how his grandfather saw, then, the man he would one day become. A true Manchu, he likes to say, to repeat, endlessly.

Many thousands of men along with a few women make the journey to Chengde, the hunting grounds. Here, tents are laid out in a symmetry that matches the Forbidden City, and each of us must give up the comforts of our palaces for a tent, however luxuriously appointed. I retreat to mine, and resign myself to the many days of boredom ahead.

From the opening of my tent I spot Lady He, standing with the

Jesuit painter, Giuseppe Castiglione. They are speaking together, smiling, as though they are old friends. I walk towards them. They do not notice me until I am almost behind them, when Giuseppe's expression alters at the sight of me. He bows deeply, his expression wary. I am certain that Niuhuru told him, years ago, the threat I made that bought me the Empress's crown. He has treated me with excessive caution ever after.

"Your Majesty," he says.

I ignore him and look at Lady He, who bows to me, her own expression fearful. Perhaps she thinks I am about to command her to my tent, to make her drink tea and eat sweets again. "Are you enjoying the hunt, Lady He?"

She flushes and her answer comes out as a stutter. "It's very interesting," she says.

"It's very dangerous," I say. "There are wild animals all around us and the hunters have been known to let fly an arrow in the wrong direction."

I wait for an answer, but she has none to give, she is all but trembling at being in my presence. The old darkness inside me rises up, a thrill of pleasure at her obvious fear of me. I turn and walk away, a smile on my lips.

But it seems the trembling concubine is not so stupid after all, not so fearful. Somehow, she finds a horse, somehow, she ends up in the middle of a hunt, and must be saved by the Emperor and his men, like something from a fairytale. I find myself wondering whether she is cunning, whether the show she puts on, of a homesick and delicate girl, is in fact a front.

For now the Emperor rides with her every day, he even neglects some of the hunting, an unheard of lack of interest. Her eunuchs work deep into the night to have her skirts altered, so that she may ride more easily, they plait her hair with tiny woodland creatures crafted from paper, which nevertheless are left dishevelled after her rides. Half the court wonders whether the Emperor has had her up against a tree or lying in a pile of leaves, like some street girl. He begins to show her other favours, having melons sent from Kashgar, in her homeland, to supposedly tempt her homesick palate. I watch her blush at a banquet when she realises the honour he has paid her, and the faces of the other ladies when they see this sign of favour. I do not taste them, only wave the platter away with disgust.

The nights grow too cold and even the Emperor must give way to the complaints of his women. We make our way back to the Forbidden City and now word reaches me that Lady He has been given another gift. A cook. Apparently, she is homesick for her own food and none of the servants in the vast Imperial kitchens have been able to feed her satisfactorily. I roll my eyes. But when I catch sight of the man, I almost gasp. He does not look like a eunuch, he looks like a man. He reminds me of Feng, his body muscular, his jaw pronounced.

"Find out everything you can about Lady He's new cook," I tell my spy.

He looks confused. "Her cook?"

"You heard me," I snap.

When he returns, the information he brings does not reassure me. His name is Nurmat, apparently, and he is a Muslim, a cook from her own country.

"He's a eunuch?" I cannot help asking.

"Of course," says the spy, looking surprised. "He sleeps in her bedroom, as a guard at night."

I pay and send him away, but something in me tells me that this is not right. This cook, I would swear, is a man, not a eunuch. And if he is a man, if Lady He has a man in her bedchamber every night, then I will ensure that the Emperor hears about it. But not yet. I need evidence.

The Emperor visits her again, this time wishing to try the work of the new cook. Briefly I wonder whether the girl, rather than belonging to our allies, does not in fact come from a family who have hidden their true nature in order to gain access to the Emperor. Is she a spy in our midst, a woman who might seek to harm the Emperor?

"Are you certain," I ask Qianlong on a rare occasion when we are alone, "that Lady He is everything she seems?"

He does not even look up, he only sighs. "I do not wish to hear of your jealousy, Ula Nara," he says. "It is not your business with whom I spend my time."

"You do not spend your nights with her," I say. "Do you mistrust her?"

"It is not becoming of you to know of such things," he says, looking up at last. His expression is cold. "An Empress should not be spying on which lady enters my bedchamber or not."

"I – " I begin.

"This is the end of our conversation," he says. "You may leave."

I have no choice. I have to bow and leave his presence.

Lady He has taken up with Qing and Ying, I see her walking through the gardens with them, watch them visit her palace, and see her visit theirs. What she makes of their forbidden alliance, I do not know, but clearly she has the ability to make friends here. I know she has visited Lady Wan, although Wan always did make friends with anybody.

It is the end of our time at the Garden of Perfect Brightness for the year, which heralds the day that I dread. When the Emperor uses the maze in the Western Palaces to show all of us who is his favourite.

The maze itself is beautiful, made of a grey stone, carved here and there with flowers. At its centre sits a pavilion, where the Emperor, during this event, will sit on a gilded throne, surrounded by lanterns. Here, in this shining, tiny palace, he will await the lady who can make her way through the dark twists and turns of the maze and ascend the steps of the pavilion at its centre. It has been an annual event, since the maze was completed. The outer walls of the maze are surrounded by Imperial yellow flowers, and on the night of this event, it is lit all around with shining lanterns of every shape and size. Each lady is given a lantern to hold, as she enters the maze, and as the first woman makes her way inside, all the lanterns, except those we carry, are extinguished. The maze will be plunged into darkness, and all we will have as our guide is the tiny flickering lanterns in our hands and the shining glow of the pavilion, which we all seek to enter.

As ever, half the court has arrived to watch the spectacle. They think it is charming to see our little lights bobbing amongst the maze, they find it romantic that one lady, one fortunate lady, will enter the Emperor's pavilion, and his arms, if she can walk the maze swiftly and surely. They do not think of the other women, those who are lost inside the maze and who suddenly see the lights of the pavilion go out, signalling that it is already too late, that a woman has made her way to the pavilion and is even now leaving with the Emperor, bound for his bedchamber. They do not think of the humiliation of those of us who must stand and wait within the maze for the eunuchs to find each lady and return us to our palaces.

I sit within my palanquin for longer than is necessary. I do not want to get out and face the court and the other women, take part in this exercise in humiliation. At last, however, I must leave my tiny cocoon and emerge to face what is about to happen. I step out, smoothing down the Imperial yellow silks that are my only protection, my only reminder that, supposedly, I am above these other women.

They are all here, of course. Even Lady Yehenara, who has recently lost a child, and is still grieving, is here. She has dressed in green, which the Emperor dislikes, and so perhaps will only pretend to walk the maze and wait quietly until this evening is over, when she can return to her palace to weep alone. I see Qing and Ying, standing nervously to one side, their hands clasped as though no one were watching. I know full well that they will make no attempt to reach the Emperor.

"Ula Nara." Ling. The only person who rarely calls me 'Your Majesty' as she ought to. I look her over. The embroidery on her robes is designed for one reason only. Bats, persimmons, peaches and cranes, all symbols of fertility, all designed to remind each and every one of us that she has given the Emperor not only two living sons but also daughters. Ling has chosen her own path. Accepting the fact that she cannot become Empress whilst I still live, instead she looks to the future, when she may become the Dowager Empress if her son is chosen as heir to the throne.

"You seem confident," I say. "Anyone would think that you knew the secrets of the maze."

"I have reached the pavilion for many years," she says.

"Since Fuca died," I remind her.

She smiles. "Indeed," she says. "Such a short time ago. And here I am, an Imperial Noble Consort already."

"It may not be so easy this year," I say.

"Really?"

I allow my eyes to flicker in the direction of Lady He, who has had the audacity to dress from head to toe in bridal red. "It looks as though someone else intends to reach the pavilion before any of us."

Ling's eyes follow mine and for a tiny moment a frown crosses her face. "Of course," she says evenly, "the Emperor likes to have a new romance, from time to time."

"He does," I agree. "And Lady He is such a young woman. Fertile, no doubt."

Again, the flicker of a frown crosses Ling's face. "Perhaps," she says. "But her fertility is untried, as yet."

"I am sure tonight will help with that," I say smiling as though I am saying something delightful and turning to leave.

"Ula Nara."

I turn back. "Yes, Ling?"

"There is no need, you know."

"Need?"

Ling sighs. "There are enough paths," she says wearily.

"Paths?"

"You are the Empress," she reminds me. "I wish to be the Dowager Empress." She pauses. "You do not seem ambitious for your... son," she adds, the tiny pause a reminder that one child is all I have left.

I step close enough that even Ling blinks and steps away. "Do not speak of my children," I hiss. "Or I will see you die."

She moves away then, head down, as though she has seen into the pain I carry for one brief moment and realised its burden. I am left with anger running through me, with a darkness that must be unleashed. I make my way to Lady He, signal her to come closer, which she does, unwillingly. I allow myself to look over every inch of her clothing and notice with pleasure the flush staining her collarbones.

"Red, Lady He?"

She bows. "Yes, Your Majesty." There is nothing else she can say.

"Do you know your way through the maze?" I ask.

She lowers her eyes and shakes her head, although there is something in the gesture that is too quick, suspiciously so.

"Have a care which path you choose tonight, Lady He," I say. "The maze is a dark place in which to be lost."

I watch her fear rising at the implied threat. It gives me some satisfaction, it takes away some of the pain that Ling's mention of my children has caused me. I move away, noting the Chief Eunuch's small gesture summoning me to take my place at the front of the women of the court, ready to enter the maze. He hands me a glowing yellow lantern and I stand, facing the dark entryway of the maze, aware of Ling behind me, and behind her all of the other concubines. I nod that I am ready and at once we are plunged into darkness. There is only the moon above our own flickering lanterns and ahead of us the Emperor's pavilion at the centre of the maze, glowing as a beacon to us. I step forward into the darkness, knowing full well that I have never learnt the ways of the maze, that I would be better off following Ling, who I am sure knows at least half of it. I hear the clatter of her shoes as she strides past me and turns right, but I cannot bear this. I cannot bear to follow her and be second. Instead I turn left, into further darkness and then left and left and left again, trying to make my way into the very darkest corners of the maze, as far away from the pavilion as it is possible to be.

I hear giggles here and there, little exclamations, sighs of exasperation and, somewhere, weeping. I stand still for a moment, resting one hand against the cold grey stone of the maze walls. Perhaps I should just stand here, I think, and wait for the pavilion's lanterns to be put out.

They are extinguished so quickly even I am surprised. Somehow one of the concubines has learned the secrets of the maze, for it is impossible to have reached the pavilion so quickly without doing so. Even Ling was never so fast. I reach up high above my head and place my lantern on the top of the wall, a signal to the eunuchs that I am here, lost in the darkness, awaiting rescue. One by one the lanterns appear, one by one they disappear again as each lady is taken from the maze back to her own palace. Some of them weep, some may rage. Some will be relieved. I do not know what I feel. A resignation, perhaps. A glimpse of the future, when year after year I will stand in the darkness of the maze and know that I have failed again at this game and that this moment will happen again and again and again, without end, until I depart this life.

It was Lady He who reached the Emperor so fast. Now he calls for her regularly, he has wooed and won her, has made her come to him of her own free will. He has created a romance and won the maiden's heart.

His gifts to Lady He become absurd. He has some notion that she is homesick. He takes this as a challenge, embarking on a quest to make her happy. First, he turns an old printing room into a bathhouse for her, insisting that we call it a *hammam*, some word from her country that no doubt pleases him with its exotic sound. I go to look at it, stand inside the small space and look up at the domed roof, run a hand across the gleaming tiles and then leave.

He goes a step further. He somehow believes that a noblewoman, if that is what she is, must miss the hustle and bustle of a street market. And so he constructs for her a *bazaar*, another exotic word for the folly he has undertaken. Eunuchs are dressed up in clothes from her home country, wearing mock beards and embroidered felt hats, the bright colours of her people. They have even been taught to pray, or at least pretend to, in a manner that mimics her own devotions. The other ladies of the court chatter over this extravagance, some even go so far as to have their hair dressed in plaits, as though they were common maids, in an effort to look like the Emperor's new favourite toy. I make my excuses. I plead illness, although no doubt everyone will whisper that I am jealous. But my curiosity cannot be held in check, and so I dress as a maid and scurry, head down, through the *bazaar* to see it for myself. No one sees me, no one expects me, they only play at their game, hoping to win the Emperor's favour by so doing. I see him with her, one arm about her waist, as though they were peasants, young lovers, instead of an emperor and his concubine. They laugh together, heads almost touching as she shows him first one delicacy and then another from her homeland. He eats the sweetmeats provided and is delighted with his illusion. I see Ling look away, lips tight, but I know that all that worries her is the possibility that Lady He might bear a child who could supersede her own as heirs. Ling plays the long game. I return to my rooms and feel the bile rising, the darkness inside me twisting. I had thought I could stay numb but I cannot. So Qianlong is to have not one but two great loves in his life and I am still denied even one? The Immortals must truly hate me, must have chosen my destiny based on some grave misdemeanour in a past life, to be so cruel in their mockery of my own desire for love.

I begin to avoid going out of my palace, I pass on my duties to other women. I am afraid of what I will do or say. The emptiness, the safe numbness, will come back, I think, I will reclaim it if I can only stay away from the sight of Qianlong and his new love.

"A visitor," announces a eunuch.

I look up. "I do not wish to receive a visitor," I tell him. I am still in my sleeping robe, my hair hangs down my back, unbrushed, unwashed.

The eunuch hovers in the doorway, uncertain of how to proceed. "It is Lady Wan," he says. "She is most insistent."

I frown. It is years since I have see Wan socially. I see her at court gatherings and she always smiles. I nod to her in return, watching the wrinkles grow on her face, noting the rumours that she is still bald, although if she is, then her wigs are a masterpiece. I do not see her socially because I do not trust myself not to wound her with my words, lash out with the hurt that is within me.

"I do not wish to see her," I repeat. "You may tell her that I am ill."

"That is why I am here," says Wan, appearing just behind the eunuch and gesturing to him to leave. He glances at me but I do not respond and so he obeys her, closing the door behind him. Wan's dog is with her, an absurdly small creature who bounces around the room as though it cannot contain its pleasure in being alive. It licks my hand and then brushes back past my fingers as though to entice caresses from me but I do not respond. Its short curly fur is rough on my fingertips.

I look up at Wan. "I cannot imagine why you would want to see me," I say, trying to keep my voice polite.

"I am worried about you," she says. She comes closer, sits down next to me, our knees touching. She is still dressed as the young girl who first came here, in a light pink silk covered with cherry blossom embroidery, her hair full of flowers. Not for her the more formal robes or stronger, darker colours favoured by the more mature women of the court. No, Wan's heart is still girlish and her appearance matches her demeanour.

"I hear that you are unhappy," says Wan. "That the Emperor's interest in the fragrant concubine distresses you."

"The what?" I ask.

"Lady He."

"What did you call her?"

Wan laughs. "'The fragrant concubine'. The ladies call her that. Because of her personal fragrance. It comes from her own skin, it is astonishing."

"Don't be ridiculous, Wan," I say. "No-one naturally smells of perfume."

Wan smiles as though she has decided not to argue with me only to keep the peace. It grates.

"I am well enough," I say.

Wan looks at my tangled hair, down at my hands, which are

grown skeletal, at my wrinkled sleeping robe, which should have been replaced by my day clothes far earlier this morning. "Oh my dear," she says, her voice trembling a little with unhappy kindness. "You are not well at all. You have not been well since you came here."

I try to laugh. "I have managed to become Empress," I say. "There are those who would say I have done well enough."

"But you have always remained unhappy," says Wan simply. "Your heart still aches."

I feel something rise up, the desire to weep at the simplicity and truth of her words, her good hearted understanding. But something warns me that there is so much to weep for that if I begin, I may never stop. Not only for the lost love of Niu Lang, but for the loss of my family and little sister, for the loss of my children, even for the loss of Feng, for Qianlong's eternal reminders that I am not loved. If I cried for everything I have been through since I was chosen, how could I ever stop? And so rather than lay my head on Wan's shoulder and let the tears fall, I only hold myself more tightly upright and give a pinched smile.

"I am sure everyone has heartache in their lives at some time or another," I say. "None of us can claim eternal happiness."

Wan only looks at me, her own eyes brimming with tears at the lie behind my words. One tear falls and she brushes it away, then rises and looks down on me. "I would always be glad to see you, whenever you cared to visit me or send for me," she says gently. "We all of us have heartache, Ula Nara, but heartache shared amongst friends is greatly lessened."

I do not answer. I do not even watch her as she leaves the room, her little dog gambolling behind her. Instead I spend several moments clenching every part of me so that the tears will not begin to fall.

So be it, I think. If I cannot rid myself of the darkness within, if I am not even free to become a nun and seek tranquillity and peace, then let the darkness rise again. I see the Emperor with Lady He. Knowing what fear I strike in her heart, I send for her again. When she arrives, I am standing looking down at my collection of *ruyis*. I see her kowtow out of the corner of my eye, but wait before I turn to face her.

"The Emperor shows you favour," I say.

"Yes, Your Majesty," she says. Her voice is very flat, she has been expecting this line of enquiry. "He has been gracious to me – as he is to all his ladies," she adds.

"I am concerned." I wait for her to ask why, but she only bows her head. "I have heard rumours," I say.

She looks up at once, frowning. Her eyes are filled with a fear I find interesting. "Rumours?"

"I have heard that the cook that His Majesty gave you is of your own country and that you speak often with him."

"He comes to me for his orders," she says, much too fast. "To agree on the dishes he should serve at my table."

I take a risk. "At night?"

Her eyes flicker. She does not deny my insinuation. "He's a eunuch," she says, then adds hastily, "there can be no harm in his attending me."

I think of Feng. I think of nights together in the dark, our bodies tearing at one another for comfort, for release, for revenge on our miserable lives. "There are many ways in which a eunuch may please his mistress," I say quietly. "It has been known before."

She gapes at me as though she cannot imagine what I am saying. "I – such things – how?" she stutters at last.

I frown. How is it she does not understand what I mean, yet her eyes are filled with fear at the idea of my questioning the status of her supposed eunuch? "Perhaps when you are older you will understand more of what can be between a woman and a man – or even a eunuch,"

I say. "You are still a child who believes the storytellers' lies of true love."

She says nothing. She does not deny, she does not pretend outrage, she does not try to protect herself. She only stands there, waiting.

I turn away. "Thank you for your visit, Lady He," I say. I hear her kowtowing behind me and then her steps as she reaches the door. I speak softly just as she is about to escape. "Lady He?"

"Your Majesty?"

"I will not fail to undo you if I find you are betraying the Emperor."

She does not answer, she only leaves me alone, gazing at the four *ruyi* as when she found me.

But her visit and my insinuations have frightened her. I hear that she has her servants whipped, that she has their rooms searched, which only turns up the fact that Ling has been spying on her also, wanting to know when she bleeds, whether she has fallen with child. This is what worries Ling. It does not worry me. I have no children, only a boy who does not even think of me as his mother. I have no-one's future to protect or fight for, not even my own.

I sit on my throne and watch.

"Lady He is promoted: she is made *Pin*, Imperial Concubine."

New allocations of silver, silks and servants are proclaimed. She stands, dressed in pink and gold, silk flowers in her hair, pearls dripping from her earrings. She is presented with a new *ruyi* in a white jade inlaid with coloured gems in the shape of flowers, which she holds as though it might break, smiling up at the Emperor, who beams back at her. She is about to complete a kowtow and leave, when he speaks.

"I have another gift for you," he says. "Something to mark the anniversary of you joining my court."

She smiles and bows. The rest of the court watches and waits.

The gifts he has given her so far have been lavish, even by Imperial standards, but they have also been unusual. We wait to see what he is about to offer this time.

"I am honoured, Your Majesty. You have done more than enough," she says.

He shakes his head. "I believe your cook has been satisfactory," he says. "I have enjoyed good meals at your palace and I even hear your clothes have been altered to ensure you can continue to eat your fill." He chuckles.

Her eyes flicker. "Yes, Your Majesty. He is a most excellent cook."

"Very good," he says. "Now I have brought you a new servant. A maid."

I catch the expressions of some of the courtiers. A maid? What sort of a gift is a maid? The Forbidden City is full of maids, indeed, Lady He has just been granted more of them. Why mention one in particular?

"A maid," he clarifies, "from your own lands. One who will remind you of Xinjiang and help you feel more at home here."

He is delighted with his idea and the court murmurs with interest, but I am watching Lady He, whose face has drained white. Her legs seem to be trembling and her eunuch attendant puts one hand on her back, as though she is about to faint. She turns to look at a small, folded up figure in the doorway, but her face suggests she already knows who the person is, before they even lift their face from the kowtow they are performing.

The girl, this new maid, is scarred, an ugly scar that comes too close to her eye and cuts her cheek in half. She stands and makes her way towards Lady He, one foot dragging in an ungainly limp. A scarred, crippled maid might be occasion for disgust, not the fear that I see on Lady He's face. The maid is dressed correctly, in a plain blue robe, her hair in a long plait, tied with a small red ribbon. Her face, despite the scar, looks similar to Lady He's, but then they are from the same country, so I suppose that is to be expected.

Lady He has still not spoken. Now she swallows, and opens her mouth. "Your Majesty's generosity knows no bounds," she says. "Thank you." She kowtows, the Emperor smiles, and she is dismissed, making her way out of the great receiving hall, the crippled maid limping behind her.

I might have forgotten about the maid, but when I think about it, it is from the moment of the maid's arrival that Lady He begins to change. She makes strange requests, such as desiring a grove of oleaster trees to be sent from her homeland, to be planted in the gardens here, claiming that they would help with her homesickness, a strange thing to be homesick for. But the trees cause more trouble than they can possibly be worth. The porters rebel against transporting them. More than two hundred men use the trunks of the trees as clubs to attack the armed guards, before going on to kill local officials and install their own leaders. This, of course, only enrages the Emperor. More trees are sent for. The men are punished.

Lady He becomes changeable in her manner: sometimes displaying unexpected coldness or rudeness to people she knows quite well. I hear that she treats the new maid as though she is afraid of her, often requesting a different maid to serve her, although one would have thought she would like to have someone with whom she can easily speak or even reminisce with about her country. I think to set further spies on her, to understand what is going on, but I am saved the trouble.

It is nightfall when a eunuch announces that I have a visitor. "A servant of Lady He," he adds, foreseeing that I will refuse to see the person in question.

I am on my feet at once. "Show him in," I say. I do not know why the personal cook of another concubine should visit me, but such a visit can only confirm my feeling that something strange is going on.

The cook hovers in the doorway and again, particularly at close quarters, I am reminded of Feng. I am reminded of a man. I would be prepared to swear that he is no eunuch. He does not walk like them. He does not talk like them, he does not even smell like them.

"My name is Nurmat," he begins, his dark brown eyes flickering around the room as though to check we are alone. He falls silent as though he does not know how to go on.

"You are welcome," I say. "Sit down."

He blinks at this unexpected offer, then takes a seat at the far end of the room from me.

"Closer," I say.

He rises obediently and makes his way closer to me, pauses uncertainly before I wave him into a seat barely an arm's length from me. For a moment, we only look at each other, before I decide to risk all.

"You are not really a eunuch," I remark, as though it were a matter of no importance rather than a treasonous offence punishable by instant death.

He could protest. He could widen his eyes and be appalled at the suggestion. But he does not. "Your Majesty is perceptive," he says.

"And you are here because you wish me to know this," I say. "Because you wish your mistress harm?"

"It is she who wishes the Emperor harm," he says.

I feel my heart begin to race. "In what way does she wish the Emperor harm?" I ask. "As far as I can see, she enjoys his attentions. And he has been most generous with both his time and gifts."

"My mistress is not what she seems," says Nurmat.

"Tell me everything you know," I say.

"What do you know about the besieging of Yarkand?"

I shrug. "The final siege of the battle to conquer Xinjiang. The Sultan surrendered. He cut off the heads of the rebel leaders Burhan ad-Din and Khoja Jihan and showed their bodies to the commander of the Emperor's army as a gesture of goodwill. The Emperor was delighted. The Empire was made a third larger by his victory."

Nurmat nods. "The girl sent here, whom he has named Lady He… she is the daughter of the family who turned traitors and helped the Emperor to victory."

"Yes," I say. "Their treasonous act to their own country finally gave us victory. The girl being made a concubine was a reward, an acknowledgement of their loyalty to us."

"But what if they had a different plan?"

"Plan?"

Nurmat pauses.

"Speak," I urge him.

"What if they thought to harm the Emperor?"

"By surrendering?"

"By *seeming* to surrender. By asking for their loyalty to be rewarded with a daughter of their house coming to court."

"And what good would that do them? What good is a woman at court?"

"A woman who hates the Emperor, who would kill for her country?"

I swallow. "Are you saying Lady He is going to kill Qianlong?"

Nurmat kneels. "I beg you to have her sent away from the Forbidden City," he says. "All of us: Lady He, myself, her maid."

"Her maid?" I think of the scarred, limping woman.

"She is here to help Lady He," he says.

My head is pounding. I think of Lady He's bright eyes looking up at the Emperor, his arm about her waist. "Are you sure of what you are telling me?" I ask. "What is your part in all of this?"

"I was to bring weapons into the Forbidden City for her," he says. "I smuggled daggers to her. Her maid sewed them into the sleeves of her jackets, so that she might use them when she has a chance, when they are alone together."

"All the court ladies are stripped of their clothing before they enter the Emperor's bedchamber," I say. "For that very reason," I add.

"But the Emperor walks with her in the gardens, he takes her hunting," says Nurmat. "It would take only a moment."

"You must leave me now," I say.

"I beg you to send her away," he repeats.

"Why do you wish her plan to fail?" I ask, suddenly suspicious. I move away from him, thinking for a moment that perhaps he, too, has daggers on him, that while Lady He kills the Emperor, he will kill me.

He swallows. "I – I love – her," he says. "I do not wish harm to come to her because of this plan."

His eyes shine with unshed tears for a moment. "You wanted her for yourself and instead she was chosen for this plan?" I ask.

"Yes," he says and I recognise grief in him, the grief I have felt all these years.

"Leave me now," I repeat. "You will do something?" he asks.

"I will think on it," I say. "She is the Emperor's favourite, I cannot simply have her dismissed."

"I am afraid," he says, his voice very low. "I am afraid she will act soon."

I am frozen. I cannot think how to even suggest to Qianlong that his favourite concubine might wish him ill. But even if I did, something makes me pause. If Qianlong were to die… I would be free. As an Empress, I would not be banished to the back palaces as would the other concubines. I would become an Empress Dowager. I would be free of obligations, for it is unlikely that my son would be chosen as heir when Qianlong has always favoured Ling. Instead I would keep my palace but be set free of any obligations, of any expectations. I might even claim that my grief for Qianlong is so great that I wish to become a nun, and no one could stop me. But if for any reason Nurmat should talk, if it became known that I was told of the danger to Qianlong and did nothing, then I would be executed for treason. And if Nurmat has lied to me and I accuse Lady He without cause, Qianlong will believe me merely jealous or worse, mad. I wonder sometimes if I told Qianlong everything and was proven right if he would reward me by setting me free, allowing me to become a nun after all, but that seems an impossibility.

I wake and these thoughts go round in my head. I sleep and dream of Lady He, of Nurmat, of Qianlong dying. I wake gasping and once again the endless thoughts circle around my mind while I try to find a way forward.

I try to eat. At every meal, my table is covered in more than one hundred dishes, yet I cannot find anything that I can swallow. Food that was once pleasing to me is now tasteless, as though my mouth no longer recognises it as food but only as ashes or dirt. It is so extreme that I wonder if perhaps I have lost my sense of taste, of smell. Yet the incense that I must burn for rituals still chokes my nose and mouth, its rich sweet smell making me nauseous. I ask my cooks to provide ever-stronger tastes, from spicy peppers to heavily salted, sharp pickles, or cakes dripping in honey. I place them in my mouth and the taste that ought to be there is gone. I eat less and less, rising from my table when the food in front of me has been barely touched. No doubt my servants eat better than they have ever done before, gulping down the lavish remains from my table, while I grow thinner than ever. When I dress in the mornings my robes fall over my shrunken frame. I see the eunuchs who dress me glance at one another. They have my robes taken in, made smaller to fit my newly narrow body, but still I grow thinner. Now when I look down at my hands, clutching bundles of incense, I can see every bone, my golden nail shields as hard and pointed as the rest of my hands. My skin turns grey. My maids take it upon themselves to rub ever-richer creams into my skin, hoping to restore some of its natural lustre, but they do not work. Even my shoes grow loose, my hair loses its shine and hangs limply down my back as the eunuchs brush and pin it each morning. I feel dizzy when I stand up, and am unsurprised when my monthly bleeding does not come, heralding not a new life within me, for I have not been summoned to the Imperial bedchamber in some time, but instead, the weakness of my body made manifest, unable to perform its natural functions.

Along with the weakness that I feel and the dizziness when I rise comes a great weariness. Even when I wake in the morning, the only thing I can think about is sleep. Sometimes I refuse to rise altogether, if there are not rituals to be carried out, instead returning to my bed, waving away my expectant servants and burrowing into the warmth of my coverlets. I feel the cold, insisting on wearing furs even when the other ladies have packed theirs away for the summer. The old nightmares that I thought had left me return. All of Ping's stories come back to me now, waking me from slumber in a sweating gasp, clutching at my covers and calling for more lights. Soon I am sleeping with lanterns fully lit in my bedroom, many dozens of them, making the night brighter than the day. Still I dream. I see the Korean concubines, lying in pools of blood, or those lucky enough to escape such an end then finding themselves obliged to take their own lives to honour the life of the man whom they must have feared and despised in equal measure. I hear things that are not there, I see things that no one else sees, starting back from shadows and refusing to be left alone. I am afraid that Nurmat will have told his mistress what he did and that now she will think to kill me first, before I can warn Qianlong, if I can ever warn him. My servants grow accustomed to keeping watch over me all night, knowing they will be whipped if I wake and find them asleep. They set up shifts amongst themselves, ensuring that there are always two of them awake, sitting in my room, watching me sleep, or rather, watching me toss and turn in the grip of my nightmares. I doubt they feel sorry for me, why would they? I have earned a reputation as the harshest of mistresses. Eunuchs and maids alike blanch at the thought of serving me, even beg not to be assigned to my palace.

My dreams and fears unnerve them. At first, they say that it is my palace that is haunted, but then I hear the whispers. They remember what Ping said, for it has been passed down, maid to maid, eunuch to eunuch. I hear them whisper about a hungry ghost, who stalks the Empress, wanting something from her, always wanting and never satisfied. They speak in whispers of Ping, whipped to death, of Feng, who took his own life. I do not dissuade them, for I believe them, although I know that it is not a ghost who stalks me, but I myself that is the hungry ghost, who searches and searches for what will fill the gaping belly of my loneliness and grief and yet cannot, will not, ever find it. I wonder that no one can see this, that no one knows what and who I am, what I have become. There are days when I remove my robes and stand, naked, in front of a mirror. I see the bones that make up my body, the grey-white of my skin and the darkened circles under my eyes, and I think, *how can you not see what I am?*

We are to embark on a new Southern Tour. I cannot help thinking back to the last such tour, when Fuca died and I made the mistake of thinking that her throne would heal me. This tour is supposedly for the good of the health of Niuhuru, so that it can be seen as the Emperor's filial duty to take her on it, although everyone knows that it is Qianlong who loves to travel. The route will take us overland through Zhili and Shandong to Qingkou in Jiangsu, where we will cross the Yellow River and continue our journey on the Grand Canal. The Canal will take us to Yangzhou, Zhenjiang, Danyang, Changzhou and then Suzhou. After Zhenjiang, we will also go on to Jiaxing and Shimen before we reach Hangzhou, our last stop, on the Yellow Sea. On our return journey, the Emperor will wish to inspect the troops at Jiangning. We will travel constantly for four months. The very thought of it is exhausting. The Emperor intends to visit the Yellow River, to ensure that barrages and ocean levees are built to avoid disastrous floods such as have happened in the past. No doubt he will enjoy inspecting the works, while we ladies will be expected to accompany him on these dull visits. Meanwhile there will be processions, with special permission granted that common people may look upon the Emperor's face and ours as we pass by, unlike in Beijing where we travel with bamboo screens along the routes we take to avoid the Son of Heaven being seen by mere mortals. There will be thousands who come to see the Emperor and, of course, his ladies. My servants spend days packing, my richest and most beautiful robes will be displayed to peasants who may never have touched silk, let alone worn it.

The court gathers in readiness for the journey and I make my way to the Emperor.

"I ask you not to bring Lady He on this journey," I begin.

"It is not your place to even make such a request," he says, and his face is already angry.

"I do not trust her," I say.

He sighs in irritation. "You don't trust anybody," he says. "You are known for it. You are known for your spying, your punishments, your jealousy of every other woman at court. It is not becoming. It is not the behaviour of an Empress. Lady Fuca would not have stooped so low."

"Lady Fuca was loved," I say.

"Are you still clinging to the memory of your lost sweetheart?" he asks.

I gape at him.

"Did you think I did not know?" he asks, standing, coming closer to me so that I have to look up at him. "Oh, I was told, I was told at once. The whole court knew. That you begged my mother to let you return to some childhood sweetheart. That when your plea went unanswered and you joined my ladies, you set your mind to grieve forever. And nothing has pleased you since. I did not call you to my bedchamber and you were not satisfied, I promoted you twice and you were not satisfied, I made you Step Empress against my better judgement and you were not satisfied. I saw to it that you bore children and you were not satisfied. You have set your mind to be unhappy, and so you are. There is nothing I can do for you, for you will not be satisfied. Now you are determined to be jealous of a woman who has done nothing to you but choose to be happy here. Can you not allow others happiness, Ula Nara? Are you not capable of it yourself?"

"My children," I begin.

"We have all lost children," he cuts me off. "There is barely one of my ladies who has not lost a child, and all of them were my own sons and daughters. You still have a son, whom you never see. You could not have him by your side all the time, and so you refuse to see him at all. You could not have your sweetheart, and so you have refused every other possible chance of happiness in your life. Do you think he has done the same?"

"I – "

"He will be married by now, Ula Nara!" Qianlong says, his voice rising in anger. "He will be married, with a concubine of his own, or maybe several. He will have children. He will never think of you, except when he has drunk too much and boasts to his friends that he once kissed the cheek of an Imperial concubine, of the woman who has become Step Empress. That is the only time he will think of you."

"He became a monk!" I retort, my own voice rising almost to a shout. "He knew the meaning of loyalty! He swore to love me for ever, and if he could not have me, he would have no other."

"And if he did!" Qianlong says, throwing up his hands, "then by now his masters will have taught him to let go of a childish love, to see beyond it and look into the infinite, not tie himself forever to an earthly need. He is gone, Ula Nara. Whether married or a monk, he is gone. And you should let him go."

"I will never let him go!" I say. "He was my true love, as Fuca was yours. And I do not think she would care to see you wooing Lady He."

I have gone too far. His face changes from exasperation to anger.

"Do not speak her name," he hisses at me. "You are not fit to speak her name."

"*His* name was Niu Lang!" I scream. "His name was Niu Lang and we loved one another! And neither of us will ever forget our first and true love. Unlike you!"

"Get out," he says. "Get out of here, before I order you punished."

I weep in my rooms for many days, and of course the servants talk. They say I am jealous. They do not know that I weep because I am afraid. Afraid that what Qianlong said is true. That Niu Lang may have married after all. Or that, as befits a monk, he may have learnt to set aside all thoughts of me. In either case, I am alone with my love, a love that is not returned, but long forgotten by my beloved.

But the Southern Tour must go ahead. The vast courtyards of the Forbidden City are filled with courtiers and eunuchs, maids and guards, palanquins in every colour, as each lady of the court and her retinue struggles to find their place in the hierarchy of the procession that is about to make its way out of the gates. My own palanquin comes close to that of Lady He, who is not yet seated within it, but is stroking a horse on which is seated Ling's son Prince Yongyan, dressed in an orange silk with stripes, a tiger costume of which he is inordinately proud. He bares his teeth at her and she laughs and makes some answer, pretending to cower. Rage rises up inside me, at this woman who finds happiness so easily, so far from home. I put out my hand from the silken drapes that cover me and say, loudly enough for her to hear, "The dogs should be at the back of the procession, especially that mongrel cur." I know that to call people of her faith a dog is a great insult, and I watch her face flush. She turns and climbs into her palanquin, seeking safety from my gaze.

And so the Tour commences. We sway along, day after day, our resting places changed each night, the servants unpacking and packing again each day. As Empress, as part of this court, I am endlessly surrounded by fawning hosts, who hope to gain favour by their treatment of me, who do not realise that all I want is to be left alone. Many of the women plead 'Southern heat' in order to avoid attending the Emperor as he visits construction sites for dykes, levees, and barrages. But I am the Empress, I am not allowed respite. In every city I must perform rituals at the temples, side-by-side with the Emperor. Local deities, sacrificial ceremonies at the mausoleums of ancestral Emperors, commemorations for historical personages of note and officials, honouring their past memories if they are dead, presenting them with tokens of favour if they are alive. My days are spent within clouds of incense, so that my lungs ache and I develop a cough. I walk up and down endless steps of temples and memorials, kowtow so often that my muscles ache. When I look in the mirror at night, my wrinkles have grown more pronounced, and I am so tired I can barely eat at the banquets we must attend. I grow thinner, and this only makes my wrinkles more evident. I feel and look far older than I am, and still there is no chance to rest.

Today we enter the city of Suzhou, almost at the end of our journey. It is something like the Garden of Perfect Brightness, criss-crossed with waterways on which boats of all sizes travel, with tiny bridges everywhere. It is famous for its gardens, some of which are built around fairytales and legends, often made of the dark twisted rocks so beloved by the Imperial Family. Expert gardeners have created mazes and placed rocks to simulate the shapes of creatures, such as those found in the Lion Grove Garden. We enter the city sailing down the Grand Canal, lined with thousands of people come to see their Emperor. There are lanterns, singers and musicians, so that there is a cacophony of different pieces of music being played simultaneously. As we pass, the people throw themselves onto their knees and kowtow, before raising their heads again to gape at our splendour. Every lady of the court, conscious that they will be seen, has outdone themselves in their selection of robes, jewels, and flowers. We look like the Imperial warehouses come to life. I sit in my Imperial yellow, wearing a diadem of golden birds and dangling pearls. I feel so tired I can barely keep my eyes open. My stomach churns, whether from hunger or the rocking of the boat, I am unsure.

"Are you sick?" asks Niuhuru, when she sees me. "Smile," she adds, conscious of the show we must put on for the watching crowds.

I fix something approximating a smile on my face and look to one side and another, so that the onlookers will be able to say they have seen the Empress and be satisfied. I put one hand out and touch the Emperor's sleeve, hoping that he may see how unwell I feel and tell me that I do not need to attend all the events that have been arranged for today. But his attention is on the high-ranking officials who are awaiting our arrival ahead, and he makes his way to them as our boat docks. A trembling official helps me disembark, and I wearily follow him, while Lady He, all smiles, follows the Emperor.

It is my birthday. Qianlong has decided there will be a banquet in my honour, there will be local officials and dignitaries. But I am distracted. I can hear endless chanting from a nearby palace, wafts of incense smoke float past.

"Lady He is having an exorcism performed," says my eunuch.

"A what?"

"An exorcism. Her eunuchs believe they saw the ghost of her dead sister in her room. So an exorcism is being carried out."

I am so tired I cannot even think this through, what it means. Ghost of a dead sister? Appearing, suddenly, in her rooms when there has been no previous mention of such a person? "I need to sleep," I say. "Close the shutters and prepare my bed."

"The Emperor expects you at your birthday banquet tonight," says the eunuch. "The maids are waiting to bathe you."

I think of the bathing, the dressing, the elaborate ministrations to my hair, the heavy headdress I must wear, the high shoes that make my feet ache. I think of the toasts that will be made, wishing me ten thousand years of this miserable life. I bite my lip so hard to stop from crying that I taste blood. "Very well," I say, as though I am a child, or a servant, to be commanded in this manner. "I will attend the banquet. But I will visit the gardens first." I need to get away from everyone, from their endless watching and from my muddled thoughts about what Lady He is doing.

Tiger Hill is warm and muggy. I almost regret coming here. I pass by the Sword-Testing Rock and then the Pond of Swords, each named after some legend or other, some myth of great deeds or words immortalised in water and stone. There is even the Magpie Bridge, named for the tale of star-crossed lovers I have clung to all my life. I turn my face away from the sight of it and call out to the bearers that it is growing late and we must make our way to the banquet, I do not wish to walk in the gardens after all. The quickest way to our destination is to pass the maze of the Lion Grove Gardens, and so my bearers make their way along a small path and then into an open area, decorated with the twisted rocks of the region, a pond and some trees. The palanquin comes to a sudden halt, as though there is some impediment to us proceeding. I draw the drapes and then, my stomach lurching what I have seen, step out of the palanquin. Somehow, I remember to gesture to the bearers to wait elsewhere. They trot away.

Lady He is standing with Nurmat by her side, both their faces flushed. Behind her, on the ground in the dust, is a crumpled jacket, as though they have been using it to lie on. But beyond the two of them stands Lady He's maid, who has turned to face me. I stare at her. She is not dressed as a maid, she is dressed in rich silks. Her scar has disappeared. What I am seeing is a near-double of Lady He. I look from one to the other in disbelief and yet what I am seeing is confirmation that Nurmat told me the truth, that there is a vast deception going on which can only mean something terrible is about to happen. A glint catches my eye and I see, at Lady He's feet, a pile of daggers, perhaps as many as seven, their blades uncovered. I step backwards, suddenly afraid for my own safety. My movement is echoed by the maid, who darts away, disappearing behind the rocks. Now I am alone with Lady He and Nurmat and I can feel my heart beating fast. Will they kill me, I wonder? Is the maid concealing herself nearby, ready to throw a dagger at me? But the two of them are kneeling to me and kowtowing, as though we are back in the Forbidden City, following the usual rules of protocol. Lady He rises, but Nurmat remains kneeling in the dust.

"How can there be so much treachery in one place?" I say at last, my voice hoarse with fear.

Neither of them answer. I turn to Nurmat, still kneeling before me. He, at least, I think, has not lied to me. "You have been loyal to me," I say. "I will not forget it."

Lady He frowns. "Your Majesty?"

"I live only to serve you, Your Majesty," Nurmat replies. His voice slurs. I think perhaps he is drunk, or maybe ill. Maybe Lady He has poisoned him, I think, has found out that he has betrayed her secrets and now means to be rid of him.

Lady He is still staring at him. "Nurmat?"

He looks up at her, his eyes bloodshot. "Now your ladyship will be punished for your transgressions," he says. "For attempting to seduce a eunuch servant of your household. For having treasonous intentions towards the Emperor, spurred on by traitorous rebels from Xinjiang with whom you secretly corresponded in Beijing. Her Majesty the Empress will see to it that you forfeit your life for these crimes."

Lady He gapes at him and then looks at me. "I–" she begins but I am already holding up a hand to stop her. There is nothing she can do to explain this situation. "You traitorous, lust-ridden bitch," I say. "I will have you executed for this and then the Emperor will see how wrong he was to care for you. He will reward those who are loyal to him."

"Your Majesty – " she begins.

"You can deny nothing," I say. "Your own servant has testified against you."

She puts out a hand but I step back. "Don't touch me," I say. "Or I will scream."

She draws back. Unsteadily, I make my way towards where my bearers have taken the palanquin, afraid that if I lose eye contact with her she will grab for the daggers at her feet and strike at me. The bearers approach as they see me coming towards them. Once I am safely inside, I address her again.

"Your country is a treacherous pit of mongrel dogs," I say, my heart still beating hard. "It does not surprise me that we have been sent two of its bitches to commit treason against the Emperor. You will all die for this."

I am carried away but as we leave the gardens I look out of my draped window and it seems to me I see the Emperor with Lady He at his side, walking together. For a moment I think of going back, of accusing Lady He in front of Qianlong but I know that my words will have more weight if there are witnesses.

I make the bearers run back to the palace. The birthday banquet will begin soon and I have not been prepared. My hands are shaking from the encounter with Lady He and her collaborators and my heart feels strange, as though wings are beating inside my chest, the rhythm of its beat uneven, first a slow beat and then two together, too fast. The maids try to wash me but I wave them away, there is no time, I will have to go as I am, even though I have been sweating, my skin feels clammy. I pull on a fresh robe, which is too large. The belt must be pulled tighter to try and shape it to my body. My hair takes a long time to style, made longer by the fact that I keep moving under the hands of my servants, my legs constantly shaking, one foot drumming out a nervous rhythm.

The eunuch painting my face does not look happy. He hesitates, before applying more pink to my cheeks, confirming what I already know, which is that I look ill. Additional trinkets are added to my hair, a longer string of pearls is hung around my neck, as though all of these things will magically make me look younger, healthier, happier.

"Enough," I say at last, seeing that he is about to put still more red on my lips.

I stagger towards the door. My head is spinning. What am I to do? Whatever the plan between Nurmat, Lady He and her maid, I believe they are about to strike. The Emperor's life is in danger. And I, who wish to be free of this life, am the only one who can save him. I stop, clutching the doorframe, and breathe heavily for a few moments. At last I raise my head. I will have to save him. There is no one else to do so and I am afraid of what will happen if their plan goes ahead. I would be a fool to think that an easy path to freedom would lie ahead for me were Qianlong to die. Why would they kill just the Emperor? They may well kill us all. I take a deep breath. I know that I look ill, but I must appear to be well enough to make this accusation against the Emperor's favourite concubine and not be thought mad or jealous. He must believe me. I begin walking towards my palanquin, when I become aware that my magpies, in their aviary, are making a strange noise. I hesitate. The banquet will already have begun, Qianlong will be angry with me for not appearing on time, and if he is angry, he may be even less likely to believe me.

But I have never heard the magpies cry like this, not even the time when one of their offspring fell out of the aviary and had to be rescued.

"One moment," I say to my hovering eunuchs. "I must see to the birds." I walk to the aviary and at once my heart falls.

Lying on the bottom of the aviary floor is the male magpie, its wings outstretched, its eyes lifeless. Above, the female magpie cries and cries again, her plaintive calling for her dead mate breaking my heart. My eyes fill with tears for her. These two birds have been my constant companions all these years. A sudden cold weight settles in my stomach. Is it a sign? Has Niu Lang died? He gave me the magpies as a sign of our love, and they have lived longer than I have ever heard of two birds in captivity living before. I had almost thought them immortal. And yet, here is the male magpie, lifeless, whilst the female grieves for her mate.

"Your Majesty," says a eunuch by my side. "We are very late. We must go."

"I cannot," I say, my voice shaking. "I cannot."

"We must," says the eunuch, "His Majesty will be expecting us."

I do not answer. I simply walk away from him, back into the palace rooms. Inside, I make my way to my dressing table, where I look in one drawer and box after another until I find what I am looking for. Scissors. The weighty golden headdress I am wearing is difficult to lift away from my hair, but I manage it. The gold and jade pins underneath are trickier. I tug and tug, feeling knots form under my fingers as I force the pins out of the elaborate hairstyle my servants have created. The floor is littered with pins, my headdress lies on its side on the dressing table, abandoned. The scissors are heavy and the metal feels cold in my hands. For a moment, I hesitate. But I am too well versed in etiquette not to know what is required of me now. The man I have considered my husband all these years is dead, and a grieving widow must take this step. The first sound of the scissors, the sharp snip of metal on metal shocks me, but I keep going. I do not look in the mirror until I have finished. When I do, I drop the scissors, which crash to the floor.

My hair is cut close to my scalp, ragged chunks still left here and there, where I could not see what I was doing. There is one long strand still left, but I am already on my feet and leaving the room. When I step out of the palace, the eunuchs turn to me. There is an audible grasp.

"We are late," I say calmly, as though nothing were amiss. "I must speak with the Emperor," I add. "We must hurry."

They do not dare to speak to me, they do not dare to ask what has happened. They will have seen me stare at the dead magpie and now they are to deliver me to the Emperor, to a formal birthday banquet in my honour, with my hair cropped by my own hand. They do not know, how can they know, that my hair has been cut for the sake of Niu Lang, the male magpie's demise a sign from Heaven that I am now a widow.

The banqueting hall is immense. I have already ignored the expressions on the faces of all the guards, servants, and minor officials whom I have passed on my way here. But when the doors are opened for me and my name is announced, there is a sudden silence as more than four hundred people turn their faces towards me and stop speaking. In the utter silence, I walk the length of the hall until I stand by Qianlong's side, with Niuhuru next to me. Slowly, I kneel, looking up into his face.

"Your Majesty," I say, my voice loud and clear, the voice I use when I must say prayers for the Empire in public, "your life is in danger."

He stares down at me. The Son of Heaven is lost for words, unable to believe what he is seeing. The Empress, disrespectfully late for a birthday banquet in her honour, kneeling at his side, her robe crumpled, her face powder caked with sweat and most shocking of all, her hair, cut as though for mourning. As Empress, there are only two people for whom I should cut my hair in mourning, and both of them are still alive, each of them only an arms' length from where I am kneeling. The silence seems never-ending.

It is Niuhuru who gathers herself first. She leans from her chair so that her mouth is close to my ear and hisses, "What are you doing, Ula Nara?"

I continue to speak loudly. Qianlong must be made aware of the gravity of the situation. "I am warning the Emperor that he is in grave danger from a woman whom he purports to love. He does not know that she is capable of treason, of taking his life in revenge for the wrongs he has done her."

I have barely finished speaking when I feel my arms pulled behind me by armed guards. I am hauled to my feet, the Emperor still gazing at me in disbelief, while the Dowager Empress quickly stands and addresses the gaping courtiers.

"Her Majesty is unwell," she announces. "You will continue the banquet without us, I must attend her."

Nobody speaks. They only stare.

"Please continue," says Niuhuru, her tone now one of command.

The courtiers look hastily back down at their plates, a few quick-witted ones begin to speak to others, in a formal and stilted manner. I admire their presence of mind.

I am being pulled backwards by the guards, towards the doors that I came through. Niuhuru is following us, her face white as carved jade, her eyes full of fear. Behind her, Qianlong has turned in his throne to watch us go.

I am manoeuvred into a palanquin and Niuhuru steps into one nearby. It takes only a few lurching moments, our bearers running at top speed, to reach my own rooms again.

"Leave us," says Niuhuru, once we are in my receiving hall. The eunuchs, their faces horrified at the sight of us, back away in silence. We are alone.

It takes Niuhuru a few moments before she speaks. Her hands are shaking when she turns to face me. "What is going on?" she asks at last.

I am so tired, so dizzy with all that has happened to me since sunset, that I sink to the floor and sit, knees folded beneath me. The room is cold, and I wrap my arms about me and rock myself a little. It feels comforting and I am badly in need of comfort.

"Ula Nara? Speak to me. What is going on?"

I can't help it, I laugh out loud. I had thought there would be questions, accusations, rebuttals. And yet no one has done any of this. They have only hustled me to this tiny shadowed room, away from everyone of importance. "I tried to tell you," I say. "The Emperor is in danger. From Lady He. Why won't you listen to me?"

Niuhuru gapes at me. "Lady He?"

"Yes."

"What are you talking about?"

"She has daggers," I say, rocking a little faster. "She means to kill the Emperor. There are two of them," I add.

"Two of what?"

"Two women," I say, realising that I have forgotten to explain this. "They look the same. But there are two of them. Lady He and her maid. Dressed the same. With daggers. And her cook," I add. "Although he is loyal to us. He warned me. He should not be punished. He loved her, you see." I add.

Niuhuru does not look as though she is listening to me. "And your hair?"

"My hair?"

"Why is your hair cut short?" asks Niuhuru.

I put a hand up, touch the ragged clumps. "Oh," I say. "No, that has nothing to do with it. I cut my hair because I am a widow now."

Niuhuru stares at me. "A widow?"

I nod.

There is silence for a few moments and then Niuhuru comes closer to me, squats down barely an arm's length from me and looks at me carefully. "You know that the Emperor is alive?" she asks.

I frown. "He is *now*," I point out. "But he is in grave danger, as I told you."

"From Lady He?"

I smile. Niuhuru is at last listening to me. "Yes," I say.

"Who you believe is aided by others?"

"Her maid and her cook," I say. "Although the cook told me what was going on, so he is loyal to us."

Niuhuru shakes her head. "Tell me again why you have cut your hair," she says.

"My husband has died," I say.

"Your husband is the Emperor," says Niuhuru, very slowly, as though explaining something to a child. "And he is alive and well, whatever danger you believe him to be in."

I shake my head. "I meant my real husband," I say.

"Your real husband?"

"Niu Lang," I say and it is strange to say his name. "You took me from him," I add, looking Niuhuru directly in the eyes. "I begged you to let me go home and you would not change your mind. You chose me for your son without wondering if my heart belonged to another."

Niuhuru's face is very pale. "I did not know…" she begins, stumbling over her words.

And suddenly the rage I have held against her all these years comes rushing out of me. I find myself gripping her face in my hands, my broken nail shields pressed into her immaculately powdered cheeks. "You knew!" I scream at her and the fear and pain I see in her eyes gives me a rush of pleasure. "You knew I did not wish to come here! I begged you to let me go back to my family, something no other girl has ever done. I was willing to bring dishonour on my family, I was so desperate not to be chosen! You knew something was wrong, you looked back and you hesitated and then you let the Chief Eunuch hurry you away, you let them drag me to join the other chosen girls, even though you saw me sobbing! You knew!"

I push her away, one of my broken nail shields dragging across her cheek as I do so, the jagged edge ripping into her skin, a line of blood welling up even as I release her. She topples backwards, her squatted stance unbalanced by the fury of my push, ending up on her backside on the floor. She puts up a hand to the stinging pain she must feel in her cheek and when she sees blood on her hand she stares at me in horror before crawling away from me as though I am about to attack her again. But I am rocking, my arms wrapped about my knees, tears rolling down my face, choking out Niu Lang's name over and over again.

"What is the meaning of this?"

I look up. Qianlong is standing over me. Behind him, Niuhuru gets to her feet, still keeping a distance, repeatedly touching her face and looking at the blood on her hand, which is shaking.

"Your life is in danger and I came to warn you even though I do not owe you any loyalty," I sob.

"What have you done to my mother?" he asks.

"It does not matter, it is no matter," says Niuhuru in a ragged whisper.

"What have you done to your hair?" he asks. "An Empress cuts her hair only for the Emperor or his mother's death. Are you cursing us? Wishing us dead?"

"I cut it for Niu Lang," I say. "He is dead."

"What are you talking about?" he asks.

"Niu Lang," I repeat. "He has died."

"You are in communication with a man outside of the Forbidden City?" asks Qianlong.

"No," I say. "I do not need to communicate with him. I know it because of my magpie."

Qianlong turns to his mother. "What is she talking about?" he asks.

Niuhuru shakes her head and does not answer.

"Is she mad?" he asks her. "Has she gone mad?"

She does not answer, only gives a tiny nod, a quick downwards jolt of her head.

"You lying bitch!" I scream at her. "I am not mad. I am trying to save your son's life even though you would not save me from the insanity of this life! I am showing you the mercy you should have shown me!"

"Be silent!" roars Qianlong suddenly. His mother whimpers while I crawl away from him, afraid. I have only seen Qianlong like this once, when Lady Fuca died and he ordered people executed for not mourning her sufficiently. I crouch in a corner, shaking, my head down, waiting for him to strike me or call the guards. But there is only silence. I hear Qianlong take a few steps and when I look up I see he has taken a seat in the receiving hall's throne. He is staring at me with an expression of combined disbelief and anger. I wait but he does not speak and now I hear running feet approaching, the familiar sound of a palanquin's bearers. There is a pause and then comes the hard click clack of heels, the sound of Lady He's shoes, a different sound to the shoes the rest of us wear. I look towards the door and there she is, framed in the light, hesitant. I do not know if Qianlong has summoned her here or whether she heard what happened, knows the accusations I have made against her. I wonder if she will strike now, if she is concealing weapons somewhere about her person.

"They want to kill you," I cry out, my voice hoarse. "I swear I am telling the truth! She has a twin, a sister! I saw them – first one with her lover the cook, both of them with daggers, embracing. And then the other one – walking with you. There are two of them and they mean to kill you!"

Lady He stares at me in horror, her eyes wide. Then she looks towards Qianlong. I wait for him to question her.

"The Empress is unwell," he says slowly, speaking only to Lady He, as though I am not even present. "She has been making accusations which I cannot believe are true. She says you are two different people, she accuses you of wishing to kill me, of drawing me close to you so that you might use these... daggers... to assassinate me in the Lion Grove."

Lady He's voice is little more than a whisper. "And you believe her?"

He shakes his head wearily. "She is unwell, as you can see," he says quietly. "I walked with you in the gardens and all was well between us, as you know. There is only one of you. She is hallucinating."

"She has hidden daggers in her clothing. Make her show you!" I scream, furious at Qianlong's dismissal. I throw myself at Lady He and grab at her jacket, tugging it off her. She fights to escape my clutches and the jacket comes away in my hands. Frantically, I turn it inside out, but still there are no daggers. I want to call for scissors but there are no servants so instead I claw at the silk with my hands and then, in desperation, with my teeth. The silk rips and the wadding inside is revealed, but still there are no daggers, no concealed weapons of any kind. I put my head to the floor and weep, rocking back and forth, still clutching at the torn silk with my bony hands. After a while, I look up at Qianlong but he is looking at me as though he barely knows me.

"You will be sent back to Beijing in disgrace," he says. His voice is low but carries as though he were shouting and suddenly I am truly afraid of him. I try to perform a kowtow, as though the ritual of the obeisance will somehow remind him of who I am. But I pitch my head forward too fast, knocking it hard on the stone floor. For a moment the room swims before my eyes and I think I will faint but I try to focus on Qianlong.

"Do not punish me, my lord," I beg through my sobs. "Punish her and her twin. They are treacherous bitches. I am your Empress and she is a nobody, a prisoner of war from a land ridden with mongrel curs." Tears roll down my cheeks. "I have been loyal to you," I half-whisper.

"I have bound myself to you since I was chosen and I have done everything in my power to deserve your favour. Do not punish me."

Qianlong is not listening, he speaks to me as he does when passing judgement in his court rulings. "You will return to Beijing under guard," he says. "You will remain there until my return and then you will be sent to the Cold Palace where you will live until the end of your days. You will no longer live within my presence."

"I am the Empress!" I shriek. "You cannot do this to me!"

"You are no longer my Empress," he says and his voice is colder than I have ever heard it. "From this moment you are stripped of your titles and privileges."

Still kneeling, I twist towards Niuhuru, waiting for her to intervene, to speak up for me, to protect me, but she stays silent, her eyes on the floor. I feel a great pain from my cramped knees, so that I slide to the floor. I can hear myself moaning in pain. Looking up I see Lady He staring at me, but she startles when Qianlong speaks to her.

"Call the guards," he says. "And a maid."

Lady He nods and backs away. A few moments later a terrified young maid appears.

"Her Majesty needs new clothes," says Niuhuru, her voice shaking.

The maid runs to my bedroom and returns clutching an armful of clothes. She stands by my side, although keeping her distance, looking down at me as though I am a wild animal. Meanwhile Lady He has reappeared accompanied by eight guards. Niuhuru turns away, as though looking out of the window, so that her damaged face cannot be seen. The maid looks about as though hoping for guidance.

"Something plain," says Niuhuru to the maid.

The maid hovers, uncertain. As Empress of China, I have very few clothes that might be called plain. She holds up a few robes but even the few I own that are not official court robes are exquisite in their use of fine materials and embroidery.

Niuhuru waves her hand without looking. "A maid's robe," she says.

The maid gapes at her. The guards remain motionless, expressionless.

"Fetch one!"

The maid hurries away and returns with a pale blue cotton robe, cleaned so many times that it has faded, still crumpled from its latest wash.

Niuhuru nods and turns away. "Dress her," she says over her shoulder, her scratched face hidden.

The maid tries, but my body is limp. She fumbles with the fastenings of the robe I am wearing and in the end Lady He joins her, the two of them kneeling at my side. Together they strip off my Imperial yellow silk outer robe and cover up my sweat-stained inner robes in the faded blue cotton. I move like a child for them, allowing them to lift my arms and legs. I do not try to obstruct them but I feel so weak I cannot really help them in their task. At last it is done. Still sitting on the floor, I look down at my body. I have never worn such an outfit before.

"Take her back to Beijing," Qianlong says to the guards.

They daren't gape nor disobey but they hesitate before laying hands on me. Carefully, three of them lift me to my feet and guide me stumblingly to the door. I have only one shoe on, the other has dropped off my foot and the difference in height of one foot to the other is causing me trouble walking. They have to half-carry me towards my Imperial yellow palanquin, topped with golden phoenixes, shielded from curious eyes by silk drapes. I am half aware that Lady He is following us.

"Stop!"

At the Emperor's voice ringing out behind us, every servant falls to their knees, face down on the ground. The guards and I stand still, prostrate bodies all around us.

"She is no longer permitted to ride in that palanquin," Qianlong orders. "Fetch an orange chair."

A servant runs out of the courtyard and returns with an intercepted chair and its bearers. I stare at it and when the guards try to make me enter it I hang back. I am the Empress. I travel in a yellow silk palanquin. This chair is orange, it cannot be meant for me, whatever Qianlong says.

Lady He appears at my side and then crouches in front of me. "Give me your hand, Your Majesty," she says in a whisper. "Let me help you into the chair."

I look down into her wide brown eyes. "There were two of you in the garden," I say in a croak.

"There is only one of me here," she replies. "Will you give me your hand?"

I take her hand, which is warm and soft. Once I am in the palanquin she reaches in and pulls the gauze curtain across, so that my vision is blurred. As the palanquin moves away, I see her outline standing watching me go. A great weariness comes over me and I close my eyes. I must rest, I think. Soon I will be back in the Forbidden City and as Empress I will be called on for many tasks. I must be ready. I must sleep so that I can perform my many, many duties.

Mountain Pass

A LURCHING. A HEAVY-FOOTED SWAYING. A juddering mis-step and then back to the swaying, no smooth rhythm to it. Grunting, panting. A muttered curse.

I try to open my eyes but the light hurts them and I close them again, feel the swaying go on and on, not soothing but startling when it fails, my body suddenly slipping one way or another. More curses. I open my eyes again and narrow them against the brightness.

A palanquin. I am in a palanquin. I close my eyes again. Of course. I travel everywhere like this, so it is familiar to me. Although there is something not quite right about this one, something my mind cannot grasp. I open my eyes and peer again at my surroundings. A palanquin should be familiar but this one is not. Why? What is wrong with it, apart from its shuddering progress, which is not as it ought to be? My bearers are the best, they are used to keeping the palanquin's progress steady, no matter how uneven the ground beneath their feet.

The colour. Orange. A plain rusted orange. I put up a hand to touch the sides. The fabric is not silk.

The colour should be Imperial yellow. I earned that colour. The walls should be made of silk. My progress should be utterly smooth.

Another jolt. I put up a hand to steady myself.

What am I doing in a palanquin that is not Imperial yellow and not made of silk? My mind is unsteady, it judders through images and stumbles over thoughts, leaving them incomplete.

Something comes back to me. Wide grey eyes in a white face, a slash of red beneath.

Someone's face too close to mine, brown eyes filled with tears.

I feel cold. I look down at my lap and see blue cotton. I frown, touch it to be sure of what I am seeing. Blue cotton? I have never worn blue cotton. That is what a maid wears. A blue cotton robe, her hair in a single plait, tied with a red ribbon. Every maid in the Forbidden City wears this. I put up a hand as though I, too, might have a plait tied with a red ribbon. But I can only find one strand of my hair and it is loose. I feel about for more of it, wondering if this one strand has come undone from its pins. But my hand touches something else. Short, rough hair.

Wide grey eyes in a white face, a slash of red beneath. Niuhuru. The Empress Dowager.

I look down at my hand. It is bony but also dirty. My golden nail shields have disappeared, my nails are mostly broken, their jagged tips lined with dirt.

Outside the bearers change over. I know the feeling, the slight dip as one man takes over the pole from another bearer. And then the palanquin rocks again as we move forward. I can hear the first bearers spit, mutter to one another about something. A laugh, cut short. Onwards. The palanquin seems to be tilted backwards, as though the front bearers are too tall for the back ones. Bearers should be evenly matched in height to serve in the Forbidden City.

Wide grey eyes in a white face, a slash of red beneath. Niuhuru. The Empress Dowager. And then, towering over me, the Son of Heaven. Qianlong. Forcing me backwards and away from Niuhuru and then...

Screaming. Orders. A maid, her eyes frightened. The blue cotton. Guards. Dark brown eyes full of tears. Looking out from an orange palanquin as I was taken away somewhere.

Where am I?

I brace myself against the sloping jolting of the palanquin and use one hand to open the curtain shielding me from the outside world.

There is only sky. How can there be only sky? Where is the horizon? Buildings? People?

I lean further forward and then my stomach clenches at what I see. A terrifying cliff edge into nothingness, a drop down – down – down to far away greenness.

I am on a mountaintop. Higher than I have ever been in my life. Higher than any mountain I have ever been to. On a tiny path, so narrow it makes my stomach lurch. I cower back in the palanquin, huddle against its rough orange sides. I am cold, very cold. Only my feet, oddly, seem warm.

Now I see that there is a blanket in the palanquin with me, it has fallen to the floor. My feet are covered, leaving the rest of me chilled. I pull at it. It is a thick padded cotton, with a greasy feel to it. I pull it up around me, feel my body stop shaking.

Now my mind unfogs a little. The greasy cotton against my skin has drawn a clearer line of thought from me. Why am I dirty? Why am I dressed in cotton: not just any cotton but a maid's blue robe? Why am I in an orange palanquin? What am I doing on the top of a mountain? Something has happened. I hold the blanket tighter in my bony, dirty hands and try to remember. But the swaying has stopped, there is a final jolt. The palanquin has halted. I hear voices far away, then closer. A hand appears inside the palanquin. I hesitate, then take it.

Coordinating my body sufficiently to get out of the palanquin seems difficult, made worse because I am still clutching the blanket to me, as though it may protect me from whatever is happening outside. My eyesight does not feel right, emerging from the palanquin I blink, the bright light of day no longer filtered through the dusky orange walls. When I can look around me better, I stare.

I am standing in a small village. Huddled wooden houses are clustered around a tiny open space of packed earth in which stands an old gingko tree. The houses are tiny and very worn, their once-brown wood now a weathered grey. They have been patched over the years: the wood is not all the same colour and the walls and roofs are crooked, sagging. There is a stink of livestock in the air.

Next to my palanquin stand the bearers. They are not eunuchs from the Imperial household, they must be local men. Their skin is burnt brown, they have wide shoulders but are short in stature.

In front of me, gathered by their houses, stand a few dozen people: men and women, a few children who peep out from behind their mothers. A baby cries and is hushed. All of them are poorly dressed in what look like layers of rags, one item of clothing over another, the bottom layers poking through here and there. Their faces are as weathered as the wood of their houses. They stare back at me.

I stand, clutching my blanket, staring about me like a lost child. Turning my head, I catch sight of two guards. Their armour and clothing marks them out as Imperial guards and they look so familiar, in this midst of all this strangeness, that I smile broadly at them. They do not smile back. I look around me again and realise what it is that seems so strange. It has been many years since my arrival somewhere was not greeted with people on their knees, their faces hidden from me as they kowtow. I wonder if this is some strange play, if I have been dressed as a maid to play a part, that once I am revealed as the Empress all these people will fall to their knees and my court robes will magically reappear, Imperial yellow silk folds tumbling over me as jade pins and flowers pull my hair back into its usual place. I put my hand up and again all I feel is roughness. I cannot think what it reminds me of, until I think of Wan's little dog and its rough fur, short and a little curly. I am not sure why my own hair would feel like dog's fur.

The guards have moved, are speaking with a man who looks bewildered, but is nodding at whatever it is they are saying. I see them hand him a large leather pouch and know that it must contain payment for something. The man is awestruck at the weight of the pouch, his nods become quicker, more eager and the guards nod back, satisfied with his enthusiasm. They speak a little more, while I stand still. The bearers pick up the poles of the palanquin and I ready myself to climb back into it. Perhaps we have not arrived where we are headed, this is only a tiny mountain village and maybe the people here were in need of help from the Emperor. It is possible that I was sent here to give them confidence that they are not forgotten. I smile at them, hoping to convey confidence and benevolence, assurance that they are not forgotten, even by the Son of Heaven himself.

No one smiles back. One little boy sticks his tongue out at me from behind his father's legs.

The palanquin moves away from me. I expect it will turn around, for there is limited space here, and then it will be brought close to me so that I can step back in. But it continues to move, the men half-trotting away, down the path we must have just come up. I look to the guards but they do not seem to have noticed.

"My palanquin," I say, although my voice hurts when I speak, I feel as if I am hoarse with shouting, although I have no recollection of shouting. "My palanquin!" I add, more loudly, as I try to command my voice. One of the guards glances at me and at the rapidly disappearing men with my palanquin and then continues talking, uninterested.

"You," I say to the guards. "Come here."

One of the two comes towards me. I wait for him to bow, but he does not.

"Where are we?" I ask. "What is happening?"

"The Emperor has ordered that you be brought here," he says.

I look about me. The villagers are still staring at me. "Why?"

The guard looks at me oddly, as though I am stupid. "You have been sent to the Cold Palace," he says, as though reminding me of something obvious.

"The Cold Palace?" I repeat. For a moment I look about me, as though there is a palace here somewhere that has been given a poetic name. But the meaning of what he is saying is seeping into me. I look down at the greasy blue cotton and my broken nails. "The Cold Palace?"

"Yes," he says and it is only now, it is only him answering me without using my title, without saying *Your Majesty* or even *your ladyship,* that suddenly breaks through my confusion.

"The Emperor has exiled me from court?" I say. I have to be certain. I have to know that I have not misunderstood a phrase that I have only ever heard applied to others.

"Yes," he says. His face is very still, there is no emotion. He has been given his orders and he is carrying them out.

"Why?" I ask.

There is a flicker now, he cannot believe I am asking this question. I think of Niuhuru, her grey eyes in a white face, a scarlet streak across her cheek but only after my hand reached out, my already-broken nail shields ripping across the whiteness, the red rising in its wake.

"I struck the Dowager Empress?" I ask, my voice shaking.

He looks at me in disbelief. "You cut your hair," he says.

I put my hand up. The rough feel of Wan's little dog. "I cut my hair?" I repeat.

He nods.

I feel a great wave of cold. I am the Empress. The Empress cuts her hair only in mourning and only for those higher ranked than herself. There are only two people in the empire for whom I would have to cut my hair. Qianlong. And his mother, the Empress Dowager, Niuhuru. "Who died?" I ask and my voice shakes.

Again the look, the disbelief that I cannot remember what has brought me here. "No one," he says and walks away from me, back to the other guard. They speak together while I stand watching them in silence.

They leave. The two guards, in the uniform that has been a constant at the peripheries of my vision ever since I was chosen at the Imperial Daughters' Draft, are gone. They walk away, down the mountain path, without a backward glance. I think of running after them but my legs will not move. I stand as though I were a statue, frozen into place, watching the last glimpse of them disappear behind a tree on the path and then they are gone.

I turn back and find that the man with whom they were speaking, perhaps the head of the village, has approached me. I wait for him to kowtow but he does not.

"Ula Nara?"

I stare at him. No-one addresses me like this except the Emperor and his mother, or Ling if she is being deliberately rude.

"Your name is Ula Nara?" he perseveres.

I nod, a slow cautious nod.

"I have been given directions that you are to live here," he says.

"Where?" I ask. I cannot see anywhere that I could possibly live.

He indicates a house among the huddle. "My niece Min lives there. Her husband died last year, so she lives alone. She will care for you." He makes an involuntary gesture towards the leather pouch, now attached to his belt. "You have been provided for."

I say nothing.

"Come with me," he says.

He walks away and I take one step and then another, the rough ground under my feet coming through the thin soles of my cloth shoes. My knees ache from being bent for so long. The villagers part to let us pass, then close up behind us.

The man pushes the door open and leads me inside. I am vaguely aware that someone else has followed us inside. The door closes on the curious stares outside.

I am standing in a single-roomed house, dominated by a mud-brick stove and a niche in the wall beside it, in which is a bed just large enough for two people to lie side by side. The floor is made of packed earth, the ceiling is barely an arm's length above my head, made lower by all the things hanging from it: dried herbs, cooking utensils, clothes and more. There is a table and a low bench, a small wooden chest. The room smells of smoke and sweat.

"This is Min," says the man, indicating someone behind me.

I turn round to face the woman who has followed me here. She is quite young, I would say mid twenties at the very most, although her skin looks older and her hands are calloused. She stares at me with undisguised curiosity.

"This is Ula Nara," says the man. "She is to live here with us. She has been well provided for and will continue to be so. She has been unwell in her mind but it is hoped she will recover. She is of no harm to others. She will live with you, Min."

I stare at him.

"How long will she stay, Uncle?" asks Min.

"For the rest of her life," says the man.

Min nods, as though it is normal for the Empress of China to be brought to a tiny mountain top village and live out the rest of her days in a one-roomed wooden shack with a sagging roof, in the company of a widow.

The man nods back at her. "The village has been given silver for her," he says. "She is to be cared for as one of us."

Min nods again and the man leaves us, the door behind him closing quickly but not quickly enough that I cannot still see curious faces outside, waiting for another glimpse of me.

I wait for Min to kowtow, to address me as your ladyship, Your Majesty, but she does neither.

"You'll need boots up here," she says. "I'll ask my uncle to make sure you have some. He's not tight-fisted," she adds. "He'll look out for you, make sure the village takes care of you. But he's a man, he won't think of such things. A coat, too, for when winter comes.. I can sew you one if he can buy me some cloth, but I don't have a lot of time for sewing so I should start soon, even if it is spring. Winter comes early here," she adds with a smile, as though I am likely to know this.

I think of my furs, of the multiple layers of silk robes I wear in winter, of the beds with *kangs* under them, the stoves kept burning all night if necessary to avoid any Imperial lady catching cold. "Where am I?" I ask.

Min frowns. "Mount Hua Shan," she says.

The only thing that comes to mind is that the Daoists claim that the god of the underworld lives under Mount Hua Shan. I try to think of the maps Qianlong was so fond of looking at, showing his empire in all its glory, especially once he conquered Xinjiang. "The Qin Mountains?" I manage at last. "Xi'an?"

She nods.

I think of how far I have travelled from the South and how far it would be to Beijing. The man spoke of me staying here for the rest of my life, he cannot have meant it. Perhaps Qianlong means to frighten me, to show me what life away from court is like. Perhaps he finds me ungrateful for not being happy as his Step-Empress, perhaps he does not realise that even that title is a daily reminder to me that I am not his true love, just as he is not mine, of all I have given up to achieve that title and yet have achieved nothing at all.

Min is still standing watching me, expecting some sort of response.

"Do you know who I am?" I ask her, a thought coming to my mind. Perhaps they have not been told. Perhaps that is why they are not behaving as they ought to.

"Ula Nara," she says.

"But do you know who I *am*?" I persist.

She shakes her head.

"I am the Empress of China," I say.

She looks at my blue cotton robe and shorn hair, my dirty-nailed fingers still clutching the blanket I have not yet let fall. I can see her thinking of what her uncle said, that I have been unwell in my mind. "I think perhaps you are mistaken," she says and her voice is very kind. "I know you have not been well. But I am sure you will recover here. It is only a little village but the people here are good people. We do not go hungry and the houses may be plain but they have always kept us warm." She smiles. "The silver your family has provided will help all of us and we will make sure you are comfortable. Are you cold?"

I nod.

She comes closer, takes the blanket away from me, placing it on the bed with other worn blankets. Then she opens a small chest and pulls out an embroidered padded cotton jacket, which she holds out to me. "It was my wedding jacket," she says, smiling. "But it doesn't get much use. It will keep you warm."

I look down at it. It's bright red, as befits a bride, clumsily embroidered with flowers. I think of the Imperial dressmakers, what they would say if they saw it. They would have an apprentice whipped for this kind of needlework. "I can't wear this," I say. "I can't wear your wedding clothes."

Min keeps smiling but tears well up for a moment before she blinks them away. "Can't have it lying around useless in a chest," she says. "Not when you're cold."

Slowly, I pull the jacket on over my thin robe. It may be clumsily made but it is warm. I try to smile. It feels like an effort but Min smiles back readily, as though I have beamed at her.

I stay in the house all the rest of that day, sitting on the low bench at the table. Even though it is still daylight I do not leave the small room. I watch Min as she breaks kindling over her knee for the stove and feeds the flames, keeping the room warm. She chatters as she works, speaking of things I do not even understand, names of people and their histories, work that must be done. She chops up a piece of mutton and puts it on the stove to cook with vegetables, then fiercely kneads a small ball of dough until she is satisfied with it. As the darkness grows outside she lights another lantern and turns the dough into noodles, adding them to the simmering pot. When she brings me a bowl heaped with noodles and chunks of fatty mutton, the whole spiced with cumin and fiery hot with peppers, I eat as best I can, although my stomach feels shrivelled. When I slow down after only a few mouthfuls I can see Min's disappointed face and I try harder, eating until I feel overly full. I do not think I have ever eaten a meal made up of only one dish.

Hungry Ghost

I STAY IN THE HOUSE FOR many days, afraid of leaving the tiny interior, huddled against the unknown world outside. Min comes and goes, she cooks for us both and we eat together. Sometimes she does work inside, mostly she leaves me alone while she goes outside, returning with flour, firewood, vegetables, clothes that have been dried outside and are now ready to put away. She is always busy, always working. Whenever she leaves the house she asks if I want to accompany her and I always say no.

"Today you need to come outside," she says at last.

"No thank you," I say.

"You can't spend the rest of your life in one room," she says. "Come." She holds out her hand. Reluctantly I rise from the wooden bench and follow her. The light outside makes me blink, I have not been in daylight for so long I had forgotten how bright it can be.

Min has tasks that take her all over the village: first to pull up vegetables, then to take some tool back to a neighbour, followed by a visit to her uncle to ask him something about seeds. I walk a few paces behind her, uncomfortable with the stares I get from the villagers.

"They'll get used to you if they see you every day," says Min over her shoulder.

Behind me trails a little boy, the one who stuck his tongue out at me when I first arrived. He has a three-legged dog, a mutt with no pedigree, a far cry from the dainty lapdogs and noble hounds of the court and hunting grounds. This one hops along with an ungainly but enthusiastic gait, faithful to her small master.

"What's your name?" asks the little boy.

"Ula Nara," I tell him.

"I am Chen," he says.

I don't answer.

"Min says you said you were the Empress of China," he says.

"Yes," I say.

"If you're the Empress of China, where's your crown?" asks Chen. "And why aren't you wearing silk? Are you in disguise? Will you tell me about the guards in the Forbidden City? What weapons do they have?"

"Shush," says Min, emerging from her neighbour's house in time to hear him. "Be off with you."

"But an Empress *should* have a crown," insists Chen.

"Little boys *should* know better than to be cheeky to their elders," says Min. "Shoo."

Reluctantly, Chen and his dog stop following us.

"I don't want to go out again," I tell Min.

"You need to," she says firmly. "You must take a walk every day."

At first I only go outside and stand, awkwardly, in the centre of the village, all but clinging to the trunk of the ancient gingko tree. But everyone still stares at me and Chen and his dog hang around me asking endless questions until I retreat back into the dark warmth of Min's home. At last I decide to walk away from the village, a little way along the mountain. The view down into the ravines below still makes me afraid. I walk as though I might fall at any moment, occasionally clutching at a bush or small tree when I feel my balance deserting me. I walk only for a few moments each day, then return to Min's house, ignoring Chen, who seems fascinated with me.

"Do you want to come with me to see the monkeys in the woods?" he asks.

"No," I say.

"The first berries are getting ripe," he informs me the next day. "Do you want to come and pick some to eat?"

I shake my head.

"Look," he says one morning, holding up a brownish dried out husk. "It's a caterpillar's cocoon. Do you want to keep it and see the butterfly come out?"

"No, thank you," I say, retreating back into the house.

He makes such offers whenever he sees me and I always refuse, hoping that soon he will stop following me.

I see Min's uncle sometimes, usually carrying an axe on his way to chop firewood or with a dangling dead chicken in one hand, still twitching from having its neck wrung.

"You are well?" he always asks gruffly and seems relieved when I nod without replying, perhaps not wishing to engage in idle chatter with a madwoman, even if he has been appointed my guardian here.

Sitting alone with my thoughts does not make for a peaceful existence. I think of my life at court, still unsure whether this exile is a welcome release or a terrifying punishment. Sometimes I laugh out loud at the ludicrous comparison between my grand palace where every room was fragranced with expensive perfumes and over-filled with precious objects and this single-roomed house, dark and full of pungent smells. I rock back and forth, laughing till I cry, then tears fall for hours while my thoughts are a jumbled whirl of Niu Lang, of my lost children, of the pain and fears and bitterness that have made up what feels like the whole of my life. Min watches me silently when I laugh, sometimes she pats me when I cry, but mostly she continues her daily tasks as though I were hardly there, as though I were some strange pet whose odd behaviour cannot be explained, only watched with interest. Her uncle brings her good cloth from the village and she spends her evenings cutting and sewing, making me warm clothes for the winter: trousers, a padded jacket, a long robe.

"He even bought both of us new boots," she says, pleased, showing me sturdy knee-high boots for herself and me. I nod, although the idea of being here all winter seems impossible, Min and her uncle are planning for a future I cannot even imagine.

I sleep badly. I am unused to a snoring body pressed tightly against me, the night noises of the mountain. Often there are strong winds and the village dogs never tire of barking when they sense some wild animal nearby. One night I lie restless and at last I rise from the bed and make my way out into the village clearing. There is a full moon, it shines as brightly as though it were only twilight. I shush Chen's little dog who is making the most noise and she subsides, which calms some of the other dogs, if only temporarily.

I stand beneath the gingko tree for a few moments and wonder whether I might sleep now that the dogs are quiet, but I already know I will not, I am too wide awake. Instead, I find myself walking down the path that leads away from the village and down the mountain, the path I was carried up, the last time I rode in a palanquin. I have never gone this way before. The villagers use it a little, for when they roam the mountain to gather firewood, or when the men descend the long way down into the valleys below, to trade. The path is not well-made, only beaten out over the years by the footsteps of those who have gone before.

The ground is steep under my feet. More than once I stumble and have to try and regain my balance. A thick, half-buried tree root proves my undoing and I fall headlong into the undergrowth, hands outstretched to break my fall. My palms sting and as I clamber awkwardly to my feet I look down and see that I have scraped them on stones and brambles. The brambles are also clinging to the bottom of my robe and it takes me a few moments to break free of them. I brush away the dirt on my hands and use my tongue to clean one particularly bad scrape. I wonder whether I should go back, but just below me the path splits and one part curves away, turning across rather than down the mountain and I wonder where it leads, why it would not follow a more direct route. *I will follow just around the corner*, I think, *then I will return to the village.*

The wind picks up. I am on a more exposed part of the mountain here and I slip again but manage to keep my footing. The path I have followed is smaller than the main path that leads downwards, not so many feet walk here regularly. I cannot see much of interest and a sudden screech overhead frightens me before I realise it must be one of the monkeys I have sometimes heard further away, the monkeys that Chen is always talking about. I twist my head upwards and see a face in the upper branches of the tree, blurred in the grey light so that it might almost be the face of a baby, bright eyes watching me. I stand still and the monkey chatters at me and then hides away among the branches, perhaps reassured that I mean it no harm. I think that I should turn back, there is nothing here, but ahead I see a darker shadow and, curious, make my way towards it. I narrow my eyes, trying to understand what I am looking at before realising that it is a rocky cliff face under which is the opening to a cave. I think of wild animals, perhaps clouded leopards, and draw back, but the cliff face catches my attention. It seems to be marked with figures. I forget the possible danger and step closer. Daubed on the cliff in what looks like a dull blood-red are human figures, their legs bent into a wide-legged squat, their arms raised up above them to mirror their stance. In the poor light, as the faint shadows of the branches move across them, they make me think that they are alive, only waiting for a command to move. I back away, noticing as I do so that the cave is not natural but carved into the face of the cliff, its straight lines betraying its human origins. I wonder what kind of person would live here, immured in rock they have carved into a tiny shelter, close to these images from another time, another world. I wonder if they were as lonely as I have been. I find my way back to the main path and to the village, crawl into Min's bed and try again to sleep, but find my dreams filled with dark caves that go on forever and red-daubed figures that dance to music I cannot hear.

My night-time walks become a habit. I wander the side of the mountain, afraid of the darkness and yet drawn to it. Some nights I can barely see anything, when the clouds cross the sky and the moon shrinks down to a tiny sliver of silver, clutching at shrubs when I fall, returning to bed with scraped knees and a fast-beating heart. Once I hear the padding of heavy footsteps and see a leopard cross the path ahead of me. It turns its yellow eyes in my direction and I hold my breath thinking it may attack me, but it only looks me over and continues on its way. Often I return to the cliff top and the cave and stare at the figures as though they might speak and tell me something. Once I scramble to the top of the cliff, following the steep mountain side round until I stand, trembling, on the crumbling edge of the cliff and look down, down, down. I wonder what would happen if I jumped, wonder how the air would feel as I fell and who would find my lifeless body, whether a hungry leopard or one of the villagers. I take a step closer until my toes are on the very edge. One step more would find me falling. Only the sudden thought that it might be little Chen to find me, that he might be hunting for berries and instead find me and be afraid, makes me pause. I would not wish to frighten him. I step away from the cliff and find my way back to the village.

Min is not one for dates and times. I am used to the court astrologers guiding my every move, their insistence on the exact time, the exact day to complete rituals or take almost any action at all. Time in Min's mind is something different. It is the time to plant seeds, it is the time to harvest them. It is the time for the goats and sheep to give birth, it is the time to kill the kids and lambs. She and the other villagers do not wait for the astrologers to tell them when to do these things. They watch the moon for themselves, they smell the wind and touch the earth with their hands and know what should be done. Then they do it.

But she does know about festivals. "It is the Festival of Hungry Ghosts tomorrow," she says, taking an empty platter and piling up fruits and vegetables on it. Later she makes noodles for us to eat and puts a portion aside for the ghosts.

I think of the vast long tables set up in the ancestral hall of the Forbidden City, covered all over with hundreds upon hundreds of fine dishes heaped with food. The thick perfume of incense everywhere as one member of the Imperial Family after another bows and lights whole bunches of incense sticks to add to those already burning. The clouds of smoke everywhere, hiding and then revealing the ancestral portraits hanging above us. I watch Min prepare the simple platter with care, heaping up different foods and arranging them as best she can into a pleasing sight.

"I will leave it outside the door when night falls," she says. "Then we will not be disturbed by those that wander."

I nod.

"The village is grateful to your ancestors as well as ours," she says earnestly. "My uncle used some of the silver to buy more livestock for each of the families, so that all would benefit from you being here. Tonight we welcome your ancestors here as well as our own."

I nod, wondering if Qianlong imagined his silver would be used to buy pigs and goats. I am glad enough for the village, it seems a better use of silver than endless trinkets such as jade ornaments no-one even notices in their rooms.

Night falls and Min closes the door after setting out the platter. I lie beside her, but cannot sleep.

At last I get up and make my way to the door. It opens with a slight creak but Min is sound asleep, she does not stir. I slip outside and softly close the door behind me. By my feet, incense burns in Min's platter. Above me, the bright moon illuminates the village square, the gingko tree's leaves trembling in a slight breeze. On the ground in front of each doorway is a dish like Min's, heaped with whatever food each household can spare. A silent clearing, waiting for the ghosts to arrive. I think that the ghosts whom the villagers expect will be their own ancestors, the hardworking men and women of the past, come to see that all is well with their descendants, well-meaning spirits who bring only good intentions and well wishes. They do not know, the sleeping villagers, that they harbour amongst themselves a hungry ghost who cannot be fulfilled with their simple plates of good peasant food, who will only bring ill fortune to them the longer I stay here.

I walk away, down the tiny path into the woods. The moon is so bright I might as well be carrying a lantern in my hand. Despite the light, I slip more than once. Creatures scurry away from me in the underbrush and the steep path causes me to tumble several times, when loose pebbles slide under my feet. My forearms sting with grazes. But I keep going down, down, down. I have never ventured this far, have always returned before I reach the foothills. Now I continue. Ahead of me, I see lights and I head for them.

The village in the foothills is far bigger than the one on the mountaintop. It seems impossibly large to me after a summer spent with Min. So many houses. Many even have tiled rooftops, the grey tiles stretching out in every direction, one house and another and another and another as far as I can see. It feels like a city to me, the size of it overwhelms me.

There are lanterns here and there, but all is quiet. It is very late, it must have taken me a long time to make my way down. I hesitate, wondering what I am doing here. What did I intend to do? Did I want a temple to pray at? Am I trying to return to the Forbidden City and Qianlong, to fall at his feet and beg forgiveness? I hesitate on the path, halfway between the mountain's forests and the first house in the village.

A chained dog barks at me. I shrink back but as it continues barking I hear its owner curse and tell it to be quiet. The dog looks at me with its ears flattened, angry at being told off for doing its duty, but it stays quiet and soon I can hear snores from the house, its owner quickly returning to their dreams. I step forward again and the dog watches me pass but does not bark again, only bares its teeth in a soundless growl.

I walk on to the next house. A lantern hangs outside, illuminating the platter of food that has been left here: a congealed meat stew, little dumplings, their white dough shining in the light, a flat bread.

The next house has skewers of meat, filled breads, dried fruits.

I feel my belly rumble. I have not eaten for many hours and in that time I have walked continuously. I am hungry. I look down at the food and wonder what will happen if I eat it. Will I be sick? Will the ghosts possess me? Will they follow me back to Min's house to reclaim what is rightfully theirs, bringing misery to the village? I shudder and walk on.

When I come to the end of the village I stop. I stand by the last house and look out across the rolling fields and hills. I could keep walking, could head for Beijing and return to the gates of the Forbidden City and ask for entry. I look down at what I am wearing and a laugh escapes me. No guard would ever let me in, they would be dismissed at once. And even if they did? I have no desire to be an empress any more. I gave everything I had to become Empress and I still could not oust Qianlong's memory of Fuca, just as he could not oust my memory of Niu Lang.

I could return to my family and beg them to take me in. My father may still be alive, perhaps Shu Fang will have a household I could join. But I think of their horror when they heard what has happened to me, their fear of retribution for their daughter's failings. They will have heard the news by now, they will know that the Empress has gone mad and cut off her hair, an unspeakable act. They will have been shocked and then ashamed to know that I have been exiled. They must have spoken my name with pride all these years, one promotion following another until the unthinkable happened and I was made Empress. Everyone in the empire knows my name, knows whose daughter I am and now everyone will know of my disgrace. I laugh again. Everyone of note, that is. To the villagers with whom I live I am no empress. I am a woman from a well to do family who has gone harmlessly but embarrassingly mad and has been sent to them so that I may live quietly out of the way, cared for but not seen by anyone of importance. I squat down for a moment, my legs are aching from the long walk. I wonder who I have left in this world. Perhaps I could find a temple where I can be a nun, as I asked Qianlong to let me be. But I do not know where I would find such a temple and it occurs to me that Min might be lonely if I were to leave. She is a widow and life is hard for a widow. I think of her sunburnt smiling face and Chen's endless questions, of Min's uncle who is always grumpy but nevertheless has not been stingy with the silver Qianlong provided him with. Perhaps the village has not been harmed by my coming after all. Perhaps if I stayed here willingly I could be a part of their lives. Certainly, my chances of happiness are greater here than they would ever be if I were to find my way back to Beijing.

I stand up, my legs cramping at the new movement. Slowly I turn back the way I have come, back through the sleeping village, to begin the steep climb up the mountain.

It is dawn when I finally make my way, panting, back into the village clearing. One or two of the houses already have smoke coming from the chimneys and I hope that Min has not noticed my absence. I am almost at her door when I see Chen emerge from his own house, to be greeted enthusiastically by his dog. I can't help smiling at the welcome she gives him, as though he has been away for a month rather than asleep a few paces away.

"You're all muddy," Chen greets me.

I nod. "I went for a walk."

"In the dark?"

"Yes."

"All night?"

"Yes."

"Why?"

I shrug. "I don't know," I confess.

He nods as though this is an acceptable answer. "Are you hungry?"

"Yes," I say, feeling my stomach rumble again.

He takes a handful of berries and a piece of bread from the platter by his own door. "Here."

I am about to refuse. The food is not to be touched by humans, it is there for the dead. But Chen means well and I am hungry and too tired to explain. I hold out my hand and he pours the berries into my palm. I hesitate but then tip them into my mouth. Their sharpness brings a rush of saliva and the hard bread he passes me is sweetened by the fruit as I chew.

Min comes out of the house, her anxious expression relaxing when she sees me. "I didn't know where you were," she says. "Are you well?"

"Yes," I say.

Fourteen days later, it is time for the villagers to light the tiny floating lanterns that will guide the visiting spirits home. They set off at dawn, carrying their little lights to a mountain stream. I pretend to be asleep, afraid that if I light a lantern my flame might not go out and it would frighten the villagers. Min tries to stir me but gives up when I turn away and pull the blankets over my head.

Summer is short here on the mountain, I can feel the first chill of autumn. I see Chen's older sister sitting on the doorstep of their house day after day, embroidery in her lap. She seems to be outlining the shapes of butterflies.

"What is it for?" I ask.

She blushes. "My dowry."

I hear myself saying, "There is a stitch I could show you. For embroidering grass stems."

She passes me the cloth and watches me eagerly as I show her a stitch much favoured at court. Its delicacy brings to life waving grass stems beneath the floating butterflies. It takes her a little while, but she makes a good job of it.

"Thank you, Ula Nara!" she calls, as she hurries to show her friends. At least, I think, being Han Chinese she will not be summoned for the Imperial Daughters' Draft, she may marry whomever she wishes to, she need only seek her parents' blessing. I raise my hand to wave her off and she beams back at me.

I stop my night-time wanderings and instead walk in the daytime. The villagers are used to me by now, they do not stare so much when I pass, only raise their heads briefly from their work and nod when they see who it is. Much of the day I sit on the doorstep, enjoying the sun's waning warmth on my skin.

"Help me pod these, would you?" Min's old neighbour, a hunchbacked woman whose own doorstep is only a few paces away, holds out a basket filled with withered bean pods.

I fumble with the pods, dropping dried beans here and there, which the straying chickens try to steal before I can pick them up again, but I manage to beat them to it just in time.

"Quick-fingered," laughs the old woman and I laugh back, proud of myself for outwitting the hens, who cluck disappointedly and return to their scratching in the dirt.

"You are well?" asks Min's uncle, passing by. He has a couple of sacks thrown over his shoulder, he must have been down to the village for supplies of some sort.

"Yes," I say. "And you?"

"Well enough, well enough," he says. "For you," he adds, throwing a small bag my way.

I catch it and open it up to reveal dried dates. "Thank you," I exclaim, surprised.

He shrugs but looks pleased. "Min said you had a liking for them," he says and walks away. I hold out the bag to the neighbour and we both munch on the dates, the rich sweet taste an unexpected treat.

"I'm still dropping the beans," I confess, when we return to the work in hand.

"Be not afraid of growing slowly, be only afraid of standing still," chuckles the old neighbour, watching me boldly shoo away the chickens.

Snowfall

AUTUMN COMES AND THE LEAVES of the gingko tree in the clearing turn golden yellow. I watch them falling from my window at dawn and then turn to Min.

"I need brushes and inks," I tell her. "In different colours."

She looks awkward. "My uncle says that you are not permitted to write letters," she says, her eyes not quite meeting mine.

I want to laugh. To whom would I send letters? To Qianlong, to beg to return? To my family, to tell them of my disgrace? To the other ladies of the court, to warn them, as if they needed to be warned, of what can happen when you fall from favour?

"I do not want to write a letter," I say. "I want to paint."

She nods, relieved, and hurries away. I wonder where she will get brushes and inks from, perhaps from a local official or her uncle. I wonder if she has ever painted in her life, if her life has allowed for such luxuries. Perhaps as a child she might have crushed red berries and smeared them on white bark or a smooth rock.

When she returns she is clutching two brushes and a few inks: blue, red, black. She also has some paper.

"Thank you," I say. "I do not need the paper." I get up and pull on my jacket, then walk out into the cold air. I make my way to the gingko tree that stands in the centre of the village and begin to collect its leaves. Min has followed me. Now she stands frowning at me.

"Why do you need leaves?" she asks.

"I will show you," I say. "Help me pick up more."

We return to the room with our hands full of the golden leaves, more than a hundred between us. I sit down at the table and take one leaf in my hands.

"Watch," I say. I take the little stem at the top of the leaf and carefully split it in two with my short nails, then pull it apart so that it forms two tiny stems where there was only one before. Min frowns with concentration, watching me as though she might miss what I am doing.

I dip the brush in the red ink and add two bright circles to the lower parts of the leaf, one to each side. Then I take the blue ink and add tiny dots to the upper half. I twist the leaf round so that Min can see it better and her eyes suddenly widen.

"A butterfly!"

"Yes," I say, smiling at her amazed face.

She quickly learns to split the stems that make the antenna for each butterfly, while I paint one leaf after another with the colours I have. I even manage to mix the red and blue to make a beautiful purple, giving me a fourth colour. Soon the rough table in front of me is covered all over with painted butterflies, the leaves transformed. Min looks to me for guidance when we have used up all the leaves.

"Now we let them dry," I say.

"What are they for?" she asks, gazing at them in wonder.

"The children," I say.

The next morning it has grown still colder. Min and I shiver, even after cramming on as many layers of clothing as possible, our arms and legs stiff with padding.

It is Chen who sees me first.

"What are those?" he asks.

I hold one out, a golden body marked with bright blue patterns.

He stares and then reaches out a fingertip to touch the quivering antenna. "What is it?" he asks and his voice is a whisper.

"A leaf," I say. "A butterfly leaf."

Suddenly he sees what it is. He beams. "Did you make it?"

"Yes," I say.

"Who taught you?"

I think of the court painters, decorating gingko leaves in their thousands to be thrown for Qianlong's bustling street scene in the Garden of Perfect Brightness, how they were barely noticed by a court too used to such marvels.

"I saw ones like these a long time ago," I say. "They were thrown into the air, so that they looked as though they were flying."

"Who are they for?" he asks.

"You," I say.

"Me?"

"You," I say and I tip the bowl I am carrying towards him so that he can see that it is full. "You and your friends." I hold the bowl out towards him and he takes it, looks down into it with wide eyes.

"Thank you," he says.

"You are welcome," I say.

He turns from me and runs away, towards a group of children a little way off, engaged in a hopping game. I stand with my hands empty, Min behind me, watching him shout out to them.

"Look what I have! Look!"

They gather round him and I can hear them exclaiming, see their hands reaching into the bowl, retrieving the little scraps of colour.

I turn back to Min. "They like them," I say, smiling.

Someone is tugging at my jacket. I turn round to see Chen's face upturned to mine.

"Aren't you going to come and fly them with us?" he demands, as though it is unthinkable that I should not go with him.

And so I find myself following the ragged band of children through the village, Min a few steps behind me. They run ahead and I have to walk quickly to keep up. In the end, I find myself half-running behind them and when they look back and see that I am keeping pace they run faster, so that I must actually run to stay with them. The cold air rushes past and my feet feel suddenly light. I have not run anywhere for years. Why would a court lady, much less an empress, run? I run and run, until we are well beyond the village and have reached the narrow ridge.

"Be careful!" I call out, panting for breath, but of course the children are sure-footed, they have been this way many times before. They look like mountain goats, bouncing and twisting along the tiny path, uncaring of the drop on either side of them. At last they stop, at the point where they can look down into the valley. By now I am no longer running. I can barely breathe, my heart is pounding and my side hurts. An empress has no need to run.

When I reach them the children are already dipping their hands into the bowl and throwing up the tiny leaves. Each one twists in the wind, spiralling first upwards with the thrust of their arms and then gently floating downwards, sometimes catching in the wind and being lifted up again, twirling briefly in the air before sinking down again, bright sparks against the pale gold and pink rays of the early sun. Each butterfly has its turn, the children watch each one begin its flight before reaching for another, until the air is full of flying butterflies. I feel the first warmth of the day's sun on my face and find that I am laughing, shrieking with delight as one leaf touches my face on its way into the valley. I look to my side and Min is laughing, begging for a chance to throw one herself, which the children grant her. I find one pressed into my own hands and throw it up high, its tiny red and yellow body setting out on a voyage of discovery. I wonder whether the children in the villages of the valley below will find them, these strange autumn butterflies, these last colourful reminders of the summer behind us, if they will wonder where they came from and think them sent down from the realm of the Immortals.

The next day Chen is waiting outside the house as soon as I step out of the door.

"Do you want to come and pick nuts with us?" he asks.

"Nuts?"

"We're going to pick birch nuts. Before the monkeys finish them off. You can come with us."

I think of my little son the last time I spoke to him, how formal he was with me, how neither of us knew what to say to one another. I have to look away for a moment, up at the sharp blue sky, while my eyes clear. When I look back down Chen is still waiting.

"So will you come?" he asks.

I smile. "Yes," I say. "Yes. Thank you."

My autumn is spent with the children. We pick birch and pine nuts, forage for kindling for the fires, turn hundreds upon hundreds of gingko leaves into butterflies. We venture down as far as the foothills of the mountains and bring back walnuts, which stain our hands when we remove their husks before we put them away in storage for winter.

Min looks at me with surprise. "Not panting?" she says one day as we reach the village, having climbed up the steep side of the mountain.

I smile. "No," I say.

"Strong lungs," she says. "Strong hands, too," she adds, pointing at my hands, which have grown calloused from carrying wood and husking nuts.

"Brown skin," I say, looking down at my forearm when I push up my jacket sleeves to wash my hands. It's true. The once pure white of my skin has grown brown in the sun. I can see my face has done the same, even in the small chipped mirror that is all I have to look at myself in now.

There is a tiny temple I sometimes glimpse, its little swooping rooftop all I can make out of it, set on the far peak of the mountaintop.

"Do the villagers pray there?" I ask Min. I have never seen any people going that way.

"No," she says. "A Daoist monk lies there, a hermit. He prays. The men take him food every few days and he prays for our village."

"Can I go there?"

She shrugs. "If you want to," she says.

It's a cold morning with a low sky. I think of turning back, of going there another day when it's less likely to rain, but I woke this morning thinking of the temple and so I set off, waving to Chen and his friends. They follow me along the tight path for a while before losing interest and diving off into the woods, looking for wild animals. I can hear them making monkey noises, crashing through the underbrush below me and smile to myself, thinking that any wild animals will go to ground at once.

The narrow path still makes me nervous. One wrong step and I would find myself clutching at thin air to try and stop a fall down the cliff-like edges of the mountain, for there are few trees sturdy enough to grab at here. The few that have managed to survive, clinging on to the rocks with desperate strength, are tiny and would be uprooted in a moment by the weight of a person. But the woods no longer frighten me. I have roamed all over them with the children these past months and I feel more at home in them than when I came here. I hear the calls of the eagle as it stretches it wings high above me and spot a flash of red and gold, a golden pheasant in the undergrowth. I hear the screeches of the monkeys and wonder what has made them so excited. Perhaps the children are chasing them again.

The temple, when I reach it, is tiny. There is a small wooden building, which I assume houses the hermit monk, protecting him from the cold. It is not the kind of highly decorated temple I grew accustomed to in the Forbidden City. This is made of simple wood, only its swooping rooftop surmounted with tiny guardian statues adds any sense of beauty. Where there would usually be a large enclosed courtyard with grand cauldrons waist-high to a man, filled with sand for burning incense, here there is only a tiny paved area directly in front of the building. There is space to take perhaps ten steps and then, abruptly, the paving ends. Two more steps would have me falling through the air, to reach the valley below lifeless. I step back a little nervously. There is a very small stand for placing incense in, with some already burning and other sticks ready to be lit. I take one and touch it to the red tip of the already burning incense, thinking of the huge bunches of incense sticks I would once have gripped as I bowed in the name of the Imperial Family. Now I am alone it seems fitting to take only one stick. I watch the tip grow red and begin to smoulder, lift it away and bow once in each direction. As I turn towards the tiny building I briefly notice that the door has opened and the monk is standing there watching me, but I continue my bows and by the time I have placed the stick in the holder and knelt before the burner he has moved to one side of me and is kneeling himself, face down.

I wonder what to pray for. Before, I was always instructed as to what ritual we were carrying out. Fertile soil, rain, sun, good crops, the health of silkworms, the wellbeing of the empire seemed to rest entirely on my shoulders and my prayers. Now that I am no longer Empress, what do I pray for?

I pray that the village will have a safe winter and enough to eat, that Chen will grow up strong and healthy. I pray that next spring the crops will grow. I pray that the animals in the woods have good deep burrows and strong nests in which to huddle come the storms of winter. Then I raise my head and look across the open air to the far horizon and give thanks that I am here and happy, that the bitterness of my life has faded from me.

For it has. I had not known it before now. Perhaps it was when I laughed at the butterflies or even when I first thought to paint the golden leaves of the gingko tree. Perhaps it was when I saw Chen peering at me and saw something other than my own thoughts and misery. Or perhaps it was the day when I opened my eyes, looked out of a swaying palanquin and felt my heart drop with terror at the view below me. Perhaps that was the first true feeling I had had for many years, a feeling based in reality rather than the tortured twisting thoughts of my mind. I think back to my belief that I was a hungry ghost and the moment when Chen fed me from a platter intended to fill the bellies of the dead. I wonder if perhaps there was something magical in that food, if it truly fed the ghost in me, or whether it was the kindness and simplicity of Chen's offer that did the feeding. I take in the cold cold air and rise to my feet looking down at the monk. I cannot see his face, for he is prostrated deep in prayer, so I only bow to him and then walk back to the village as a fine mist of rain begins to fall on me.

The cold grows sharp now and even the children prefer to stay indoors. I sit near Min as she does her chores and help her when I can. The first time I do so she looks startled, and more startled still when she sees that I have never chopped vegetables in my life and that I am likely to cut my fingers. She shows me how to hold the sharp knife properly and slowly I grow more useful to her. I help her wash clothes and marvel at my wrinkled fingertips, chop mutton and learn to roll and hand-rip noodles for the fiery cumin-spiced stews she makes. I squeeze stored pomegranates for their juice and suck my fingers clean, the sweet-sharp taste a welcome reminder of summer's fruits, now that fresh fruits and vegetables are hard to come by.

I teach Chen to write his own name and to read a few characters. He wants to know how to write *horse* and *dog*, *sheep* and *house, monkey, berries* and *noodles*, the words that make up his life here. He does not want to compose poetry and read up on illustrious ancestors, for he has none. He wants the words that feed and house him, the words for friends and family, the words that tell of his adventures roaming across this mountain.

Every day I walk to the temple. I grow used to the pathway, although there are days when fierce winds remind me of my fears and with good reason. I take with me a stout stick, so that I can use it for balance if the path is slippery with rain. When I reach the temple I light a stick of incense, watch the red tip glow and breath in the sweet smell. I pray for little things: for Min's cut finger to heal, for Chen's mother's cold to get better soon. I give thanks for a full belly and for a warm hearth to sit by. It is a relief to pray for little things and not feel the weight of an empire's expectations crushing down on you.

From time to time I see the monk. Not every day. Sometimes I catch a glimpse of him practising his martial arts a little way off, or praying, more often I do not see him at all. He is often busy carrying or cutting firewood or making repairs to the wooden building. I do not speak to him, nor do I really look at him: he seems to want to keep himself apart and after all he is a hermit, so I do not wish to disturb him. But he is a comforting presence. Sometimes I bring the food from the village for him and leave it outside his door, where he will find it, taking back to the village the empty basket he leaves there. I like the silence and smallness of this temple and I like that there is only one monk here, that he cares for it as his own home. It seems a more humble way to approach the Immortals than with vast pomp and ceremony as though we were equal to them, as though the

Emperor were indeed the Son of Heaven instead of what I know he really is: a man, like any other.

Thick snow falls. The children play in it, building up great heaps and trying to sculpt it into the shape of people, of little houses, of animals. I watch them from the window and then join them, only to be pelted with snowballs that they have made and stored up behind a snow wall. I give satisfying yelps as they hit me and they collapse laughing when my own poor attempts miss them entirely. Chen's three-legged dog barks hysterically, overexcited by the children's enthusiasm. I make more and more snowballs, my aim improving until I manage to get Chen exactly in the chest, at which he staggers and plays out a convincingly dramatic death scene, which has the dog worried.

The snow seems too thick to risk walking to the temple but after a few days I ask Min whether the monk will have enough supplies.

"He has enough for two or three more days," she says. "After that one of the men will have to make their way there or he will have to fast."

"I can go," I say.

She looks at me doubtfully. "If you slip now, we'll never find you," she says.

"I have my stick," I say. "And the poor man must have some food." I do not say what is also true, which is that I miss my walks to the temple. I can pray in the village of course, I can pray by the warmth of the fire if I wish, but the little temple draws me. I like to say prayers by the cliff edge, as though they have nowhere to go but straight to Heaven. I like to feel the cold air flowing over me as though it takes every bad feeling away, every fear and worry, every bad memory and replaces it only with the cold and purity of the air, sweeping away all that is not good and leaving a fresh surface, like new-fallen snow. I enjoy returning refreshed and purified, as though I have been blessed by the Immortals.

And so when a few more days have passed I take up my stick and Min helps me put a basket onto my back filled with food for the monk.

The snow has fallen more than once and it is thick. Each step I take pushes down layer upon layer of the snow with a satisfying crunching sound. Despite Min's worries, the thick fresh snow actually gives my boots something to grip onto, unlike the wet muddy days of autumn, although I think that if it turns to ice I will have to rethink my confidence in coming here.

The temple has almost disappeared into the snow, from a distance one might not even see it, or think it was just a hilly mound. The doorway and a tiny path has been cleared of snow, but the rest is entirely white. I twist round so that I can take off the basket, gratefully releasing its heavy weight onto the ground with a little grunt. I roll my shoulders and then consider whether or not to knock at the door. But I have never spoken with the monk and I do not want to disturb him if he is at prayer or meditating. So I simply leave the basket in front of the door and then turn to the little altar at the cliff's edge. There is no incense today, so I only stand before it and make my four bows, then kneel in the snow and kowtow. When I stand I brush down my clothing and stand for a few moments, looking out over the valley below and the mountains beyond. It is a scene of exquisite beauty. The mountains are endlessly white. The tiny villages that I know sit in the valleys below are gone, lost in the snow somewhere. It is as though a painting has been wiped away, the colours and shapes I knew taken away, revealing the white silk canvas beneath it, fresh and clean, ready for a brush again, for a new image to be painted. I feel the cold air rush through me, imagine it taking away everything that has happened in my life, taking me back to a moment in my life when all was good, to snowy mornings when Shu Fang would whisper in my ear that Niu Lang was waiting for me in our garden. I think of everything after that moment floating away from me, leaving me here in the white snow, purified and blessed, my burdens released. When I turn back to the tiny path, passing the hermit monk's hut, I am smiling.

Stormy days follow, with snow blizzards so heavy that we can see nothing at all and have to spend our days huddled indoors. Sometimes we scurry to a neighbour's house and spend time together, the old people telling stories while the children crack nuts between two stones at our feet, munching and giggling at funny stories from the past or sitting wide-eyed at legends featuring great deeds of heroes and Immortals. I hear the story of the Cowherd and the Weaver Girl and for once, it does not hurt my heart. My thoughts turn to Niu Lang, wherever he is, and I hope only that he is happy, that he is surrounded by good people, as I am.

At last, the storms clear and a sun-sharp day dawns, the glitter on the snow so bright that we have to shade our eyes, walking about like moles newly-emerged from the earth, bedazzled.

"The monk will need food," says Min and I nod. This job seems to have become mine and I am glad to do it, it pleases me to have a task that is mine, a task that otherwise someone else would have to do. I feel useful doing it, part of the village's life. I take my stick, hoist up the basket and set out.

When I get to the temple I leave the basket by the door, then make my way to the altar, which has been swept clean of snow. Set on it is a round object like a ball. It looks like something encased in ice, perhaps a forgotten tool or a stone. I get closer to it and set down my stick before reaching out my hand, which is shaking.

The ball is a carving in ice. Two magpies, their bodies intertwined to form a spherical shape. I stare down at it in disbelief.

"Ula Nara."

I don't turn. I don't need to. I would know his voice anywhere, even after more than thirty years. I look down at the carving in my hands, the two birds just as I remember them, trembling between my fingers as though they have come to life.

"Niu Lang."

The Bridge of Magpies

I DO NOT KNOW HOW LONG we stand on the cliff edge together. At first we stand side by side and do not speak, do not even look at one another. I look forward but I can see the shape of Niu Lang at my side, close enough that I could reach out my right hand and touch him. The cold wind blows through us and I wonder whether it has been sent down from the Immortals, if this snow is the magpie bridge that I have spent three decades waiting for, if the Immortals have finally relented.

"I thought I had learnt patience," he says at last. "I thought I would wait until you saw me for yourself." He laughs a little. "But you were too wrapped up in your own world, Ula Nara."

I think of the glimpses I saw of him: kneeling, carrying wood a little way off, his graceful movements as he practiced martial arts with his back turned to me. Now it seems incredible to me that I did not see it was him. "I was wrapped up in my own world," I echo. "I felt only my own pain."

"I have spent thirty years praying for your happiness," he says and his voice cracks.

"Your prayers are granted," I say.

"But only now," he says and I can hear the sadness in his voice.

I am about to say yes and then I pause. "Before now," I say at last. "Before now."

"When you came here?"

"Yes," I say.

I catch a movement of his head, a nod. "I saw you change," he says. "I could have waited for you to see me for yourself. But I was still too impatient, even after my years of training, even after all my masters have taught me. And the snow would have melted. I could not wait another year to make you an ice sculpture."

I laugh. I laugh out loud and then I turn to him even as he turns to me and I see him for the first time.

"You are the same," I say in surprise.

He laughs. "Older by thirty years. And without hair."

I shake my head. "You forgot the wrinkles," I tell him, still laughing. "But you are still you."

"Who did you think I would be?"

"A monk," I say.

He snorts with laughter, his eyes shining with tears. "I am."

"That is not what I meant."

"I know." He looks at me for a moment, then looks down. "Your hands must be frozen."

I am still holding the icy magpies. I place them back on the altar.

"Come inside and get warm," he says.

I follow him to the little building. Inside it is much like Min's house, but less cluttered. I sit on a little wooden bench while Niu Lang makes tea and serves it to me.

"When did you first see me?" I ask.

"In the woods."

"The woods?"

"You were walking in them alone, at night. I think you had only been here a little while."

"Did you recognise me?"

He looks at me in disbelief that I would even ask the question. "I thought it was your spirit. I thought you had died and that you had come to bid me farewell."

I think of the grief I felt when the male magpie died, my certainty that it was a sign that Niu Lang had died. "What did you do?"

"Watched you walk away and came back here."

I wait.

"And wept for you. For us."

I look down, my own eyes brimming. "I wanted to become a nun," I tell him. "As you became a monk."

"We do not all arrive at the same place by the same means," he says.

"You remained true to who you were," I say. "You remained pure in your mind and in your body. You practised a spiritual path that kept you whole. And sane," I add. "While I was dragged into court life, and all its darkness. It warped me. My love and grief for you became something twisted. It lost whatever was good and pure and became something bad. It made me into someone else, a dark person. A bad person." I shake my head, as though to release something stuck in it. "It drove me mad. I saw things that could not have been true, things I wanted to see. I saw the secrets that everyone keeps and hated them because I had secrets of my own that I could not speak of." I look down at my hands. "I became nothing but skin and bones, as though there was a terrible hunger in me. Gnawing at me all the time, begging to be fed and yet I could not find anything that would satisfy it. It made me ill."

He nods. "Ying is the spiritual self," he says. "Yang is the physical body. The two are equally important, they cannot be separated. Your feelings affect your body whilst your body affects your mind. They are two parts of the whole."

I give a little laugh. "You are a physician," I say. "Did becoming a monk make you happy?"

"Not at first. I was angry all the time, I refused to obey orders, I would try to pick fights with the other boys, even with my masters.

At last my master taught me that we do not simply achieve peace. We must *practice* the Dao. We try to build a path between who we are and who we want to be, but it requires effort. It requires learning. It requires planning and thinking about who you want to be."

"Tell me about your training," I say. "About the early days."

"I started my training late. Many boys had already begun their training on Wu-Tang Mountain by the time they were thirteen. It was exhausting. Before dawn we would run up and down the mountain carrying heavy sandbags before attending morning prayers. We spent more than nine hours every day learning ancient forms, drilling with weapons, stretching and praying again. We were taught herbal medicine and massage, even acupuncture. We chanted sacred texts. We had to study Daoist Scripture. We slept ten to a room and when we were not training we would walk in the mountain eating wild berries or play board games together in our dormitory. It took me many years to complete the training. Once ordained I left my master and became a wandering monk. I travelled from temple to temple, year after year. I sought out other masters, learned their skills and practised what I had been taught when I was alone. Along the way I learned to play the bamboo flute and cook for myself." He laughs. "I am not a bad cook now, Ula Nara."

"You live here all year round?"

"Yes."

"It is a hard life," I say.

"I am used to it. Most of our practice when I was a trainee was outside. We trained in the sun and in the cold. If it rained or snowed we could practice indoors." He looks around at the thick snow surrounding us. "Although I have always liked being in the snow," he smiles.

"It is such a tiny house," I say.

He laughs. "I have two sets of practice clothes, some street clothes, a bowl to eat from, and a cup to drink from. Bedding. A basin for washing myself. There is a bed, a table, the bench and a chest for my belongings, such as they are. I am not sure what I would do with a larger house."

"If you enjoyed the company of the other students," I say, "why did you leave the temple and come here? Wu-Tang Mountain is close enough, you could have returned there."

"I struggled to master my sense of loneliness," he says, looking away. "Even when I was surrounded by others, I thought of you and felt alone. In the end my master suggested that I explore what it is to be truly alone, with one's thoughts, one's feelings, one's physical body." He looks down into the valley below us. "And so I came here, to this tiny place."

"How long ago?"

"More than ten years." He grins. "I think the villagers thought I would not last the year, especially once the snows came. But I surprised myself, and them."

"What made you stay?"

"The people, at first. They were so kind. They brought me food, they watched out for me, the children were forever peeping at me from behind the bushes. They made me laugh."

I think of the children leaping in the air and shouting at the sight of the ginkgo butterflies and smile. "And then?"

"Then the mountain, I think."

"The mountain?"

"When I first came here, I spent days and days wandering all over the mountain. Months. I saw all its secrets and all its beauty. I saw the living spaces of hermits before me, who had come here and found peace. And before them, people from so long ago we do not even remember their names."

"The caves," I say. "And the paintings."

He nods. "Yes. At first they frightened me, I did not know what they were."

"Do you know what they are now?"

He laughs. "No, but they no longer frighten me."

"And what else?"

"Everything." He thinks for a moment. "The trees, the berries, the animals. The way the seasons pass and things change but are the same."

I think of the ginkgo leaves changing from green to gold and then into painted butterflies. Of the berries I ate from Chen's hand, so different from the over-ripe berries steeped in honey I was served at court, how their sharp-sweetness awoke something in me and laid something else to rest. I nod.

Spring comes. The snow and ice melts away. Tiny streams make their way down the mountain's sides, to join rivers in the valley below and make their way to the Yellow River. I have a cough, which Min fusses over, but I tell her it will be gone soon, it is only the change in weather.

"You shouldn't spend all that time out in the cold," says Min. "Let the men take food to the monk."

"It makes me happy to go there," I say. She calls me stubborn and has me wrap up more warmly, but she lets me go. Every few days I walk to the temple as I have done these past months and take food to Niu Lang. Then we sit together and look out over the valleys below, watching the seasons change.

"Tell me about your life," he says one day.

I think. We have never spoken of my years in the Forbidden City. What do I tell him about? The pomp and ritual? The splendour? My children, lost to me as soon as they were born? Feng? Ling? Qianlong? Lady He? All the petty rivalries, which now seem so meaningless even though they were all I had to live for? "I was a hungry ghost," I tell

Niu Lang. "I wanted what I had lost and I did not know how to find it. I searched and searched but each time I thought I had found something to feed on it was only an empty bowl and my hunger grew greater."

He nods.

"I cut my hair because I thought you had died. I had come to the end of my search," I say. "I realised I would never fill that need. I was mourning for myself as much as for you."

We sit in silence for a little longer.

"I ate food from the bowls left out for the hungry ghosts last summer," I say. "I thought I was one of them."

"And then?"

I shake my head and smile. "Perhaps it fed the hungry ghost in me," I say. "I thought of going back to my family or to Beijing to beg for forgiveness. But I came back to the village that night because it felt like my home. One of the children offered me food from the ghost dishes and the food seemed meant for me, as though I belonged here. The people felt like my family. And they did not care about who I was before. They don't even know who I was," I add with a laugh.

"They know who you truly are," says Niu Lang.

I nod. "I was afraid that the hungry ghost would never leave me," I say. "There was a Hungry Ghost Festival many years ago in the Forbidden City and when we set candles afloat afterwards to guide the spirits home, my flame alone did not go out. I thought it was a sign that there was still a ghost wandering in my life and then I thought it must be me. That I *was* the ghost and that I would wander forever, unhappy and seeking what could not be found."

Niu Lang gets to his feet and walks away, to the little house. I wait for him, watching the clouds moving across the sky. When he comes back, he is holding a tiny round candle and a scrap of paper. He folds the paper this way and that until he has made a little boat, into which he sets the candle, wedging it firmly into place.

"What are you doing?" I ask.

He goes to the altar and lights the candle, brings it back to me and indicates the little stream running down past the altar, the last of the winter's snows.

I look down at the boat cupped in my hand. "The lanterns are supposed to be sent out fourteen days after the Festival of Hungry Ghosts," I say quietly. "It is too late."

"It is never too late to set a spirit free," says Niu Lang.

I take the boat with its tiny flame and kneel by the side of the stream. I set it gently in the fast running water and watch as it bobs its way around obstacles: a twig, a stone, moving now fast, now slow. It reaches the edge of the cliff and just as it tips over the edge a gust of wind catches it. The flame flickers and goes out.

I look up at Niu Lang, who smiles.

"It is never too late to be set free," he says.

Many of the characters in this book recur in my other novels set in the Forbidden City. Ladies Ling, Ying and Qing are the main characters in *The Consorts*, the Emperor's mother Niuhuru and the Jesuit painter Giuseppe Castiglione are the main characters in *The Garden of Perfect Brightness* while Lady He is *The Fragrant Concubine*. The Emperor Qianlong features in all the books, at different points in his life, as does Ula Nara.

If you have enjoyed this novel, I would be very grateful if you would write a brief review: it really helps a book find new readers. Thank you!

Author's Note on History

Ula Nara features in all four of my books set in China, and I have mostly cast her as a villain: a frightening rival or presence for many other characters. But the more I wrote about her, the more I wanted her to have her own story. Her real name is lost to us, as most concubines did not have their real names recorded, only their clan names. I have therefore chosen to use her clan name as a given name rather than make one up.

Ula Nara came from a military family and was chosen as a concubine for the heir to the throne, known as Prince Bao (later the Qianlong Emperor) at the age of sixteen (he was twenty-three and his Primary Consort Lady Fuca was twenty-two). I always thought that there must have been many young girls attending the Imperial Daughters' Draft who were already in love with someone but who were then selected for the Imperial Family and had no choice in the matter, so I gave this back story to Ula Nara. To aid with the comparison between Ula Nara and Fuca's experiences, I have them enter Qianlong's life together, although in reality Fuca would have already been his Primary Consort for a few years when Ula Nara arrived.

Looking at her records suggests that Qianlong was not very interested in Ula Nara. She was promoted on the occasion of his coronation (this was standard) and then twice more for no obvious official reason. She had no children at all until two years after she became Empress, a full sixteen years after being married to Qianlong. She then had three children in only four years, which means she was not infertile but strongly suggests she had not been favoured until Qianlong felt he ought to call for her since she was now his Empress, indicating duty rather than fondness. Ula Nara lost two of her three children very young, while they were still toddlers. Her eldest child lived only into his early twenties, dying about ten years after she did. It was standard practice for a concubine's child to be raised by a different concubine.

Qianlong was very much in love with his Primary Consort Lady Fuca, who was made Empress after his coronation and whose sons had been chosen as heirs before they both died. Chinese emperors did not necessarily use primogeniture when choosing an heir: they chose the son they believed was the most appropriate for the role or the one of whom they were most fond. Qianlong did not wish to have a new empress appointed after the death of Lady Fuca, but his mother Niuhuru apparently intervened and insisted that a new lady be made Empress, forcefully backing Ula Nara, who was said to be extremely well versed in court etiquette. After a stubborn delay of two years of mourning, Qianlong gave Ula Nara the unheard-of title of Step Empress rather than Empress, again indicating a rather reluctant appointment.

On a trip to Southern China, Qianlong apparently celebrated Ula Nara's birthday but then suddenly and dramatically demoted her from Empress. She had cut off her hair, a huge breach of protocol, which could be interpreted as cursing the Emperor and his mother, as cutting off her hair suggested one of them had died. She was sent back to Beijing, where she had only two maids (what a very low-ranking consort would have had). She died a year later, aged forty-eight. To this day no-one is certain why this incident occurred. After her death she was buried with only minor ceremony more suited to a medium-ranked concubine. When, after her death, both a historian and a scholar pleaded with Qianlong to give her a better burial or re-instate her position, one was exiled and the other executed.

After Ula Nara's death Qianlong flatly refused to ever appoint another empress. Lady Ling acted as Empress where required but was not given the title. Her son (raised by Lady Qing) was chosen as the next Emperor (Jiaqing) but she did not live to see him on the throne.

Magpies have been known to live for more than twenty years, I stretched this a little further for Ula Nara's pet pair.

Lady Wan outlived Qianlong by eight years and lived to the grand old age of ninety. She was made a Dowager Noble Consort by his heir, the Jiaqing Emperor, in recognition of her age and service.

Lady Wang suffered demotions twice for being abusive to her maids. However, she was reinstated both times because she had a daughter of whom Qianlong was very fond, saying that she should have been his heir.

Being exiled from court, as Ula Nara was, was known as being sent to 'the Cold Palace', which is an expression, not a real place, but in this book I created a real exile for Ula Nara, so that I could re-unite her with her fictional long-lost love. I based her place of exile on a slightly-fictionalised Mount Hua Shan, a very beautiful but isolated place with terrifyingly narrow mountain-top ridge pathways, caves carved by hermits, strange red ochre paintings of human figures on rock faces (some of which are 16,000 years old) and temples set on the clifftops. The mountain is considered sacred by Daoists, whose mythology says that the god of the underworld lives under it.

I used the Qixi or Lovers' Festival as a structure and theme for Ula Nara's fictional love story, but also used the Hungry Ghost Festival (which takes place just after) because I felt there was something of the hungry ghost to Ula Nara's unhappiness, forever craving something that could not satisfy her. She died in August, the month in which both festivals take place.

We know so little about the women of the Forbidden City, yet the glimpses of their lives are fascinating. From what I could piece together I felt Ula Nara had an unhappy history. This book is partly my apology for always casting her as the villain, as well as an attempt at guessing what might have happened in her sad life from the tiny fragments left behind. It gave me pleasure to create a little fictional happiness and peace for her at the end of her life, however unlikely.

Biography

I mainly write historical fiction, and am currently writing two series set in very different eras: China in the 1700s and Morocco/Spain in the 1000s. My first novel, *The Fragrant Concubine*, was picked for Editor's Choice by the Historical Novel Society and longlisted for the Mslexia Novel Competition.

In 2016 I was made the Leverhulme Trust Writer in Residence at the British Library, which included writing two books, *Merchandise for Authors* and *The Storytelling Entrepreneur*. You can read more about my non-fiction books on my website.

I am currently studying for a PhD in Creative Writing at the University of Surrey.

I love using my writing to interact with people and run regular workshops at the British Library as well as coaching other writers on a one-to-one basis.

I live in London with my husband and two children.

For more information, visit my website www.melissaaddey.com

Current and forthcoming books include:

Historical Fiction
China
The Consorts (free on Amazon)
The Fragrant Concubine
The Garden of Perfect Brightness
The Cold Palace

Morocco
The Cup (free on my website)
A String of Silver Beads
None Such as She
Do Not Awaken Love

Picture Books for Children
Kameko and the Monkey-King

Non-Fiction
The Storytelling Entrepreneur
Merchandise for Authors
The Happy Commuter
100 Things to Do while Breastfeeding

Thanks

My grateful thanks go to Professor James Millward for his expertise on the Qing era and encouragement. Mark Elliot's book *Qianlong: Son of Heaven, Man of the World* is a fascinating book for character information on members of the court and contains the poem Qianlong wrote to celebrate conquering Xinjiang. www.daoistgate.com and in particular the blog on the site was my main source for Niu Lang's life as a monk. Their collective scholarship gave my imagination a wonderful basis to work from, although of course all errors as well as deliberate fictional choices are mine alone.

Thank you to Rob Gifford, author of *China Road*, a great travelogue where I first read about the Chinese legend of the Fragrant Concubine, which kick-started this series.

Thank you to my beta readers for this book, Etain, Helen and Martin, for their questions, ideas and reminders that made the story and the writing better. To all the readers who review my books: I read every word and I am so grateful for your time in sharing your thoughts.

I am immensely grateful to the University of Surrey for funding my PhD: a very precious gift of three years of creative freedom to explore not only this series and my craft but many other creative outlets as well.

To all the scholars, artists and photographers on whose work I have drawn in the many years I have spent writing novels set in eighteenth century China: thank you for opening up the gates of the

Forbidden City to me, it was a world beyond imagination and I am sorry to leave it behind as I complete this series.

Thank you to Streetlight Graphics and the illustrators who helped make the world come alive in my own books.

Thank you to my family and friends who continue to offer encouragement along the way. To my children, for their inspiring enthusiasm in writing their own books once they realised what I do for a living.

And always to Ryan, who makes all things possible.